Jessica Huntley

THE DARKNESS THAT BINDS US

Book 2 of The Darkness Series

First published in 2023
Copyright © Jessica Huntley 2023

Jessica Huntley has asserted her right under the Copyright, Designs and Patents Act 1988 to be identified as the author of the work.

This is a work of fiction. Unless otherwise indicated, all the names, characters, businesses, places, events and incidents in this book are either the product of the author's imagination or used in a fictitious manner. Any resemblance to actual persons, living or dead, or actual events is purely coincidental.

All rights reserved. No part of this publication may be reproduced, transmitted, or copied by any means (electronic, mechanical, photocopying, or otherwise) without the prior permission of the author.

ISBN: 978-1-7397697-6-5

First edition
Website: www.jessicahuntleyauthor.com

Cover Design: Get Covers
Edited and proofread by: Jennifer Kay Davies

About Jessica Huntley

Jessica is, and always has been, a huge fan of psychological and suspense thrillers. Her favourite authors are Chris Carter and John Marrs. She loves the twists and turns and shocking reveals and uses the books she reads as inspiration to write her own.

Jessica wrote her first book at age six. Between the ages of ten and eighteen, she had written ten full-length fiction novels as a hobby in her spare time between school and work.

At age eighteen, she left her hobby behind and joined the British Army as an Intelligence Analyst where she spent the next four and a half years as a soldier. She attempted to write more novels but was never able to finish them.

Jessica later left the Army and became a mature student at Southampton Solent University and studied Fitness and Personal Training, which later became her career. She still enjoys keeping fit and exercising daily.

She is now a wife and a stay-at-home mum to a crazy toddler and lives in Newbury. During the first national lockdown of 2020, she signed up on a whim for a novel writing course, and the rest is history. Her love of writing came flooding back, and she managed to write and finish her debut novel, The Darkness Within Ourselves, inspired by her love of horror and thriller novels. She has also finished writing the My ... Self trilogy, completed a Level 3 Diploma in Editing and Proofreading and has worked with four other authors on a collaborative horror novel entitled The Summoning.

She is now working on a new novel in her spare time, reads every day (thrillers...obviously).

Other books by Jessica Huntley

The Darkness Series
The Darkness Within Ourselves
The Darkness That Binds Us
Book 3: Title TBC (Out early 2024)

My ... Self Series
My Bad Self: A Prequel Novella
My Dark Self
My True Self
My Real Self

Standalone Thrillers

Jinx

Writing in collaboration with other authors
The Summoning
HorrorScope: A Zodiac Anthology

Acknowledgements

First, I'd like to thank the readers who read my debut novel, "The Darkness Within Ourselves" and convinced me to write a sequel. The Darkness Within Ourselves was never supposed to be part of a series, but I'm so glad you all hounded me until I gave in because without you, then this book wouldn't exist, and I think it's one of my favourites I've written so far.

As always, thanks go to my husband, dad, sister and best friend who always support me, even though they don't know the ins and outs of what I do as an author now, they're still always there for me. And to my son, who is always my inspiration and I hope I'll make him proud one day. Seeing his face when he saw my book recently in Waterstones was an incredible moment I'll never forget. "Look, Mummy, it's your book!"

To my amazing bookstagram friends and fellow authors who constantly support me and lift me up when I'm down: Mariette Whitcomb, Amanda Jaeger, Jamie Lee Fry, Harriet Everend, and Hayley Anderton ... Honestly, there are so many, I'm sorry I can't list you all! Your continued support means everything to me.

A special mention goes to my wonderful Beta readers who read this book before it was finished and offered me some amazing advice, and guidance and pointed out some continuity errors; Hayley Anderton, Kimberley (@thearieslibrary) and Sophie Jones.

To my wonderful editor, Jennifer Kay Davies, who, although didn't edit my debut novel, has been with me since my second book and is invaluable in helping me ensure my books are polished and ready to be read. Thank you for sticking with me along my self-published journey.

To the incredible indie author community, especially on Instagram. We have it tough at times, but we all support each other and I'm proud and honoured to be a part of such a community.

Finally, to you, the reader … Without you, my stories would be unread and untold. Thank you for reading and being a part of my author journey.

Connect with Jessica

Find and connect with me online via the following platforms.

Sign up to my email list via my website to be notified of future books and receive a twice-monthly author newsletter and also receive a **FREE thriller novella called My Bad Self.**

www.jessicahuntleyauthor.com

Follow me on Facebook: Jessica Huntley - Author - @jessica.reading.writing

Follow me on Instagram: @jessica_reading_writing

Follow me on Twitter: @jess_read_write

Follow me on TikTok: @jessica_reading_writing

Follow me on Goodreads: jessica_reading_writing

Trigger Warnings

Anxiety, disappearance, depression, grief, hallucinations, murder, suicide, fire, blood, profanity, cheating, child loss, alcohol use, a person with a substance use disorder, mental health illness, physical assault, death, car accident, body injury, bullying; mentions domestic abuse, child molestation, rape, overdose, and cancer.

Cherry Hollow and The Creature:

A True Horror Story or a Terrifying Hoax?
By Stephen Mallow
Date: 5 May 2022

The Lake District is a national park in England, renowned for its sheer beauty and tranquillity. From its rugged mountains, glacial ribbon lakes and historic literacy associations, there isn't an area of the district that doesn't draw awe and wonder. Tourists travel from all over the United Kingdom and indeed, the world, to experience all it has to offer, including the views, walks and, not forgetting its inns and pubs, perfect for unwinding at the end of a long day exploring.

But there is one town situated within this picturesque landscape, between two mountains in the Hope Valley and not far from Lake Peace, that tourists visit not for the beauty or the tranquillity, but because of the true horrors that have happened there over the past two and a half decades.

This town is called Cherry Hollow.

The locals have a saying: *Cherry Hollow is a place where, if you leave to live elsewhere, you never return, and if an outsider moves in, they never leave.*

What exactly has happened to turn this quaint country town into a living nightmare?

Let me tell you a story and then you can decide for yourself whether you believe it or not.

On 20 July 1998, Cherry Hollow was the setting of an unimaginable tragedy.

The disappearance of twelve-year-old Kieran Jones. On the cusp of becoming a teenager, loved by his friends and family and renowned for his mild-mannered and friendly personality, the boy's disappearance sent shock waves through the close-knit community, ripping his family apart and turning his four best friends against each other, never to speak to one another again.

He and his friends would later become known as The Fated Five.

But his disappearance was only the beginning.

The local police searched for years, keeping the case open for as long as possible, but the boy had vanished, leaving no leads or clues behind. Had he run away? Had he been kidnapped? Had he succumbed to a tragic accident and perished? Or had he been brutally murdered and his body buried somewhere it would never see the light of day again?

His disappearance remained a mystery.

His four best friends were the last to see him alive.

His body was never found.

Until twenty years later …

In July 2018, a watch once belonging to Kieran Jones was discovered at the bottom of Beaker Ravine, a steep, treacherous crevice located just outside the town's borders, despite having been thoroughly searched years before. The only way to reach it was through a thick expanse of trees and brambles.

Beaker Ravine would be the setting for many more tragedies to come.

A new police investigation was launched, urging anyone with any information, no matter how small, to come forward.

However, so many years had passed. The children of twenty years ago were now adults, including the four who had last seen Kieran alive. They were now estranged from each other, having grown apart over their two decades of grief.

Having spoken to several members of the local community, who wished to remain anonymous, it appears that the remaining four had hidden a dark secret which they bore alone for many years … and, over time, it slowly ate them alive, turning them into mere shells of their former selves.

Brooke Willows used to be a blonde-haired, blue-eyed beauty who oozed self-confidence and had dreams of living in London and becoming a make-up artist to the stars. She later became a prisoner in her childhood home, being cared for by her poor mother. Suffering from an aggressive form of agoraphobia, Brooke kept herself locked away from the outside world, claiming she was plagued by a fear so intense, it refused to allow her to be free. Brooke became a terrified, skeletal woman, too afraid to take a step outside her front door or even pull back the curtains to let in the light. Was this fear real or was it all in her head, created by her own imagination and guilt?

Jordan Evans, a gentle and loving teenage boy who every girl wanted to date and every boy wanted to be like, became a hate-filled, aggressive man who abused and cheated on his wife. His father, who owned the local plumbing business, was forced to apologise daily for his son's actions.

Jordan blamed his outbursts on a violent sensation that took him over at will, refusing to accept responsibility. He promptly pushed everyone who had ever loved him away, including his ailing mother, who could no longer be around him and moved out of the area. Was this violent *sensation* a true mental health condition or something more sinister?

Tyler Jenkins was no longer a confident and headstrong young man or the life and soul of the party. He was swallowed by a dark pit of depression and wallowed in his own self-pity for years, becoming a recluse whose only means of having a connection or relationship with another person was by paying for it. He wished he had the ability to end his life, but his depression wouldn't let him escape that easily. Did he truly have severe depression or was his guilt so strong that he couldn't bear to live with it, and he made up this condition as a way to justify his actions? Years later, after his confession, his darkness finally allowed him to take his own life, something he'd wanted all along.

On the outside, Amber Walker appeared to have it all; she was a loving wife and a caring mother, but she, quite possibly, had suffered the most over the years. Once a happy young girl who dreamed of becoming a doctor or scientist, she soon began to suffer from severe insomnia, which robbed her of her beauty and zest for life. Not only that, but it was believed she had lucid hallucinations of a dark entity she called The Creature who hunted her in her dreams and, eventually, in the outside world. Was this creature a true representation of a medical condition or was it a vivid hallucination she made up to punish herself for what had happened all those years ago?

And this is where the real story of The Creature and Cherry Hollow begins …

A few days after the watch was discovered at the ravine, Tyler Jenkins confessed everything on tape, revealing that he had been the mastermind behind Kieran's death, that he'd killed him because he'd threatened to reveal Tyler's family secret; a secret so dark that no child should ever have to keep. Tyler's parents were child molesters and rapists and they conducted their sordid affairs on their own son, making him swear using a blood oath that he'd never reveal their true personalities.

Tyler confessed that he had pushed Kieran into the ravine, burned his body, and scattered his remains so that even the wildlife would never find them. Satisfied that his revelation would make everything right, his *depression* finally allowed him the sweet release of death. He jumped from the same fallen tree that Kieran had fallen from, down into the depths of Beaker Ravine, which claimed its second victim.

But it was never going to be that easy to hide from the darkness within …

Because, according to some of the locals, that's not what really happened back in 1998. Guilt has a way of following the guilty forever.

Rumours began to fly. People talked. Children gossiped. The only people who knew the truth were Amber Walker, Jordan Evans and Brooke Willows, all of whom continued to keep silent on the matter.

Now, several years after Tyler's confession and subsequential death, life appears to have returned to normal. No longer a married woman, Amber has found love with none other than Jordan Evans, who has changed his ways and is no longer gripped by anger. Brooke has moved to London and has never returned to Cherry Hollow, cementing the local saying as gospel.

But Amber, according to locals, has started acting strangely. No longer afraid to speak her mind, she's apparently convinced that The Creature is still after her and is even targeting her daughter.

But hang on …

Why is The Creature back? Does it mean that Amber still has something to hide? Or is The Creature merely a figment of her overly exhausted imagination and she truly does have a disturbing mental health condition that warrants further investigation?

Now, a new rumour is in town.

The locals say Beaker Ravine is haunted by the ghosts of those who have plunged to their deaths. They even say that The Creature will call out to you and make you jump into the deep chasm if you visit it.

This journalist decided to test this theory for himself.

Having never been one to shy away from a haunted house or jump at scary movies, I pride myself on my ability to get to the bottom of this truly fascinating story once and for all.

However, upon visiting Beaker Ravine, I decided not to further pursue this strange phenomenon. I do not wish to cause alarm or spread any further rumours around the already plagued town, but The Creature is something that will haunt me for the rest of my life.

I will never be returning to Cherry Hollow …

I did indeed see a dark shadow pass over the ravine, and everything turned cold.

It was the most frightening experience of my life …

And anyone who moves to this haunted town should reconsider their life choices …

If you do visit Cherry Hollow … <u>do not visit Beaker Ravine.</u>

It may be the last thing you ever do.

The question remains: is Cherry Hollow the location of a true horror story, or is it simply a terrifying yet fantastic hoax?

This journalist will no longer be pursuing this line of enquiry.

Prologue
Halloween 2023

As Olivia guided the car around a street corner, Emma's eyes locked onto the eerie orange hue in the distance, just over the brow of the road. It was made even more prominent by the growing darkness of the autumn evening. Since she'd heard the shocking news, the darkness had engulfed her as well, gripping her insides and not releasing its hold.

Emma leaned forwards as far as the seatbelt would allow, clenching the edges of the passenger seat with so much force her nails dug into the thick material, leaving miniature crescent shapes when she removed them. The belt dug into her shoulder, but her brain barely registered the sting.

'What's going on?' she asked. 'Why are you stopping?'

Olivia slowed the car to a stop and applied the handbrake, blowing out a breath. 'I'm sorry, Emma, but I can't go any further. They've cordoned off the whole road.'

Emma looked again and, sure enough, she saw the yellow crime scene tape stretched across the road along with several police officers dressed in uniform, patrolling the area. They had stern looks on their faces as they held up their hands, stopping the throng of pedestrians and onlookers from passing through. It looked as if the entire town had turned up to watch the events unfold.

Emma flung open the car door, leaving Olivia in the car, and sprinted towards the nearest police officer, a petite woman with black hair tied neatly in a bun. 'That's my house!' she screamed as she grabbed the flimsy tape and shook it.

The officer stepped in front of her. 'Ma'am, I'm going to have to ask you to please step back. The fire brigade is tackling the flames as we speak and—'

'My son! Where's my son? My house is on fire. I demand to be let through! Please!'

The officer nodded. 'Okay, one minute. Wait here.'

Emma watched, her patience waning by the second, as the officer spoke to her colleague nearby, who then stepped forwards, taking over the situation. He was exceptionally tall, and Emma had to crane her neck to look at his face as he spoke.

'Ma'am, I can take you a little closer so you can speak to Detective Williams. He's in charge. We don't know where your son is, but—'

Emma's world crumbled and she let out a garbled shriek. 'No! Alex! Please, let me through.'

The officer waved her through and lifted the yellow tape to enable Emma to duck under.

'Come with me. Everyone else needs to stay back.' He lowered the tape again and nodded at his female colleague. 'Make sure no one else comes through. I'll be back in five minutes.' He then turned to speak to Emma, but she was already halfway up the road.

Emma had never run so fast in her life. She didn't care her lungs were burning and felt like they might explode at any moment. She didn't care her legs were filled with so much lactic acid she could barely feel them.

As she reached the brow of the hill, the devastating reality hit her like a punch to the face as she saw her home being ravaged by flames. Thick plumes of smoke billowed into the air. Police lights pierced the gloomy darkness, illuminating the surrounding houses on the street in red and blue tones. The sirens had stopped blaring now, but she still had ringing in her ears on top of her pounding heartbeat.

By the time she arrived puffing and panting at the edge of her street, her legs were ready to collapse underneath her, but she pushed forwards. She could hear the officer running to catch her, telling her to stop, but she ignored him. There was no way she was stopping now.

There it was …

Her home …

The home that, less than a week ago, she'd moved into with her wife and children; the home that was supposed to have been a fresh start for her family. It was now engulfed in a blazing inferno of brick, wood and all her earthly belongings.

A fire engine was parked on the street, along with an ambulance and two police cars. Numerous people wearing an array of uniforms relating to one of the emergency services were milling about, but there was no sign of the only person she wanted to see.

Emma stared up at her house.

Huge jets of water were being hosed onto the flames by two firefighters, but even Emma knew that the house was too far gone to be saved. Only a crispy, black shell remained.

Her only thought was of Alex.

Emma had never felt more useless in her life. She sank to her knees and wept hysterically, screaming Alex's name over and over until a paramedic came and draped a silver foil blanket around her trembling shoulders.

Chapter One
EMMA

Six Days Earlier
Thursday 26 October 2023 – 11:02 a.m.

'Cherry Hollow is a place where if you leave to live elsewhere, you never return, and if an outsider moves in, they never leave.'

That was what Emma Smithson had been told by the local estate agent ten minutes ago when she'd picked up the keys to her new home on Baker Street.

At first, she'd merely smiled at the man, who looked to be closer to fifty than forty and was doing his best to combat the ageing process by dyeing his hair jet black, but then he'd locked eyes with her, almost as if he were sending her a warning message. Her smile faltered and her stomach was left feeling unsettled as she walked out of the office, clutching the keys to her new house in her left hand. She stood at the edge of the pavement for a full five minutes, wrestling with her overactive imagination, before getting in her car. She drove the short distance to Baker Street, which was situated near the outskirts of the town, on the south side.

Maybe it's one of those things the locals say to try and be funny …

Emma had to admit, from the little she'd seen of the town so far, it seemed a pleasant and wholesome community, a beautiful place to live and raise a family. She passed a coffee shop, a plumbing business and a community centre, all of which were bustling with smiling customers.

Cherry Hollow was situated in the middle of the Lake District, a dream location for Emma who had always preferred the countryside to the hustle of the busy city. This area would be the perfect place to quiet her mind and relax and enjoy watching her children grow up, even though the oldest was midway through his teens already. Childhood was so fleeting.

Luckily, her anxiety dissipated when she set eyes on the house that she and her wife of three years, Linda, would now call home, along with her sixteen-year-old son, Alex and seven-year-old daughter, Phoebe.

Number 6 Baker Street was her dream home. A stunning modern property with four double bedrooms, two bathrooms, a large and light kitchen diner, a spacious lounge and a playroom.

The garden was enormous, with enough space for her growing children, complete with a wooden treehouse situated in a large oak at the end of the lawn. Emma wondered if the big garden and wide-open countryside surrounding the town would be enough to convince Linda to let them have a dog. A canine companion would be the perfect final piece in her family jigsaw puzzle.

Emma smiled as she gazed up at the house and its many windows. It reminded her of one of those show homes she often saw in glossy magazines. She wondered if it had been a happy home for its previous occupants. It had been sold cheaply, thousands under what it was worth, but the owner had been in a hurry to sell.

Emma didn't know a lot about Sean Walker, only that he was a single father to his twelve-year-old daughter, Bethany. Emma secretly hoped the house would be her own fresh start for her and her family, which was why she'd snatched it up without even looking at the property in person. The photos on the website had been beautiful, highlighting its light and airy living areas and its many bedrooms. Linda, of course, had told her she was crazy for buying a house without looking at it, but eventually had agreed that even if it did need a bit of work, the price was too good to be true. By the looks of it though, the house was in perfect condition, a real gem of a find.

As Emma walked up the light grey stone steps towards the front door, she stopped to admire the red rose bushes growing on either side. She bent down and sniffed the nearest bloom. It filled her nostrils with a wonderful floral scent, but as she attempted to snap a flower from the stem to present to Linda when she arrived, a thorn stabbed her middle finger. She flinched, yanking her hand away and sucked at the small wound, which released a bud of blood.

Not a great start.

She left the rose dangling from its stem and climbed the remaining steps to the front door. A strong wind whipped around the house and caught her off-guard. For a moment, she considered heading back down the steps to her car and grabbing her jacket, but Linda would be along in a moment with Alex and Phoebe and Emma wanted to ensure she'd opened the house and checked everything was in order before they arrived.

The key slid effortlessly into the lock and the door opened with a long groan. It seemed the hinges needed oiling. Emma grinned like an excited schoolgirl as she took in the wide hallway and the large kitchen diner beyond. The house was cold, and she shivered as she closed the door. It may have been near the end of October, but there had been an unusual cold snap lately, especially in this area of the Lake District. She'd kept an eye on the weather for a few days prior to arriving here. One of the first things she needed to do was locate the boiler and ensure it worked. Her wife enjoyed scalding hot showers every morning and, if she didn't get one, her mood was generally unpleasant for the entire day.

Linda was very different to Emma's ex-husband. Chris had enjoyed cold showers; flicking the hot water to cold at the end for a duration of thirty seconds was, apparently, his way of boosting his immune system.

A lump formed in her throat as she thought about Chris. She'd tried desperately to make things work with him, but over the course of their decade-long marriage, she realised she didn't love him, not in the way he truly deserved. The children had come along early in their relationship, and they had brought so much joy into her life that it felt as if nothing could top the feeling of being a mother.

But then she'd met Linda on a rare night out in Blackpool and her life had spiralled since then. That had been five years ago and now, here she was, divorced from the father of her children and married to the woman of her dreams. It hadn't been an easy five years by any means.

At first, Chris had been horrified to learn that his wife had fallen in love with a woman and had stormed out, leaving her alone with the kids for almost a week, before returning and asking her to tell him everything. Emma didn't know what had happened or who he'd spoken to during that week away, but he'd listened as she'd poured her heart out, sobbing over the fact she felt like a terrible person and begged for his forgiveness. She explained that she'd known she was bisexual almost her entire adult life and had been too afraid to date women, scared what her parents would say. Then she met Chris and had fallen in love with him, but as the years went by, she realised she didn't love him enough to want to spend the rest of her life with him.

Chris had listened patiently, only interrupting to ask her to elaborate a little more on various details. Chris accepted her new life decision and agreed to meet Linda. Emma couldn't believe it. What had she done to deserve such an understanding husband?

Even Alex and Phoebe had accepted Linda as part of the family, although they both refused to call her Mum, which was fine.

Everything was perfect.

And then one day ... it wasn't.

Emma's perfect world crumbled, and she'd been left to pick up the pieces.

But that was then, and this was now.

Cherry Hollow was their new start and the children, although they missed their father, were excited to move to the country and start afresh. At least, she assumed they were excited. Alex, as a teenage boy, rarely communicated anything more than a grunt or a snort, or sometimes she received a half-hearted 'yeah' or 'fine'. Phoebe, on the other hand, had jumped up and down and squealed, exclaiming she wanted a big garden so she could have rabbits, guinea pigs and a dog.

The kitchen diner was calling her name, so Emma headed in that direction first, but as she stepped into the room, she sensed something wasn't quite right. She swivelled her head in the direction of the sink and immediately spotted the reason for her unease; there was water all over the kitchen floor. Emma sighed as she paddled over to the sink and opened the cupboard door underneath. The culprit: a leaking water pipe.

Emma turned the water off using the valve and stood up, surveying the damage. Luckily, the floor was lino, but the water had crept over towards the carpeted area where the dining room would be. It didn't look like there was too much damage, but she needed to get this water soaked up quickly. Emma had brought a few boxes in her car and remembered that one of them held a load of towels and sheets, which would do nicely.

Nothing was going to phase her today, not even a leaking pipe.

Two hours later, Emma had made a considerable dent in unpacking the boxes from the car. She'd mopped up the water with numerous towels, which were now hanging in the garden to dry, and she'd begun to put away some essential kitchen items that she'd brought.

Linda would be along any moment with the suitcases and children in their second car, and then the moving lorry was due to arrive first thing tomorrow morning with all their furniture and general appliances. They'd have to rough it for a night, but that was the whole point of moving house; it was supposed to be fun.

At the sound of wheels crunching against gravel, Emma stopped unwrapping the plates from their paper prisons and ran to the front door, excitement fluttering in her chest at seeing Linda's reaction. She flung the door open just as Linda got out of their white 4x4 and shut the door. Linda stood for several seconds, staring open-mouthed at the house. She didn't notice her wife standing at the top of the steps until Emma spread her arms open and said, 'Well ... what do you think?' Emma positively beamed with pride and happiness.

Linda covered her mouth with her hands to stifle a laugh. 'It's huge! It's wonderful! I can't quite believe all this is ours.'

Emma jogged down the steps and the women hugged and kissed. 'I told you it would be,' replied Emma, squeezing Linda's hands in hers. She loved her wife's hands; delicate yet firm, smooth yet rugged.

Linda smiled and nodded in the direction of the 4x4 behind her. 'Try telling Alex that.'

Emma flicked her eyes over to her teenage son in the front passenger seat. His head was down, the hood to his favourite jacket was up and pulled low over his head, and his eyes were glued to his phone.

'Did he say anything on the drive over?'

'Only to say that the signal out here *sucks*. What time did you arrive? Have you checked out the house properly yet? Any issues?'

Emma was glad about the change of topic. 'Other than a leaky kitchen pipe, it all looks in good order. I turned off the main water supply and cleaned up, so it won't be an issue now. The tools are in the moving lorry, aren't they?'

'Yeah, but I saw a place as I was driving through the town called Fix It All. I'll pop back and get something from there to sort the leak.'

Emma nodded, remembering that she'd seen that business earlier too. 'It can wait till tomorrow.'

'No, it can't. We need running water, Emma.' Linda's deep tone of voice told Emma all she needed to know. What Linda was saying was that *she* couldn't deal without running water for her shower in the morning.

'Okay, fine. You pop into town and leave Alex and Phoebe with me.'

'What do we need to fix the leak?'

'Looks like a new valve or something. I'm not too sure. Maybe the whole pipe needs replacing.'

'I'll take a quick look in a minute and then get going before the shop closes.'

Emma nodded as she opened the passenger door. 'Welcome to your new home, Alex. Hey, Phoebe, there's even a treehouse at the bottom of the garden and a playroom too.'

'Cool!' came a high-pitched squeal.

A second later, the door behind Alex was flung open and, wearing a pink jumper and blue leggings, Phoebe jumped down from the 4x4 and ran up the steps towards the house.

'Be careful you don't trip!' Emma sighed as she watched her daughter wave a hand in the air to show she'd heard. She was already halfway through the house. 'She's going to love it here,' said Emma with a smile.

Linda returned the smile, but it didn't reach her eyes. She walked around to the back of the 4x4 and opened the boot to unload the cases, then carted them towards the house.

'Are you getting out?' asked Emma to her son.

Alex sighed. 'Is the Wi-Fi up yet?'

'No, the Wi-Fi is not up yet and won't be until sometime tomorrow or maybe the day after. It won't kill you to spend a few hours away from your phone.'

'Maybe not, but do you really want to risk it?'

Emma rolled her eyes. 'I'll take the risk. There's nothing I can do about the internet until the suppliers come and install it. Will you come and help me unpack?'

Alex heaved himself out of the car. He towered above Emma by three inches, all gangly with long limbs and messy hair. His clothes looked too big for him. He stared at the house and sighed again.

'I'll help later. I saw some people my age in town as we drove through. I thought I'd go and introduce myself and make some friends.'

'We literally just got here.'

'So?'

'So … Do you need to go and make friends right this second? I'd appreciate some help unpacking and your sister won't be able to help very much.'

'Funny that. See you later, Mum.'

Emma watched as her firstborn child turned his back on her and walked down the road, his head bowed over his phone again. It was a wonder he didn't walk into lampposts more often. Her worst fear was him stepping out in front of a car because he was too engrossed in a TikTok video.

No … that wasn't her worst fear.

Her worst fear was—

'Fuck me, have you seen the size of the garden!'

Her wife's voice echoed from inside the house, causing Emma to laugh. It wasn't often Linda swore. Usually, it was when she was extremely angry or surprised and, by the sound of it, she certainly wasn't angry.

Emma grabbed a suitcase from the boot and hurried up the steps, excited to see her family (minus the grumpy teenager) exploring their new home. As soon as she stepped into the kitchen diner, she dropped the case on the floor and watched Linda as she walked around the garden, brushing her fingers against every plant within reach.

Linda was the more green-fingered of the two of them. Yes, Emma liked to potter about in the garden from time to time, but she usually ended up killing a plant or two, so had left it to Linda to tend to their garden back in Bedford. It hadn't been huge, but Linda had made it a beautiful and inviting space where they could hold family BBQs and gatherings. Although Emma couldn't remember the last time they'd hosted a family BBQ. It had been a couple of years at least. But she couldn't wait to see what Linda would achieve with this garden. Maybe she'd dig a vegetable patch? Linda had always talked about growing her own vegetables one day but had never had the space to be able to do it. In this garden, the possibilities were endless; potatoes, carrots, kale, runner beans …

Linda ran up to Emma and threw her arms around her neck with such vigour that Emma stumbled backwards several paces. 'It's my dream garden. You're amazing. I love you.'

'I told you that you'd change your mind about this place once you'd seen the garden.'

'I still think buying this house without seeing it was risky and crazy, but for the time being you're in the clear.'

'Oh, good! That's a relief.' Emma laughed with her wife.

'Right, I'm going to take a quick look at the kitchen pipe situation and then get into town.'

'If you see Alex hanging around, can you try and convince him to come home and help unpack.'

'I'll try, but I've never been one to perform miracles.'

Emma had just finished putting away the last of the plates when the doorbell rang. Her immediate thought was maybe their new neighbours were popping by to introduce themselves, so she quickly checked her reflection in the oven door before jogging to answer. She'd looked better, but there wasn't time to worry about those dark eye bags and hollow cheeks now.

A man in his mid-to-late-thirties stood on her doorstep holding a bouquet of fresh flowers, and a little blonde girl of around twelve stood next to him. He gave Emma a kind smile, but his face was sullen and the bags under his eyes told Emma he probably hadn't had a decent night's sleep in a while. Probably about the same amount of time that she'd not had one.

'Hi, I'm sorry to disturb you. I know you've just moved in, but Bethany wanted to stop by and say one last goodbye to the house. I'm Sean Walker.'

Emma gasped as the name registered. 'Oh! Hello! It's so lovely to meet you. Yes, please come in.' She stepped aside. Sean handed her the flowers, looking a little awkward as a faint blush rose on his cheeks. 'Thank you,' said Emma, taking them.

Sean nodded and made his way into the kitchen diner. Bethany was still standing on the doorstep, staring at Emma with unblinking eyes.

'Would you like to come in?' asked Emma.

Bethany lowered her head and stepped over the threshold. There was something in the way Bethany held herself, the way she moved, that told Emma she wasn't a particularly happy child. Emma couldn't help but wonder where her mother was and immediately felt a strong tug in her heart at the thought of a little girl being without her mother.

'Can I make you a cup of tea or anything?' asked Emma, following Bethany into the kitchen area where Sean was standing by the patio doors, staring out across the garden. 'I've just unpacked the mugs.'

Sean turned around on the spot. 'Thank you, but no. We can't stay long. We have a couple of hours drive ahead of us down to Manchester.'

'Is that where you're moving to?'

'Yeah, my parents live there. It's where I grew up. Thought Bethany could do with being around family.'

Emma nodded and turned to Bethany. 'My daughter, Phoebe, is playing in the garden. She loves your tree house. Maybe you can show her around it?'

Bethany looked over at her father who nodded. 'Don't be long,' he said.

Emma and Sean watched Bethany walk down to the end of the garden. They stood in awkward silence for ten seconds before Sean sighed heavily and said, 'I'm sorry about Bethany. I didn't want to come back to the house, but she insisted on one last goodbye.'

'It's completely fine. Honestly! She must have had a happy childhood here.' As soon as the words left her mouth, she wondered if they'd been the wrong ones to say because she saw Sean's body tense out of the corner of her eye.

'Yes, well … it was happy until … I'm sure you've already heard.'

Emma shook her head. 'No, I haven't heard anything.' Her heart rate increased.

'It won't be long until you do, thanks to the local gossips in this town, so you may as well hear it straight from me … Bethany's mother, my ex-wife … Amber … She died and this house was the last place Bethany saw her alive.'

A lump formed in Emma's throat as she fought the urge to gasp. She knew it would come across as rude if she did, so she attempted to not react at all, but a question formed on her lips before she could take it back.

'Did she die here?'

It wasn't like she was superstitious about people dying in houses and leaving their ghosts behind, but if Amber had died in this house, its low price made a bit more sense.

'No, she didn't die here, but after she did die, I just wanted the house to sell quickly so I lowered the price and kept my wife's death out of it.'

Emma nodded. 'Of course … I understand. I'm so sorry.' Emma made a mental note not to mention this new piece of information to her own wife, otherwise the phrase 'I told you so' would more than likely turn up in that conversation.

Sean sighed again. His shoulders were hunched forwards, as if it were a huge effort to remain standing upright.

Emma could practically see the weight of the world resting on him, digging him into the ground. She, of course, knew all too well what that felt like.

'Can I ask how—'

But Emma never finished her sentence because Bethany came running through the house. She stopped in front of Emma and, before Emma knew what was going on, the child wrapped her arms around her and squeezed her tight.

Emma's body froze; she didn't quite know how to respond.

The warmth from Bethany's little body seeped into her own skin through her clothes and warmed her heart. She felt tears bubbling under the surface as Bethany pulled away slightly and whispered in her ear, 'I'm sorry.'

Emma wanted to ask the girl what she was sorry for, but the question got stuck in her throat as Bethany continued, 'Don't look under the floorboards in the spare room. You might not like what you find.'

Chapter Two
LINDA
Thursday 26 October 2023 – 13:43 p.m.

Linda's head throbbed as if a hammer was pounding against the inside of her skull as she pulled up outside Fix It All. She'd taken pain relief over an hour ago while on the road, but they hadn't made a dent in numbing the pain.

Her headaches were getting worse. Sometimes, she had a headache on top of a headache that then morphed into a mega migraine. Those days were the hardest to slap on a fake smile and pretend she wasn't living in constant agony. She'd been able to hide her pain and discomfort from Emma, who often lived in her own little world. Usually, a couple of painkillers were enough to dull the misery, though not enough to get rid of it completely, but not today. It seemed today was a bad day. Just as long as she didn't take too many painkillers again. It had been an accident, of course, and she'd been able to call an ambulance before she passed out and they'd rushed her to the hospital. Thankfully, Emma had been at work and, when she'd returned hours later, Linda was tucked up in bed and had been able to pass off her illness as a stomach bug.

Linda couldn't remember the last time she'd been headache free. Often, the pain would travel from her head, down the back of her neck and across the top of her shoulders.

She had her own special name for it … but there was an official diagnosis.

Tension headaches.

That's what the doctor had called it back in Bedford. Apparently, she just needed to relax and do some breathing techniques, which might have helped during the first year, but now, approaching the second year of pain, Linda realised it wasn't as simple as that. She'd told her doctor when they'd started, but not the reason. She couldn't tell anyone the reason because …

It was obvious why she couldn't.

She'd lose everything; her wife, her new home, her family …

The headaches would just have to continue.

In fact, by some twist of fate, the painkillers finally seemed to be doing their job.

The constant pressure and pain were manageable as she swung her legs out of the 4x4 and hopped down to the ground. Moving here would be worth it in the long run, she was sure. Emma was right; it was good to have a fresh start, and maybe Emma would start to feel better too. Maybe things could go back to the way they used to be.

A high-pitched bell signalled her entry into the business. Within a second of stepping over the threshold, a bounding black Labrador charged towards her, tongue lolling, tail wagging.

'Morgan!' came a stern, male voice from somewhere in the back of the building.

Linda leaped backwards just in time to avoid the enormous dog crashing into her. The black tail was wagging so hard that the dog's entire back end was shaking from side to side. It wasn't that she was afraid of them, but dogs (especially those she didn't know) could be temperamental and get over-excited, and that's how accidents happened.

Linda knew Emma longed for a dog to add to their family, and in their previous house she'd been able to use the excuse of not having a big enough garden, but now she'd have to come up with a new excuse … or run the risk of *getting* a dog. Maybe just a small one … like a French Bulldog, or something along those lines.

A man with short brown hair and a strong, chiselled jaw ran towards her and grabbed the dog by its red collar. 'I'm so sorry about that. He's friendly, but Morgan gets a bit over-excited. Morgan, come!'

Linda let out a breath. 'That's okay. He's lovely,' she replied with a forced smile.

The man directed the canine towards the back of the shop and then turned to Linda with a friendly smile. 'I'm guessing you're one of the new residents of the town. I pretty much know everyone in Cherry Hollow.'

Linda chuckled. 'Yes, I'm Linda. My wife, Emma, and I have just moved into the house on Baker Street that was up for sale.' Linda could have sworn she saw a dark shadow pass over the man's face as she spoke the name of the street.

'Lovely to meet you. Welcome to Cherry Hollow. I'm Jordan Evans. I own this business and I'm the local handyman.'

'Ah! Then I'd like to hire you immediately. There's a leaking pipe in the kitchen and I don't have the first clue about fixing it, even though I told Emma I did.'

Jordan laughed. 'I can be over in twenty minutes.'

'You're a lifesaver. Thank you.'

'Don't mention it, and hey, it's on the house. Consider it a welcome gift.'

Linda raised her eyebrows. 'Are you sure? That's wonderful, thank you. Do you need me to give you the exact address?'

Another dark shadow passed across Jordan's face and his smile faltered. 'No, I know the place well.'

'Perfect. See you soon.'

Linda pulled into her new driveway (which was large enough for two cars parked side by side) and turned off the engine. She sat for a few minutes, alone with her thoughts, before heading inside.

Jordan had been a pleasant enough man. He'd smiled and made her feel welcome and was even on his way over right now to fix her leaking kitchen pipe, but there was something off about him. At times, she thought she had a sixth sense for picking up on a person's insecurities, and this house (her house) appeared to be one of Jordan's. But why? Looking up at the handsome building, a cold shiver ran up her spine and her tension headache increased.

As soon as she pushed open the front door, she walked towards the sound of rustling paper and found Emma unpacking a box in the lounge.

'You're back quick! Did you get something to fix the pipe?'

'Yes, I enlisted the help of a handyman.'

'How very un-feminist of you.'

Linda stuck her tongue out at her cheeky wife. 'He will be here in a few minutes.'

'Oh, you're serious? Who is this knight in shining armour?'

'Jordan Evans. He owns Fix It All in town and offered to help free of charge.'

'How lovely.' Emma screwed up a ball of packing paper and threw it in a nearby empty box. 'Oh, by the way, Sean Walker and his daughter popped by to say goodbye to the house just after you'd left. You've only just missed them.'

'The guy who sold us the house?'

'Yes. Bethany, his daughter, seemed like such a lovely girl. She went and played with Phoebe in the garden for a while.'

Linda flicked her eyes to the garden and then back to Emma. 'What did they want?'

'Bethany wanted to say goodbye to the house. Apparently—' Emma stopped and turned away, but not before Linda noticed her cheeks blushing.

'Apparently what?'

'Nothing. Bethany just grew up here so wanted to say goodbye, that's all.'

Linda narrowed her eyes. As well as having the ability to notice someone's insecurities, she could also tell when people were lying. Not all people, but her wife was the easiest person to read. She couldn't say anything though because Emma would overreact and take it the wrong way. It was really time to start seeing a couple's therapist again, but that was an issue for another day.

Chapter Three
JORDAN
Thursday 26 October 2023 – 13:51 p.m.

He watched the door close and let out a long sigh, relaxing his shoulders as best he could. Linda, the new owner of Amber's old house, seemed nice, and he was happy to help her out with the leaking pipe because there was nothing worse than moving into a new house and having something go wrong with it on the first day. It was what his dad would have done to welcome a new resident into the town. His dad had always gone out of his way to help others and, now that he was gone, it was Jordan's turn to continue his legacy.

Jordan had inherited his dad's business after he'd passed away, and now ran it single-handedly. His dad had died of a sudden heart attack one evening after work almost a year ago. He'd been alone at the shop and hadn't been able to reach the phone in time to call for help. Jordan had found him later that night after returning to the shop to look for him. He'd been on the floor, on his back, his face frozen in agony and fear. He'd died alone. All alone.

Jordan blamed himself. If he'd only offered to help him lock up, he would have been by his side when the heart attack had occurred, and he'd have been there to save him. But that night, he'd been distracted and had rushed over to see his girlfriend at the time, who'd also needed his help.

What Jordan needed right now was to hire some help to assist with the paperwork side of things, or at least someone to handle the walk-ins at the reception desk. He was now the front man, the person everyone spoke to when they walked through the door, the man who visited people's houses to fix their leaking taps or busted doors, and yes, the accountant too. He barely had time to sign delivery forms and check inventory, but at least this job kept him busy. He'd learned it all from his dad and had worked here since he was a teenager, although had only started taking it seriously in the past few years. Before that, he'd not cared about the job or helped his dad out without being asked. And when he'd spent a short stint in jail for robbing a local store, he'd not cared about how his dad had coped with the business on his own. He'd been selfish and arrogant and had taken his dad for granted.

Now, it was up to him to keep the business going. It's what his dad would have wanted, and he hoped that, even in death, his dad would be proud of him. At thirty-seven years old, Jordan finally felt as if he had his life under control, to a certain extent. At least his busy schedule stopped him from thinking about—

He looked up at the sound of the bell.

Two people entered: one was the last person he wanted to see, and the other was the only person he wanted to see.

Bethany ran up to him and threw her skinny arms around his neck, squeezing so tight he couldn't draw in a breath at first, but he didn't care and hugged her back, lifting her off the ground with ease.

'Hey, pipsqueak.' He locked eyes with Sean as the girl released her grip from his neck and he placed her back on solid ground.

'Bethany wanted to say goodbye,' muttered Sean. He had his hands stuffed into his pockets and his head drooped forwards. It seemed he didn't want to be here almost as much as Jordan didn't want him here, but this wasn't about what they wanted. Jordan was overjoyed that Bethany had come to say goodbye in person.

Jordan nodded his thanks and turned to Bethany. 'Morgan would have been gutted if you hadn't said goodbye before you left. I'm not sure he ever would have forgiven you.'

'Where is he?'

'I had to put him out the back for a bit. Why don't you go and get him?'

'Okay!'

Bethany sprinted towards the back of the building, through the door behind the reception desk, calling the dog's name.

Jordan stood up straight and faced Sean. 'So, you're off then.'

Sean nodded once. 'Yep. Good riddance to this fucking town.'

'Will you bring Bethany back to visit?'

Sean laughed. 'Why the hell would I do that? There's nothing left for her here. We're never coming back. Ever.'

'I'm here.'

'You're not her family.'

'No, but Amber—'

Sean's head snapped up. 'Don't! Don't you dare say her name in front of me.'

Jordan raised his eyebrows as his whole body flexed, ready for a fight. 'Excuse me? Amber was *my* girlfriend.'

'She was *my* wife!'

'Ex-wife.'

'Whatever.'

'You're the one who cheated on her, Sean.'

'Oh please! She always had a thing for you even when you were an arrogant, angry twat who went around acting like some big tough guy beating up every person who looked at you funny. You're lucky I even let you anywhere near my daughter. It's only because she likes you that I'm allowing her to say goodbye.'

Jordan clenched his jaw. Not so long ago he would have leaped across the room and beaten the shit out of Sean Walker, leaving him with a broken nose and a black eye, or worse, but he wasn't that man anymore.

He wasn't ... *The Bad Man*.

That's what he called the overwhelming surge of anger that would pulse through his body without warning. Years ago, he'd been officially diagnosed with Intermittent Explosive Disorder, brought on by the severe trauma of losing a childhood friend, but Jordan knew it was more than that. It might have had a medical name, but he called it The Bad Man. Plus, he hadn't *lost* a childhood friend. He'd helped cover up his murder, but that was in the past now. He'd put those demons behind him and now he was a changed man.

No, The Bad Man no longer had control of Jordan. Jordan was the one in control and he intended it to remain that way. Nothing Sean said was going to change that.

'Well,' said Jordan, swallowing his anger, 'I appreciate you letting me say goodbye.'

Sean snorted a response and stepped aside as Bethany and Morgan came galloping back into the room.

'Are you and Brooke going to come and visit me soon in my new house?'

Jordan ignored Sean's warning glare. 'Of course! I've always wanted to visit Manchester. And I'll write letters to you all the time and send you pictures of Morgan.'

'No one writes letters anymore. It's 2023.'

'Right. Okay ... then I'll text you.'

'No one sends texts either.'

'Then what do they send?'

'WhatsApp messages.'

'Right ...' Jordan nodded. 'Of course.'

'And we'll Facetime too,' added Bethany.

'Cool.'

'But you do promise you'll visit, right? Dad says we won't be coming back here again.' The disappointment was clear in her voice as she rolled her eyes in her father's direction. Jordan fought hard against the urge to do the same.

'Yes, we'll visit. In fact, I'll call Brooke soon and discuss it with her. We'll let you and your dad settle in first though.'

'And you'll bring Morgan?'

'Of course I will.' Jordan ruffled Bethany's hair. She dodged away, pretending it annoyed her, but her smile told him otherwise.

'I'm going to miss you, Jordan.'

Bethany wrapped her arms around him again and he had to use all the strength in his body not to let the tears flow. Having the love of a child was something he'd never experienced with his own son because he hadn't survived more than a few hours after being born. Alfie had been born prematurely and his tiny lungs hadn't been strong enough. Jordan never brought up that topic of conversation because it hurt too damn much. It was a part of his life he hadn't shared with anyone except Amber. His ex-wife had long since left him and started a new family. He was happy for her. He was. But feeling Bethany clinging onto him now made his heart ache almost as much as losing his son had. A piece of his own heart had died that day too.

'I'm going to miss you more, pipsqueak.'

Bethany looked up at him with her big blue eyes and leaned in close to his left ear. 'Keep an eye on the new family in our house. I have a feeling that things won't go well for them.'

Jordan's mouth went dry. He was used to Bethany saying weird stuff, especially lately, but that had been unexpected. 'Why'd you say that?'

'Because it's still here.'

'What's still here?' whispered Jordan, but he already knew the answer. Like mother, like daughter. He locked eyes with Bethany, willing her to say the words, but she remained silent and shook her head slowly.

'Come on, Beth Bug. We have to go.' Sean's abrupt voice jolted Jordan upright.

Bethany gave him one last solemn look and ran to her father. 'Bye, Jordan. Bye, Morgan.'

And then she was gone.

Just like that.

Sean and Jordan stared at each other, but neither said another word. They didn't need to.

Jordan stared at the closed door for a while, mulling over what Bethany had said. Her words chilled him to the bone. He knew exactly what she meant.

It had been weeks later, after he and Amber had sat side by side on their bench and after they'd finally confessed their true feelings for one another, that Amber had told him the truth. They'd been walking hand in hand along an overgrown path through the local woods.

'I'm glad you decided not to confess,' said Jordan, squeezing Amber's hand tighter. He knew how hard it had been for her to change her mind about confessing her part in hiding the watch that had belonged to Kieran for twenty years and hiding the body of their dead friend at the bottom of the ravine. She'd been adamant it was the right decision for her and her daughter, but, thankfully, her best friend Brooke had been able to talk her out of it, but now Amber seemed distant and withdrawn. The dark shadows under her eyes told a story that no one wanted to hear.

Amber cracked a weak smile. 'Me too,' she whispered.

Jordan hoped she was happy, but it was a daily struggle to read her moods. She appeared distracted most of the time. Yes, she'd smile and laugh, but that smile never reached her eyes, which remained lifeless.

'I feel like there's something you're not telling me,' said Jordan.

Ahead of them on the path, Morgan barked at a mysterious sound in the long grass and then continued on his way, sniffing everything in sight and never missing an opportunity to practise weeing with one back leg cocked. He was maturing and growing every day, no longer a gangly puppy whose paws were too big for him, but now a sleek, adolescent dog. He still had a lot of growing to do, but at least he'd stopped weeing in the house.

Jordan allowed the silence to linger for a few minutes, but then broke it by stepping in front of Amber. He placed his hands on her shoulders and held her eye contact as he spoke.

'Please, tell me. Whatever it is that's eating you up, I want to know. We've been through too much over the past twenty years to spend one more second suffering alone.'

Amber blinked as tears filled her eyes. She shook her head. 'I can't. I don't want to cause trouble, Jordan.'

'You causing trouble? Never.' It was meant as a joke, but neither of them smiled.

'It's still here,' she whispered. Her shoulders trembled beneath his hands.

'What's still here?'

'The Creature.' Amber placed one of her hands over his and squeezed it. 'I didn't confess to the part I played in Kieran's death and the planting of the evidence. I'm still not free from it. You and Brooke are free from your demons and I'm so happy that you are, but I'm in danger and so is Bethany.'

'But Brooke and I didn't confess either. We might be free from our guilt and be able to live our lives now, but I still get moments where anger threatens to overwhelm me. I don't know about Brooke, but I'm sure she still has some issues with The Fear. Our mental health was damaged so severely that maybe we'll never be truly free from our torment.'

'Maybe ... but why is The Creature still hell-bent on destroying me? Why is it still here? Bethany has seen it, you know.'

Jordan frowned. 'I don't understand what Bethany has to do with any of this. The Creature is your issue, not hers. And how could she see it? I thought we figured out that it was just a figment of your imagination due to being sleep deprived for two decades?' Amber had also told him that, years ago, the doctors had diagnosed her with hypnagogic and hypnopompic hallucinations. That had been their answer to what The Creature was, merely strange hallucinations usually seen as a person fell asleep or as they were waking up. They'd never said there was any cause for concern.

They had been wrong.

Amber shook her head. 'I don't know either, but it's still here and it's still haunting me. I can't let it hurt Bethany. I can't, Jordan.'

Jordan's heart ached as he watched Amber sink to the ground in tears, her whole body shaking from the uncontrollable sobs. He bent down next to her just as Morgan came charging up to them, tongue lolling. He jumped on Amber, licking her face, and she laughed through her tears as she stroked the young dog.

Jordan placed his arm around her. 'I promise you. I won't let anything happen to you or to Bethany. I'd rather die. You have my word.'

Jordan picked up the keys to the van and whistled for Morgan to come. Thinking back to the moment when Amber had warned him about The Creature still haunting her filled him with an overwhelming urge to punch something, because he hadn't done what he'd promised her. He hadn't kept her safe. He'd broken his promise.

And now Amber was dead, and he was truly alone.

As he sat down in the driver's seat, his phone vibrated, alerting him to an incoming call. A familiar name flashed at him on the screen, a name he always associated with bad news. He sighed as he swiped up to answer.

'This had better not be bad news.'

'Well, it's not good news,' came the gruff reply of Detective Graham Williams, the local police detective who'd worked on all the high-profile cases in the area, including Kieran's disappearance and death, as well as Amber's. 'It's about Amber's death,' he said. 'We've recently come to believe that she may not have taken her own life.'

'What do you mean?' Jordan inhaled as deeply as he could despite his chest feeling constricted.

'Jordan … I shouldn't be telling you this, but I feel like I owe it to you to tell you the truth. I've been there from the start with all of this. My whole professional career has revolved around you and your friends and what happened all those years ago. I don't want you doing anything stupid or jeopardising the investigation into Amber's death.'

'Wait … you're opening up the investigation again?'

'Yes. We have evidence to suggest that Amber was murdered.'

Chapter Four
EMMA
Thursday 26 October 2023 – 14:15 p.m.

Emma listened as Linda happily hummed her favourite tune while sorting out the suitcases and unpacking clothes, putting them away into the new built-in wardrobes in the master bedroom. She watched Phoebe still playing outside in the treehouse with her dolls and smiled as her excited shrieks and laughter echoed through the house, filling her with the most wonderful warmth. Her heart had ached, physically ached, before coming here after losing someone so special, but now … now things could start to settle down.

They could be happy here.

They *would* be happy here.

She would make sure of it.

Emma smiled as she climbed the winding staircase, carrying a heavy box full of books. She was an avid bookworm and planned to start a book club in the town (or join one if they already had one set up) once she'd gotten to know a few people. It was something she'd always wanted to do but had never had the motivation to do it. She dreamed of having close friends round for tea (or something stronger) of an evening, to chat about and discuss books and maybe start up a heated debate over a controversial topic. She loved a good cosy romance, something that made her feel warm and fuzzy after she finished the last page, but she also used to enjoy a decent thriller, something that was fast-paced and kept her glued to the page long into the night. Emma was a mood reader, not choosing her next read based on what the most popular book was at the time, but instead based on how she felt. Lately, she'd needed those happy, cosy feelings that came from romantic comedies. She hadn't picked up a dark, disturbing thriller in nearly two years. Maybe it was time to start, but thrillers were usually full of stories of missing children, dead siblings or murdered spouses. Emma shuddered at the thought. Maybe she wasn't ready quite yet …

It seemed Linda had already assigned the rooms upstairs. The largest room was obviously the master bedroom, full of light with blue walls and a spacious en suite (what a luxury!). Phoebe's room was the smaller one at the front, which had a little built-in wardrobe painted pink inside, and Alex's room would be the one at the back of the house, the one furthest from everyone else.

There was also a fourth bedroom. Emma kicked open the door to this room, which would work nicely as an office and library. Eventually, she'd find another job and perhaps work from home. She missed working, but her previous job as a Human Resources Administrator hadn't allowed her to work from home, so she'd quit. Well … maybe she hadn't technically *quit*; more like, she'd been coerced into taking redundancy. But that was fine because now she had a generous pay out, which would last them for a few more months until she could get back on her feet.

Bending her knees and performing a squat, she placed the box on the floor and then stood up straight, rubbing her lower back. She wasn't as fit as she used to be, having given up on exercise two years ago, so she often noticed new aches and pains that shouldn't be there in her mid-thirties.

She turned in a circle, staring at the bare walls, imaging shelves and shelves of books colour coordinated, or maybe arranged by genre or author. Just another fifteen boxes of books to go, but they'd arrive in the lorry tomorrow. She'd only brought her special edition books with her in the car, just in case they got damaged en route. She hadn't trusted the moving men with her precious sprayed-edge and signed collections.

Emma turned to begin her trip back downstairs and then stopped as she remembered what Bethany had said earlier. Was this the spare room she had spoken about or was it another of the rooms? Phoebe's room perhaps, or Alex's? She scanned the floor, but there were no boards on show due to the cream carpet.

Bethany's words echoed in her mind. 'Don't look under the floorboards in the spare room. You might not like what you find.'

Had she hidden something inside this house? Why would she do that? And if she had, then what could she possibly have hidden … and why wouldn't Emma like it? Surely it had nothing to do with her. She was a stranger after all, and Bethany couldn't possibly have known she'd move to this house.

A loose corner of carpet in the far-right corner of the room caught Emma's eye. Her heart skipped a beat and thudded hard in her chest, causing her to lose her breath for a moment. She took a step closer to the loose carpet …

No.

No. No. No. No.

She wasn't going to get caught up in some silly, childish prank, which was probably exactly what it was, after all. Bethany seemed like a switched-on, serious young girl, but she was still a child, and maybe she'd just wanted to scare Emma a little. The girl obviously had a deep connection to the house. It was the last place she'd seen her mother alive.

Emma left the room with the vague idea of suggesting to Linda to rip up all the carpets on the top floor to reveal the lovely floorboards underneath. Maybe she'd hire that handyman from the store who was coming over to fix the pipe …

The sound of crunching gravel alerted her to the arrival of said handyman. Emma jogged down the stairs and met him at the front door with a friendly smile. She heard a dog whining and peered past the man and saw a beautiful black Labrador staring longingly out of the window of the van, tongue lolling out the side of his mouth. His breath was causing fog to appear on the window.

Emma chuckled. 'You can bring him in with you if you like,' she said, nodding towards the vehicle.

'You sure? He's a bit of a whirlwind. He likes to break stuff.'

'The garden's big enough. My daughter would love to play with him.'

'Okay thanks, as long as you're sure.'

Emma watched as he went back to the van, unlocked the door and freed the dog from its metal prison. The Labrador bounded straight up to her, tail wagging faster than she'd have thought possible.

'Oh my goodness, he's gorgeous. What's his name?'

'Morgan.'

'And you must be Jordan. I'm Emma. You met my wife earlier. Thank you so much for coming to help.' Emma ruffled the dog's fur and showed Jordan into the house.

'No problem at all. It's always a nightmare when things go wrong on day one of a house move.' Jordan paused at the door for a split second before stepping inside. He headed straight for the kitchen, clearly knowing his way around. Maybe he'd known Sean and Amber well.

'Linda! Your handyman's here!' Emma called up the stairs. She then went to the kitchen where she found Jordan with his head in the cupboard under the sink.

Morgan darted through her legs, straight outside and relieved himself on the grass. Emma heard a squeal of delight and watched as her daughter began playing with the dog, but he didn't seem to want to play fetch with her, happier instead sniffing the bushes and running around her in circles.

Emma's attention turned back to Jordan. 'Have you lived in Cherry Hollow long?' she asked, immediately cringing at how corny her small talk sounded.

'All my life,' came the quick reply.

'Did you know the previous owners of this house at all?'

Jordan banged his head as he came out from under the sink. 'You could say that.' There was a tightness to his voice that told Emma he didn't want to continue talking about it, so she switched tact.

'Where's the best place to meet people here?'

Jordan grabbed a spare part from his toolbox. 'Well, the community centre's a good place to start. There's a coffee morning each week on a Saturday at ten. Maybe you could pop by this week to take a break from unpacking. I'm sure everyone would love to meet you.'

'Perfect. Thank you. My son, Alex, is already searching out people his own age somewhere in town.'

'I'm sure he'll fit right in. I had a great childhood here until ...' Jordan seemed to realise he'd said something wrong and quickly turned back to his work. 'There you go. All done,' he said a few seconds later once he'd tightened the nut around the pipe.

'Wow, that was quick work. Are you sure we can't pay you for your time?'

'Not at all. Happy to help.' Jordan nodded at her with another tight smile, whistled for the dog and was gone from the house within thirty seconds, leaving Emma somewhat speechless and confused at his strange manner.

Later that evening, Emma ordered pizza from the local takeaway for dinner because the kitchen utensils weren't in the boxes they'd brought and there hadn't been any time to buy fresh food. There wasn't even anywhere to sit to eat their meal, so she, Linda and Phoebe sat cross-legged on the lounge floor with the various pizza boxes spread out in front of them. They'd have to sleep on their respective bedroom floors in their sleeping bags tonight too, which Phoebe found extremely exciting.

'It will be like camping!' she exclaimed, tucking into her Hawaiian pizza, her favourite.

'It will be exactly like camping,' replied Emma with a smile.

Linda took a bite of her spicy pepperoni pizza and sighed with pleasure. 'Wow, they do good pizza here. Screw Dominoes.'

Emma nodded with her mouth full. 'It's a shame Alex is missing it.'

'Did you message him to come home for dinner?'

'An hour ago.'

Linda sighed and shook her head. 'I hope moving here will be good for him.'

'Me too. We just have to give him more time,' said Emma, placing her right hand over Linda's arm and squeezing gently.

'How much more time do we need to give him? He barely says two words to us and when he does, he doesn't even look us in the eye.'

Emma glanced over at Phoebe who seemed oblivious to the way the conversation had taken a more serious turn. She envied her daughter in a way. What she would give to be a child again and not have any worries or issues. All Phoebe cared about were her dolls and playing and learning exciting things at school. Speaking of which, Emma made a mental note to pop into town tomorrow and visit the local school. She researched it online before visiting the school to meet the headteacher and was satisfied with the exceptional OFSTED rating. Both her children had been accepted into the new term, albeit slightly late. They would start after Halloween.

While Emma chewed a mouthful of pizza, she heard the front door open and close, which was followed by footsteps down the hall. Emma and Linda looked at each other at the same time and raised their eyebrows.

'The prodigal son returns,' Emma said to Alex. 'Your pizza's getting cold.'

Alex kicked off his shoes and shrugged out of his jacket, casually throwing everything in the corner. He then slumped down next to Phoebe and grabbed a pizza slice. Emma and Linda held their breaths, waiting to see if he would engage them in a conversation of his own accord and then, as if by magic, he did.

'I met a kid my age in town, and he told me that, apparently, something weird happened in this town twenty-odd years ago.'

Linda choked on her mouthful of pizza and Emma froze mid-chew, not because of what he had said, but because it was the highest amount of words he'd uttered in a single sentence in ... Emma couldn't even remember how long. She'd almost forgotten what his voice sounded like.

'What happened?' asked Linda. She looked at Emma and they both smiled, delighted that he was initiating a conversation for once and not the other way around. Normally it was like trying to get blood from a stone.

'Well, apparently, some kid called Kieran disappeared twenty-five years ago and his best friends were the last ones to see him. The kid I met showed me a newspaper article about it. Some random journalist came here and wrote a story on it. Turns out, one of Kieran's best friends murdered him and hid his body and the rest of them never spoke to each other until five years ago when one of them confessed to the whole thing. Apparently, he pushed Kieran into a ravine. And the woman who used to live in this house also jumped into the ravine and died, so I'm going there tomorrow to check it out. It sounds cool.' The entire speech had been spoken on a single breath and, at first, Emma hadn't managed to take in exactly what he'd said, but clearly Linda had as her mouth dropped open, and a small piece of masticated pizza fell out.

'She took her own life! That's awful. I just assumed she and her husband had split up and that's why they were selling the house. Emma, did you know about this?'

Emma gulped back a lump in her throat. 'Um, no, I didn't. It's the first I'm hearing of it.' It was partly true. Sean hadn't said anything about his wife ending her own life and she certainly hadn't known anything about a suspicious death before she'd bought the house.

'What happened to the person who confessed to killing that boy?' asked Linda, clearly enthralled yet shocked by the story.

'He jumped into the ravine too. I'm telling you, that place must be cursed or something. There's even talk of some sort of creature haunting it.'

'Okay, now that's just ridiculous,' scoffed Linda, picking up a new slice of pizza. There was a moment of silence and then she asked, 'What sort of creature?'

Alex spoke with his mouth full. 'Dunno, but if you visit the ravine, apparently it can make you jump into it.'

'I'd rather we didn't talk about ... *ending one's life* ... in front of young ears.' Emma tilted her head in the direction of her daughter. Phoebe, luckily, was more interested in feeding her dolls some pieces of pineapple that she'd picked off her pizza.

Alex merely rolled his eyes and continued, 'Three people have died in that ravine. One of the friends left and never came back … Brooke somebody, but the other friend still lives here. Some people still suspect him, but others believe his story. Jordan Evans. He works at some plumbing place in town.'

Linda choked on her pizza again. 'Oh my God! Jordan … the nice man who came to fix our pipe earlier? Are you serious?'

Alex laughed as he bit into his second slice, the first having been practically inhaled at lightning speed. 'He's not the murderer. I'm sure he's nice enough, although apparently a few years ago he had a bit of a temper on him. Everyone hated him, but now he's like the nicest guy in town and helps everyone. His girlfriend was the woman who used to live here.'

Linda frowned. 'I thought she was married.'

'I guess they got divorced,' replied Alex with a shrug.

Linda blew out a long breath. 'Yeesh, and here I was thinking we had moved to a quaint little town where nothing ever happened that was remotely interesting. How do you know all this?'

'I told you. The kid in town told me and showed me a newspaper article about it.'

'And who is this *kid*?'

'Just a boy from school.'

'It might all be rubbish,' interrupted Emma. 'Gossip can spread fast, especially in a small town like this. Sometimes journalists write this stuff to try and bring in tourists.'

'Well, I'm just saying what I heard and read. I'm going to check out the ravine tomorrow.'

'Please be careful,' said Linda.

'I will. Thanks for dinner.' Alex got up from the floor and brushed the crumbs off his top. 'Is the internet sorted yet?'

'No, not yet,' said Emma with a sigh. Alex groaned. 'It's not exactly a priority at the moment, Alex.'

'Maybe not to you.'

'Why don't you help your sister with her reading tonight instead?'

'Pass.' With that, Alex walked out of the room and headed upstairs, leaving his shoes and jacket on the floor where he'd left them.

'Well,' said Linda, once he'd left the room, 'he went from forming full, complete sentences to his usual one-word answer, but I'd still say it was a success, despite the morbid topic of conversation. I can't believe that the woman who lived here took her own life. What was her name again?'

'Amber Walker,' replied Emma.

A knot formed in her stomach and stayed with her for the rest of the evening.

Chapter Five
BROOKE
Friday 27 October 2023 – 05:58 a.m.

The grey light of the morning peered through the blackout curtains of Brooke's London studio flat, which she'd lived in since moving to the capital four years ago. This rental was situated on the top floor of a dilapidated building which should have been demolished years ago, but had somehow managed to pass its inspections year after year. It was all she could afford. It was small, and smelled slightly damp, but to her it was merely a place to sleep. She spent most of her time working or outside experiencing the busy London lifestyle, having spent two decades cooped up in her childhood home in Cherry Hollow, a prisoner to The Fear. It's what she used to call her crippling terror of the outside world, otherwise more professionally known as agoraphobia. It had started when she was almost thirteen, after the incident with Kieran.

It was a time in her life she didn't like to think about, especially now that she'd managed to escape The Fear. She loved living her life in the capital city and was working for a small television company and hoped to progress her career to bigger and better things.

Brooke hadn't returned to Cherry Hollow since she'd left, not even to visit her best friend, Amber. Not even when she'd received the devastating news that Amber had died; worst of all, that she'd ended her own life. Brooke had done her best to distance herself from her past. She loved her parents, and she'd loved Amber and Jordan, but they reminded her too much of the trauma she'd suffered over the years. Leaving Cherry Hollow had been the best decision she'd made. Yet every morning she woke up with a solid lump in her throat and a heavy heart that she quelled by going for a run.

Brooke sat up in bed just as her alarm erupted, alerting her to the fact it was six o'clock and time for her said run, a routine she'd adopted almost straight away. She could have worked out inside her flat, but she found it more freeing and enjoyable to run outside, especially around Hyde Park. If she stuck close to the perimeter, she could run for three miles around it and then, depending on the time, she could do another loop and return for a shower before heading to work.

Putting on her running trainers, which were getting a bit scruffy, she flinched when her phone went off again. Had she forgotten to turn off the alarm? Leaning over, she saw a friendly name appear on the screen and she couldn't help but smile. Since Amber's death, they'd spoken a lot more on the phone, sometimes long into the night. It was nothing romantic, but their friendship was evolving and there wasn't a day that went by when she didn't think about him and how he was doing.

'Jordan? Do you realise what time it is?'

'Don't give me that. You're always up at the crack of dawn. Did I catch you before you went for your run this time?'

'Barely. To what do I owe the pleasure of this early morning call? It's not like you to be up this early.'

'I've been awake all night for a couple of reasons.'

'The first one being?'

'They've gone.'

Brooke relaxed her shoulders and sighed. 'Ah. I'm so sorry, Jordan. Did Sean at least let you say goodbye to Bethany?'

'Yes, but he wasn't exactly shy about letting me know how much he hates my guts.'

'That's expected, I suppose.'

'What, because he thinks I stole his wife?'

'Something like that. You've got to face it, Jordan. You and Sean will never see eye to eye and get along. And you didn't steal her, silly. Sean cheated on her with a woman who worked for him, and you were there for Amber when she needed you.' Brooke gulped back the solid lump in her throat at the mention of her name.

A few seconds of silence passed.

'I miss her,' said Jordan in a low voice.

'I know, so do I. Every day.'

'There's another reason I couldn't sleep last night. I had a call from Detective Williams yesterday afternoon. He told me there's been some new evidence to suggest that Amber didn't take her own life.'

Brooke almost dropped her phone. 'W-What?'

'He didn't give me any other details. He said he shouldn't have even told me, but he thought I deserved to know … He thinks she was murdered.'

Brooke's stomach dropped and nausea threatened to overwhelm her. She covered her mouth with her free hand and attempted to push down the anxiety that was now rising in her body.

No … Not today.

'Brooke, did you hear what I said?'

'Y-Yes, I'm sorry. I did. I don't know what to say. Do the police have any leads?'

'If they do, the detective didn't say, and I doubt his generosity extends that far.'

'Who would want to kill Amber? She was the most generous, likeable, and the gentlest person in the world—'

'Who helped cover up a murder twenty-five years ago,' added Jordan.

'Okay, well we all did that, didn't we? Do you think this has something to do with that … with Kieran's death, I mean?'

'I have no idea.'

Brooke allowed the silence to build again. She was about to ask another question, but Jordan broke the silence by saying, 'There's something else that's happened too. A new family has moved into her old house. Emma and Linda. They have a teenage son and a young daughter. I went to the house yesterday to fix a leaking pipe in their kitchen. It was so weird being back in that house. I could almost feel her presence. It was weird and gave me the creeps.'

'Maybe you did. After what we all went through a few years ago, it's entirely possible that she's still here with us.'

'I don't believe in ghosts, Brooke.'

'No, maybe not …'

'Also, Bethany said something to me before she left. She said that it was still here. Not *she*. She didn't mean her mother. She said *it*.'

The unmistakable slither of fear crept higher up her body, reaching the back of her neck as she heard that word.

It.

But that wasn't what Amber had called it.

'The Creature,' whispered Brooke, clutching the phone tighter to her ear.

'Yeah.'

'But what's it still doing here? Amber's gone and now so has Bethany.'

'Beats me. Have you … I mean … is your issue definitely gone?'

'Yes. In fact, I can't wait to get outside every day. I barely spend any time in my flat.'

'Good. That's good.'

'What about you?'

'Well, yesterday I certainly felt like beating the crap out of Sean, but that's no surprise, considering the guy is a complete twat. I didn't even raise my voice, so I think it's safe to say that I have The Bad Man under control.'

'So, why's The Creature still hanging around?'

'Maybe it has something to do with the new family who've moved into Amber's old house.'

'You think?'

'I don't know, but if The Creature is hanging around that house for some reason, they're all in danger. You don't happen to have any holiday to use up, do you?'

Brooke laughed, but then her face fell as it dawned on her what he was asking her to do. 'No, you know I can't go back there.'

'Amber has been murdered, Brooke. *Murdered.* You didn't even come back for her funeral. You're supposed to be her best friend.'

'Are you trying to make me feel bad on purpose?'

'Is it working?'

Brooke sighed. 'Yes. But you have to understand what you're asking me to do. You want me to go back there, to that place I spent twenty years trapped in. I haven't set foot inside that town since I left. I can't go back to that house. I can't stay with my parents.'

'Then stay with me … Please?'

'And do what? What do you want us to do when I get there?'

'Figure out why The Creature is still haunting us and who killed Amber.'

Brooke sighed heavily and stared towards the ceiling. Her brain was shouting no, but her heart was screaming yes. Unfortunately, her brain won, and she shook her head slowly as she blinked away tears.

'I don't think I can do it, Jordan. I can't come back to Cherry Hollow. I'm sorry.' She was afraid Jordan might explode back at her, but he didn't. She heard him sigh at the end of the line. She could tell he was disappointed in her.

'It's okay. I understand.'

'I'm sorry,' she whispered.

'Don't apologise. It was wrong of me to ask such a big thing from you. You're the lucky one to have escaped from this place when you did. I shouldn't be trying to drag you back under. I'm sorry.'

'You're still going to try and figure it all out, aren't you?'

'Yes.'

'And there's nothing I can say to make you change your mind?'

'No.'

Brooke shook her head. 'Okay, well if you need anything, call me, okay? Day or night. If you need to talk things through. I may not be there with you, but I can help discuss things and come up with ideas.'

'Okay. I will, thanks. Oh … and one more thing. I promised Bethany that once she was settled, we'd visit her.'

'You think Sean's going to let you know their exact address?'

'No, but Bethany will.'

'Okay. Yes, of course I'll go and visit her with you. Look, I have to go and get out running or I'll be late for work. We'll chat soon, okay?'

'Bye, Brooke.'

'Be careful, Jordan. Bye.'

Brooke pressed the disconnect button and immediately switched to her music app, pressing play on her favourite running album as she fished her earphones out of the cabinet beside her bed and placed them in her ears. She tied her blonde hair back with a black elastic band and headed for the door.

It wasn't until she reached the gates of Hyde Park that she stopped and performed a few stretches after her brief warmup jog. It hadn't been the nicest of starts to the morning. The weather was overcast and grey, which did nothing for her state of mind after that phone call. Guilt was already gnawing away at her insides, the anxiety brimming just under the surface.

Running would help.

As she started jogging, Brooke thought back to the last time she'd seen Amber. She tried to block their last conversation from her mind, but it was impossible and played out like a movie in her head, as clear as if she were watching it in high definition.

Amber was visiting Brooke in London for a girly weekend, and it was almost time for Amber to return home. They were having coffee at Brooke's favourite coffee shop, which was just around the corner from her flat. It was September 2022, and the air was still warm enough to sit outside in the courtyard without a jacket. Brooke loved to feel the sun on her face and, while she waited for Amber to return from using the facilities, she closed her eyes and smiled as the warmth lit up her cheeks.

'Here we go.' Brooke opened her eyes just as a waitress set the tray on the glass table.

'Thank you,' said Brooke.

The waitress walked away and, a few seconds later, Amber arrived at the table. The weekend break had invigorated her as she was much bubblier than when she'd arrived, but as Amber sat down at the table and reached for a coffee cup, Brooke noticed her hands were shaking, which Amber then attempted to cover up by setting the cup down as quickly as possible.

'Wow, this coffee smells amazing,' said Amber, leaning forwards and inhaling the aromas.

'Well, they export the beans fresh from Colombia, I'll have you know,' replied Brooke, pretending to put on a fake posh accent.

'Oh, really? And what's this amazing coffee called?'

Brooke shrugged. 'No idea, but it tastes good though, right?'

The women shared a laugh and spent the next few seconds in silence while they poured the coffee from the cafetiere and added milk and sugar from the array of pots.

'So,' said Brooke, leaning back in her chair, 'what do you think of my neck of the woods?'

Amber glanced around at the already bustling London streets. 'It's ... different than Cherry Hollow, that's for sure.'

'Just a bit.'

'How do you sleep with all this noise? Then again, I'm one to talk seeing as I spent twenty years unable to sleep while living in a town that's so quiet at night you can hear mice scuttling in the bushes.'

Brooke watched as Amber took a sip of her coffee. Her friend looked as if she had the weight of the world on her shoulders. 'Is everything okay?'

Amber smiled. 'Yes, of course it is.'

'It's just that we've spoken about your divorce, we've spoken about Jordan, and Bethany, but we haven't actually spoken about you. Is everything okay with you, Amber?'

Amber's shoulders dropped a fraction of an inch. 'I'm ... not good.'

'Talk to me.'

'I'm not sure I can.'

'Remember when you knocked on my bedroom door after twenty years and dragged me out of my room for the first time and told me that you were going to help me?'

Amber's lips twitched into a smile. 'Yes.'

'Then this is me returning the favour. Let me help you.'

Amber held her friend's gaze for a moment. 'I want to confess.'

Brooke stopped her coffee cup just before she took a sip. 'Amber, I thought we went over this four years ago when you originally had this idea. Jordan and I talked you out of it and explained what a crazy idea it was. And guess what, it's still a crazy idea, and a dangerous one too. You'd be risking everything. You'd get put in jail. Sean would get custody of Bethany.'

'I know that, but it's still here, Brooke. The Creature is still here.'

Brooke placed her cup on the table. 'I don't understand. Jordan and I haven't had any problems with our ... issues.'

'I think it's because I feel guilty that Tyler took the blame for us. I wish he'd spoken to us about it first.'

'You shouldn't feel guilty, Amber. Tyler made his choice, and it saved us all.'

'But he shouldn't have had to make that choice alone.'

Brooke sighed, trying but failing to hide the annoyance from her voice as she spoke. 'The fact that you'd rather put your own guilty conscience ahead of your daughter is something I'm really struggling to accept.'

'This isn't about me,' snapped Amber. 'This is about Bethany. I'd be doing it for her. She's already mentioned seeing it and I can't risk it hurting her. She's been through so much already and is now struggling with school.'

'What if The Creature has nothing to do with you anymore?'

Amber tilted her head to one side. 'What do you mean?'

'I mean … what if … what if it's not here for you and you're the one that's holding onto it? Jordan and I have accepted what's happened. We've realised it's no longer in our control and there's nothing we can do about it now. The Bad Man and The Fear have gone. If you move on and accept that what Tyler did is final and nothing you do will bring him back, then The Creature will leave. You're the one that's keeping it alive, Amber. You're the one who's putting your daughter at risk. I'm sorry to be so harsh, but it's the truth and I can't just sit around and let you dig up the past and put everyone in jeopardy.'

Amber sat up straighter. 'You mean put you in jeopardy. You haven't even been back to Cherry Hollow since you left.'

'No. This isn't about me. I've dealt with my demons and put them behind me. It's about time you did the same.' Brooke stood up, accidentally knocking into the table and spilling her coffee. Amber reached out to grab her hand, but Brooke flinched away. 'Please, Amber, why can't you just leave things in the past where they belong? We went through enough.'

Amber stood up and cried as she said, 'I can't Brooke. I can't live with myself anymore.'

Brooke turned away from her friend without uttering another word.

That was the last time she saw Amber.

A few months later, she was gone.

Chapter Six
LINDA
Friday 27 October 2023 — 07:31 a.m.

She woke up with a stiff neck and an aching back, thanks to camping on the floor in a sleeping bag. Gone were the days when Linda could spread out on a random pull-out sofa or find a spare corner of a room to curl up in and sleep (a story from her university days). Despite her ageing body groaning in protest, she had slept solidly. She'd always been a good sleeper, able to sleep anywhere, often drifting off on the sofa during a film, something that annoyed Emma to no end, but the fact they'd recently moved to a new house was bound to play on her mind. Apparently not though. She hadn't even thought about the strange story Alex had told them last night, about the woman who used to live here taking her own life by jumping into the local ravine. But it was the first thing she thought about when she opened her eyes, though she didn't dwell on it.

The second thing she thought about was having a hot shower in her new home.

Linda knew Emma would already be up and doing whatever she did early in the mornings. Today was the day all the furniture would arrive along with the rest of their boxes and possessions, so they would no doubt be busy sorting out the house all day, which was a good thing because Linda liked to keep busy. It stopped her from mulling over the past and overthinking things, which usually caused her headaches to worsen, making it difficult to focus.

Speaking of headaches …

Linda let out a soft moan as the dull ache crept up the back of her neck and over the top of her head. It slithered down and over her eyes and settled there. Sometimes it felt as if a hand was trying to suffocate her. Linda fought against the urge to close her eyes and keep them closed forever.

There was no escaping it …

She started her new job in a few days. She'd managed to grab the only job that was going – working as a barista at a local coffee shop called The Bean Café. She'd been hired straight after the Zoom interview. She'd been interviewed by the manager, a woman called Hayley, who looked young enough to be her daughter (if she'd had her at sixteen). No, it wasn't a glamorous job, nor was it what she'd dreamed of doing when she was a little girl, but it would pay the bills until Emma got back on her feet.

And she would get back on her feet one day.

One day soon …

Hopefully …

Linda scored her shower a seven out of ten. The water pressure could have been stronger and the water a little hotter. It steamed up the bathroom mirror, which had been left hanging above the sink by the previous owners. A foggy mirror was always a good sign of a decent shower temperature.

Linda wiped the condensation away with her hand and, as she did, a black shape emerged behind her. Her breath caught in her throat and she spun around on the spot, clutching the tiny towel she'd packed against her naked body.

What the hell was that?

Her heart rate spiked.

She could have sworn it was …

But no, it couldn't have been.

It must have been a strange shadow. Her own shadow, perhaps.

'The moving people are here!' shouted Alex from downstairs. 'Bye!'

Linda cursed under her breath at the lack of willingness to help from that boy. He wasn't her biological son, but he may as well have been. They'd been through a lot. When she'd first met him, he had just turned eleven and, although he had his moody moments, he was a lot more polite and pleasant to be around than he was now. Then again, could she really blame him for acting out after what he'd been through over the past two years? After what they'd *all* been through. No young boy on the cusp of manhood should have to witness such an awful ordeal.

Forgetting about the weird black shape in the mirror, Linda got dressed without drying herself properly into her usual uniform of jeans and a t-shirt and jogged down the stairs to meet the moving company at the door. There were only two men on the team, but both seemed fit and up for the job.

'Can I make you a cup of tea or coffee?' she asked, mainly because she was going to make a strong coffee for herself anyway.

'Two teas please, milk and sugar in both. Many thanks.' The older of the men nodded his head at her and then they both walked back down the front steps to the large lorry that was parked at the end of the driveway.

'I can move our cars if you like so you can bring the lorry closer.'

'That won't be necessary, ma'am.'

Linda cringed at the phrase. *Ma'am.* Who the hell called women that anymore? Clearly, he was old-fashioned or just trying to be polite.

A strong wind whipped around the house and straight through the open front door. Linda shivered and struggled against the gust to close it. She still hadn't seen Emma this morning. Maybe she'd left already to visit the school, like she said she wanted to do first thing today.

Luckily, Linda knew she wouldn't have to do any humping and dumping of the boxes. The moving men had labelled them all clearly and were already traipsing in and setting them down in the various rooms. They'd laid out a sturdy mat on the hall floor to protect the cream carpet, which Linda was thankful for. She didn't want to imagine how much scrubbing it would take to get out trampled-in dirt from a cream carpet.

She flicked on the coffee machine and filled up the kettle for the two teas. She'd insisted on bringing those two appliances with them. She couldn't function without coffee. A hot shower and a cup of coffee. That was what she needed every morning to survive.

That, and ... one other thing.

She popped her head up to check where the men were and then, happy they were out of sight, reached into the back of the cupboard underneath the sink for her secret stash, which she'd managed to smuggle in yesterday when Emma wasn't looking.

Linda topped up her coffee with a splash of vodka and hid the bottle again. She was running low, so a trip to the shop would be in order soon. The warmth of the coffee and the sharpness of the vodka numbed her tongue and she instantly felt more relaxed after her fright in the bathroom earlier.

Right … Time to get on with the day.

Three hours later, the moving men were on a break. They told her they'd be finished in another three hours. The house looked like a bomb sight with stacks of boxes piled in every possible corner, but it was nice to see the furniture in the rooms.

A glass coffee table now stood proudly next to the grey corner sofa, which took up the entire back wall of the lounge. The large, flat-screen television was propped up against the wall opposite, ready to be hung. After Phoebe had managed to knock it over once several years ago, she knew Emma now liked it to be mounted on the wall out of reach. Linda's pride and joy, a Queen Anne Chesterfield Wingback chair in oxblood red, dominated the room with its presence. It was the only piece of furniture that belonged solely to her. Everything else had originally belonged to Emma, but now they were married, she guessed she owned it all too. Sometimes she still found it strange to think that she was married. When she'd realised she was gay, back in her teenage years, she imagined she'd never be able to get married the way a man and a woman usually did, but times had changed. And here she was. A married woman.

And the best thing was that people barely blinked an eye when she told them she had a wife. Yes, there were the odd few who raised an eyebrow or stuttered over their next word, but overall she felt completely accepted for who she was and had never been ashamed of herself. Never.

When she first met Emma, she knew she was the woman she wanted to spend the rest of her life with. Yes, it was a cliché, but it had been love at first sight for Linda. Of course, back then Emma had been married to Chris and hadn't yet come out as bisexual, so they'd started out as friends, but there had certainly been a spark of something between them.

During their first meeting at a club in Blackpool, they'd swapped numbers and danced the night away. Linda had wanted to kiss her right there on the dancefloor, but Emma had been cautious. Alcohol had allowed her inhibitions to flow, and Emma had grabbed Linda at the end of the night and kissed her as they had said goodbye. The next morning, they started texting and then … their relationship bloomed from there.

Linda had never pressured Emma to come out, never pushed her into leaving her husband. It had happened naturally once Emma had realised she no longer loved Chris. Linda had never meant to break up a family, but if she hadn't then she wouldn't be here today. Maybe things had a way of working out for the best …

Linda couldn't lose what she had fought so hard for.

Not now … Her secret would have to remain hidden.

Linda was about to open another box of lounge 'stuff' when there was a knock at the front door. She guessed it was the moving men back from their break but was taken by surprise when she opened the door to find two women of around her own age standing on the doorstep.

One of them, the lady with short brown hair cut into a neat bob with heavily mascaraed eyes, was holding a beautiful autumn bouquet of flowers and ferns.

The other, a larger woman wearing stylish workout clothes, was clutching a basket filled with different items, including bread and milk and cheese.

'Oh!' Linda exclaimed, placing a hand over her heart.

The woman with the bob smiled widely, showing off her perfectly straight teeth. 'Hello! My name's Trisha Sharp—'

'And I'm Lucy Forrester,' added the other woman.

'And we just wanted to welcome you and your family to the neighbourhood. We weren't sure if you'd managed to get out and about for supplies yet, so we brought a few things along. And these flowers are ones I picked from my own garden.'

Linda gasped. 'How lovely! Thank you so much. That's so generous of you. I'm Linda and my wife's name is Emma. We have a teenage son called Alex and—'

'Oh! My son is called Alex too! How lovely!' said Trisha. 'We'll have to get them together. My Alex is seventeen.'

'Our Alex is sixteen.'

'How lovely. Did you say your wife's name was Emma?'

Linda's stomach tightened. Maybe Trisha would be one of those rare people who raised an eyebrow or made some sly comment about gay people. 'Yes, that's right. She's not here at the moment. I think she's popped into town.'

Trisha's jaw twitched as she attempted a forced smile. 'We've never had a gay couple live in the town before … not that I know of anyway. How lovely.'

Linda saw Lucy subtly kick Trisha in the shin and all three women smiled awkwardly.

Lucy cleared her throat. 'By the way, I have a daughter called Harriet who's also sixteen. You probably don't know this yet, but there's a coffee morning on a Saturday at the community centre, which is on the main high street. You can't miss it. You should pop by tomorrow and I'll introduce you to everyone.'

'Thank you. That would be great. Actually, I have heard of the coffee morning. Jordan mentioned it too.'

'You've met Jordan Evans already?' asked Trisha.

'Yes. He came to fix a kitchen pipe. It was leaking.'

'What a fine man he is. Well, *now* at least. He never used to be.'

Linda frowned. 'What do you mean?' Linda's memory flashed back to the previous evening and what Alex had said about Jordan and how he'd had a bit of a temper a few years ago.

Trisha lowered her voice as she spoke, despite there not being another person around. 'Well, you didn't hear it from me, but Jordan Evans was as bad as they came. He was a nasty piece of work. Always swore, was rude to customers, cheated on his wife and treated his poor father terribly, but then … one day he changed.'

'What … just like that?'

Trisha nodded. 'Just like that.'

'What do you think happened?'

Trisha shrugged and readjusted the bouquet of flowers she was still holding. Linda stepped forward and took them from her. 'Ooh, thank you. No one knows. It's a mystery, but it's always been a bit strange. One day a man has a terrible temper and abuses his wife and father, and the next … he's a new man. Of course, I think Amber had something to do with that. She was such a lovely lady. She always looked so tired though, and sad, very sad.'

'Amber was the woman who lived here, right?'

'Yes, that's right. Poor woman. Her husband cheated on her too, and she got together with Jordan once her divorce was finalised and she seemed okay for a while, after that whole Tyler issue.'

'The man who jumped into the ravine?'

Trisha raised her eyebrows. 'You know about the tragedy already?'

Linda shook her head. 'Only what my son found out yesterday, but I wasn't sure whether to believe him. You know how teenage boys can be.'

Trisha laughed. 'He probably heard it from my Alex. What else did you hear?'

'Just that … um … Amber died.'

Both women nodded slowly.

Lucy finally spoke. 'Yes, poor Amber. Such a shame she decided to end her life. Oh, look at us, telling you such awful stories. This town really is a lovely place to live. We aren't all killers and crazies! Although, I must say I'm quite glad that Sean and Bethany decided to leave. Bethany was a lovely child, but towards the end she became a bit … intense.' Lucy looked at Trisha as she spoke, and Trisha then nodded her agreement.

'Intense?' pressed Linda. 'What do you mean?'

'Well … she … at school, she spread around a rumour that upset quite a few of the children, especially the younger ones. She said that …' Lucy leaned in closer to Linda and whispered, '… that a creature was after her and her mother.'

Linda's heart skipped a beat. Alex had said the same thing last night, but she'd assumed it was just a joke. 'A creature?'

'A big, black creature that visited her at night and watched her sleep.'

'Did she have some sort of sleep disorder?'

'Oh, heavens, no, I don't think so, not Bethany, but I think Amber did. She never told anyone about it, but it's common knowledge. She saw a therapist about it to start with, but it didn't help. She always looked as if she'd never slept a day in her life. Anyway … I apologise if I've scared you. That wasn't my intention at all.'

Linda forced a smile. 'No, you haven't. It's fine. Thank you both for the lovely flowers and the basket. I'll be sure to come along tomorrow to the coffee morning.'

Lucy nodded. 'Please do!' she exclaimed as she handed over the basket of goodies.

Trisha smiled. 'It would be lovely to meet your … *wife*.'

Linda tried hard to hide the twitch in her left eye as she took the basket, something that always happened when she was biting her tongue.

'See you both tomorrow then,' she said before closing the door. She let out a long sigh. It seemed wherever they went, drama always followed.

Death by suicide.

Creatures.

Cheating allegations.

What next?

They'd moved here specifically to try and get away from drama. Back in their previous hometown of Bedford, everything had been fine at first. Even when she'd moved in with Emma, after Emma's ex-husband had moved out, there hadn't been any drama as such. More like … whisperings. No one talked about the fact that a happily married woman had suddenly come out as a bisexual, kicked her husband out of the house and divorced him. Everyone just ignored it and pretended things were normal, and that was how Linda liked it.

But here in Cherry Hollow it seemed everyone had an opinion on everything, and even an incident that happened over twenty years ago was still being talked and gossiped about as if it had happened yesterday. It seemed she and Emma were the talk of the town; or at least they would be once Trisha and Lucy had spread the word.

Linda rummaged around in the back of the cupboard under the sink for a vase, which she'd unpacked and put there earlier. She spied her hidden stash, took a quick sip, and returned to her task of filling the vase with water and arranging the flowers as best she could. She placed them pride of place in the middle of the dining room table. She didn't know what sort of flowers they were, but the pinks and reds were beautiful and caught the afternoon sun just right, shining at their brightest. The green ferns were lovely too.

As Linda stared into the abundance of colour, her mind cast back to two years ago to a day she promised herself she'd never dwell on again, but there it was: drama.

And it had followed her here.

It was the morning of Halloween and Phoebe was begging her mother to take her shopping again for more spooky decorations. Apparently, the graveyard in the front garden, the fake ghosts on the roof, the spider webs hanging from the windows, the array of bloody fingers on the doorstep and the fifteen carved pumpkins weren't enough to satisfy the Halloween-obsessed child.

'It's fine,' Linda said to Emma, who'd been trying to convince her daughter that they had plenty of decorations and it was a waste of money to buy more, 'I don't mind taking her shopping. I know you have to pop into work this morning.'

So that's what she did.

Emma kissed her, telling her she'd make it up to her later, then hugged her daughter goodbye, warning her she wasn't allowed to buy more than three items, all having to cost under ten pounds each, to which Phoebe agreed.

Spooktacular was a shop in town that sold the biggest and best selection of Halloween decorations a child could ask for. Even Linda was quietly shocked and impressed when she stepped through the double doors and was immediately attacked by an automated witch who cackled and said in an evil, high-pitched shriek, 'Welcome, my pretties! You may enter, but you can't leave!' She then proceeded to screech hysterically. Phoebe, of course, loved it, but Linda frowned as she side-stepped the witch and entered the shop properly.

'Where do you want to start?' she asked Phoebe, but there was no answer. The girl had run off and was nowhere to be seen. Linda's heart lurched as her eyes darted around her immediate surroundings. 'Phoebe?'

Linda dodged past a couple of teenage boys who were checking out the fake blood and vampire teeth and searched down the aisle of dressing-up outfits for children. But Phoebe wasn't there. Neither was she by the half-price sale on witches' brooms and hats.

'Phoebe!' she called again in a firmer tone. Her heart didn't stop hammering until she finally spotted the girl checking out the range of zombie decorations. 'Oh my God, Phoebe, please don't run off like that. You nearly gave me a heart attack.'

Phoebe looked up at her. 'Sorry, I didn't mean to.'

'It's okay. It's fine.' Linda put a hand on her heart as if to steady it and took a deep breath. 'There's a lot of stuff here, huh? Have you found anything you want yet?'

'Not yet, but these zombie masks are cool, right?'

'Yes, very cool.' Linda tried to give Phoebe her best enthusiastic face as she glanced at the freaky masks. She'd never been a huge fan of this holiday, but then she'd never had children of her own to celebrate it with, until now. 'What is it you're dressing up as later for trick or treat?'

'I have three outfits.'

'Oh. Really? Three?'

'Yes. Alex said he'd take me out with his friends first, so I'm going as a witch. Then Mummy is taking me out, so I'll do a quick change into my zombie costume and then Poppy's mummy is picking me up and taking me out with them for a *little bit over on Bedford Road, which is apparently the street for the best chocolates and sweets. I'll be going as a princess for that trip.'*

'A princess? That's not very Halloweeny.'

'A dead princess.'

'Ah. Gottcha.'

'But I like this zombie mask better than the other one I have, so I think I'll get this one. It's scarier, don't you think?'

'It's definitely scary. Okay, so what else?'

'How about some fake skulls to decorate the lounge?'

'Sounds good. Lead the way!'

Linda followed Phoebe through the throngs of people towards the back of the shop, but Phoebe was smaller and nimbler so by the time Linda made it out of the crowd, she'd lost sight of her again.

'Fuck's sake, this child,' she muttered under her breath.

No, that wasn't fair.

She was just an excited kid at Halloween, hyped up on the prospect of chocolate and sweets. Linda tried not to let her heart race as she began her search, once again, for Phoebe.

Chapter Seven
EMMA
Friday 27 October 2023 – 14:51 p.m.

'Hunny, I'm home!' Emma went to close the front door, but a strong gust of wind caught it and slammed it shut, which caused the hairs on the back of her neck to stand on end. It was almost as if someone had grabbed the door from her grasp.

Weird.

Linda appeared from the kitchen looking a little flummoxed, as if she'd been caught out doing something she shouldn't. She wiped her mouth with the sleeve of her top and rolled her eyes.

'Uh, let's not go down that route again. Remember when we went through the whole "hunny bunny" and "sweetie" fiasco?' She kissed Emma hello.

'Right, yes, sorry. It was just an expression. How's your day been so far? I see the moving men have almost finished.'

'My day has been … enlightening. Where've you been?'

'Oh, just out.'

'It's nearly three in the afternoon.'

'I lost track of time.'

Emma's cheeks heated as the feeble attempt of an excuse poured out of her mouth. She knew better than to lie to Linda, who'd always had the ability to see straight through her, although Emma reckoned she wasn't as good at reading people as she thought she was.

'Sorry,' added Emma. She walked past Linda and into the kitchen. 'Ooh, who are the flowers from? They're beautiful.' She sniffed the blooms and stroked one of the long fern leaves.

'Neighbours. Nosey neighbours.'

'Ah, well, I guess that was to be expected.'

'I'll tell you about it more later.'

'Can't wait. Well, Phoebe and I enjoyed our trip into town. She's playing outside again now. There's a lovely park with slides and climbing frames. She didn't want to leave.'

Linda's eyes flicked towards the garden to where Phoebe was playing. Emma smiled when she saw her daughter sitting in the middle of the expanse of grass, playing with one of her favourite dolls. The sun was shining upon her beautiful face and lighting it up as if she were an angel.

'Well,' said Linda with a hint of annoyance in her voice, 'all the furniture is in the appropriate rooms and the moving men are close to unpacking the last of the boxes.'

'Great. I grabbed some food from town for dinner tonight. Does a curry sound good? I also bought a bottle of wine; thought we could celebrate our successful move tonight.'

'Perfect.'

'I'll finish putting away the kitchen stuff.' Emma turned to the two remaining boxes just as one of the moving men walked in.

'We're all done now. The garage is pretty full, but it's all in there.'

Linda nodded. 'Thanks very much.'

'Bye now. Oh … thought you should know that while I was unloading the lorry, I saw a person peering over the hedge that's next your driveway.'

Emma raised her eyebrows. 'Our new neighbours, by any chance?' She directed the question at Linda who shrugged.

'I expect so. Thanks for letting us know.' She smiled at the moving man, who nodded his goodbye and walked out of the house, allowing the door to gently close behind him.

'Should we be worried about these new neighbours of ours? They're spying on us already,' said Emma as she peeled off the tape, which was sealing the box lid together.

Linda shook her head. 'No, it's not the neighbours we should be worried about.'

She didn't expand and Emma didn't press her for further details. In fact, it wasn't until several hours later when she was cooking dinner that Linda's words sunk in.

What or who exactly *should* they be worried about?

The curry was a complete success with the family. Well, with three-quarters of the family anyway. Alex, as usual, was nowhere to be seen when Emma set the plates out on the dining room table. He'd sent her a text earlier in the day saying he'd be home after dinner and to leave him some and reminded her that she needed to sort the internet out soon or he'd run away from home forever. Emma had smirked slightly when she'd read that. He'd always been a dramatic child.

One time, as a ten-year-old, he'd threatened to hold his breath until Emma bought him a cheap Spiderman toy. Emma had stood in the toy aisle of Tesco and watched as her son turned red in the face, his cheeks puffed out, his jaw clenched. A few parents had given her a knowing glance as they passed, a silent acknowledgement to stay strong and that they'd all been there. Alex had finally released his breath, stamped his foot and stormed off, proclaiming that his own mum didn't love him enough to buy him a toy. He'd even tried to get a woman with a baby to adopt him on the way out.

Phoebe had been much easier. In fact, she was the epitome of the perfect child. She'd always slept through the night, hardly ever threw tantrums and mostly did as she was told. She even said please and thank you without having to be reminded. Emma often felt the pang of 'mum guilt' whenever she wished her oldest child could be more like her youngest. It wasn't that she loved Phoebe more. It was just that Alex was very difficult at times. What was wrong with wishing he was a bit different? Did that make her a bad mother? Was it her fault he'd turned out so rude? Surely all mums felt that way with their first child. It wasn't like children arrived with an instruction manual.

'Thank you, Mummy. That was yummy,' said Phoebe as she took her plate to the sink and slid it into the soapy water.

Emma smiled. 'You're welcome.'

'Is there ice cream for pudding?'

'Of course. You were there when we picked it out, remember?'

'Oh, yes, I forgot.'

'I'll get you some now. Linda … a top-up?' Emma nodded at Linda's empty wine glass, but Linda didn't reply. She was staring at the wall just past where Phoebe was now sitting at the table, seemingly oblivious to what was going on around her. 'Linda? More wine?'

Linda's whole body jumped as if she'd been electrocuted. 'Yes! Sorry. What did you say?'

'Would you like more wine?'

Emma frowned at her wife, who looked as if she'd seen a ghost. Linda did look a little pale. Maybe she was exhausted from the move and all the unpacking she'd done today. More guilt flooded Emma's thoughts as she realised that she'd left her here alone to do it all herself while she'd been out with Phoebe visiting the school and sightseeing.

'More wine. Definitely more wine.' Linda held out her glass and Emma noticed a slight tremble in her hand.

Emma walked to the fridge for the bottle of white and took out the ice cream from the bottom drawer of the freezer while she was at it. She dolloped two scoops into Phoebe's pink bowl and set it on the table in front of her. She then topped up Linda's glass, followed by her own before returning to her seat opposite Phoebe, who already had chocolate ice cream smeared across her lips and chin.

'Are you okay?' asked Emma, keeping one eye on Phoebe and the other on Linda, who picked up her wine glass without even looking at it and drained half of the contents in one gulp.

'Yes. Fine. Tired, I guess. Sorry … I'll tell you about it later once you've … put Phoebe … to bed.'

Emma nodded and began clearing away the dirty plates, putting them in a pile beside the sink. 'Have you heard from Alex today? He texted me, but I have no idea where he is or what he's been doing all day.'

'No,' replied Linda. 'Not since he shouted bye at me this morning.'

'I hope he's okay. At least I can tell him the good news that the internet is being installed tomorrow.'

Linda grunted in response, which told Emma that she had an opinion on the subject but didn't want to put her foot in it.

Alex and Phoebe weren't Linda's children, so Emma knew that she sometimes had a hard time keeping quiet about how Emma raised them. Linda didn't have children of her own. She didn't understand that Emma questioned herself every single second of every day about whether she was doing the right thing for them, whether she was making the right decisions for their futures. She prayed daily that they were happy and had always hoped to have the type of close relationship with her children where they could come to her about anything that was troubling them, or for advice on any issues. But Alex had started slipping away from her grasp years ago and Emma hoped she'd brought him up well enough to know the difference between right and wrong. He was going through a hard time right now. She knew she needed to give him space. That was it. He just needed more space and more time and then he'd be the Alex he used to be; the fun, cheeky, loving little boy who used to run up to Emma, give her a big squeeze and say, 'I love you to the moon and back again, Mummy,' but he wasn't a little boy anymore. He had a deep voice, he had facial hair, he was taller than her and he clearly had sexual urges, which Emma had attempted to ignore one day when she'd found a stash of dirty magazines under his bed while she'd been cleaning.

An hour later, Emma tucked Phoebe into bed. The main lights were off and her small nightlight was on, giving off its soft, ambient glow from the corner of the room. Phoebe's pink unicorn duvet cover was tucked up around her chin and her vast array of stuffed animals were lined up precisely along the left side of the bed nearest the wall, each in their specific spot.

'I like it here, Mummy.'

Emma tucked a strand of her child's dark hair behind her ear. 'I'm glad you do. I think we're going to be very happy here. Shall I sing you your favourite song?'

'Yes, please. From the top.'

'Of course.'

Emma cleared her throat and began singing 'A Million Dreams' from Phoebe's favourite movie, *The Greatest Showman*. Emma had been made to sit through it so many times that she knew all the songs off by heart, but this one was a particular favourite. She watched as her daughter's eyes fluttered closed like the delicate wings of a butterfly, a smile across her face as she drifted off to dreamland.

A squeaky floorboard made Emma look up towards the bedroom door, which was cracked open. Alex leaned against the doorframe with his arms folded across his chest, watching them. His eyes were fixed on Emma, and when she looked at him and waved he tutted and rolled his eyes before walking away. She heard him open and slam his bedroom door. Phoebe stirred briefly but otherwise remained asleep.

Once Emma had sung the last line of the song, she kissed Phoebe on the forehead, straightened up and walked towards the door. She turned for one last glimpse of her precious child and saw a huge, black shadow standing over the bed, like a hideous beast with claws and fangs.

A scream lodged in her throat as she stumbled against the wall. With her heart still in her mouth, Emma raced downstairs and into the kitchen where Linda was doing the washing up.

'Linda! Come upstairs. Quickly!'

Linda dropped the plate she was scrubbing and ran after Emma. 'What the hell is going on?'

Emma dragged Linda towards Phoebe's bedroom door. 'There … by the bed … do you see it?'

Linda peered into the room, taking note of the night light and scanned her eyes over the bed. 'What am I supposed to be looking at?' she whispered.

Emma looked around the room, but the shadow – whatever it was – was gone. 'N-Nothing … I guess it was just a trick of the light.'

'Are you sure?'

'Yes, sorry, I must be tired or something.'

Linda turned and headed back downstairs, leaving Emma panting as if she'd sprinted a hundred metres. Emma stayed by the bedroom door for a few more minutes before realising it must have been exactly that; a trick of the light.

She pulled the door to and stood for a few moments, listening to the soft snores of her daughter before heading back downstairs.

Emma and Linda sat side by side on the sofa, their legs intertwined with each other's as they drank their wine. Emma's heart had finally stopped racing ten minutes ago. Alex had emerged from his room long enough to heat up his dinner and grab the tub of ice cream. Emma told him to keep his music low or use his headphones so as not to wake up his sister. A grunt told her he'd heard her.

'So,' said Emma with a sigh, 'tell me about these nosey neighbours of ours.'

'Well … Tracey is a homophobic bitch and Lucy is the town gossip.'

'Brilliant.'

'However, I did learn one thing.'

'Oh?'

'Alex was right about Amber and Jordan and what happened twenty years ago, but there was something else they said too, which really freaked me out.'

Emma took a sip of the crisp white wine, allowed it to tingle her tongue for a few seconds and then swallowed. If she was being honest, her mind wasn't fully focussed on what Linda was saying. She was too distracted by what had happened in Phoebe's room earlier and was fighting the overwhelming urge to get up and go and check on her.

'Lucy said that Bethany, Amber's daughter, kept telling the kids at school that something was after her.'

At the word *something*, Emma felt a familiar tightness in her chest. 'Some*thing*, not some*one*?'

Linda nodded. 'I think she must have been suffering from PTSD or something after her mother died. It's very common when children lose someone they love at a young age.'

'Mmm, maybe.' Emma could feel the unspoken words hovering in the air above them, but neither woman spoke them. 'She certainly seemed like a normal girl when I saw her yesterday.'

'She didn't say anything weird to you?'

Emma opened her mouth to tell Linda about what Bethany had said about the floorboards in the spare room, but then filled her open mouth with wine instead, shaking her head. 'No. Nothing.'

Again, the unspoken words floated around the room.

Emma hated lying to her wife, but it was the only way to protect her from the truth which would surely rip the family apart, and Emma had sworn to herself, after what had happened two years ago, that she'd do whatever it would take to keep her family together.

And that meant keeping secrets.

Chapter Eight
ALEX
Friday 27 October 2023 – 20:05 p.m.

He chucked his ragged backpack into the corner of the room and flopped down on his bed, making the slats creak under his ever-growing weight. He was getting too tall for the bed now, his feet often dangling over the bottom edge. He'd outgrown it at least two years ago, but his mum had been too busy having a mental breakdown to worry about silly things like her son growing up.

He glanced around his new room. It was bigger than his old one, which was cool, and all his boxes and clothes were piled in the corner ready to be transferred to the built-in wardrobe. He couldn't be bothered to sort them out now. Maybe his mum would do it for him if he left them there long enough. Then again, when had she ever noticed anything other than her precious daughter?

When he'd returned home, he watched her sing Phoebe to sleep, like she did every night, silently disappointed that she never tucked him in and said goodnight anymore. He may have been sixteen, but couldn't she at least acknowledge his existence occasionally rather than spend all her time focussing on Phoebe? He knew he didn't make things easy for her. Maybe he'd pushed her too hard and she didn't love him anymore. He often noticed the look of disappointment in her eyes whenever she looked at him. Was that what he was to her now – a disappointment?

Alex tucked one arm behind his head as he stared at the ceiling. There was a small crack in it. Earlier today he'd met up with that local kid he'd met the day before, the one who shared his name. He'd also introduced him to an extremely cute girl his own age by the name of Harriet who had shockingly natural red hair. No, it wasn't ginger. It was red and it was the most spectacular colour he'd ever seen, and it made her green eyes pop. She'd given him a coy smile when he'd introduced himself. His heart fluttered as he thought back to meeting her earlier in the day.

'I'm Alex,' he said, standing up a little straighter, exaggerating his almost six-foot frame even more. Maybe she didn't like tall boys, he didn't know, but it couldn't hurt to try.

'Harriet,' she said back. Her cheeks were flushed, and she batted her long eyelashes at him. Oh yeah, she was into him already. 'You've just moved into the old Walker place, right?'

'I guess so, yeah.'

'It's a nice house. Have you heard about what happened to the previous owners?'

'Alex the First filled me in on some of it yesterday and showed me that newspaper article. I'd like to check out Beaker Ravine today. Can you point me in the right direction?'

Harriet raised her eyebrows. 'Alex the First?'

Alex chuckled. 'I'm Alex the Second. You know, since I was here second.'

'Got it. But ... um ... we don't go to Beaker Ravine anymore. It's cordoned off for safety. People say it's haunted by everyone who's jumped into it. It's not exactly a great place

to visit anymore. Years ago, before it happened, kids went there all the time. There's even a little cave at the bottom, but no one's been down there for over two decades.'

'And you believe that shit about it being haunted?'

Harriet shrugged. 'I don't know. It's enough to freak me out, I know that much.'

'Want to find out for sure?'

'Why do you want to see it so badly? It's just a ravine.'

'Just curious about the history of this place. Plus, what else is there to do around here for fun?'

Harriet kicked a small pebble into a nearby bush. 'We usually just hang out by the shops and chat.'

'And as riveting as that sounds, I'm going to pass and go and explore the ravine. Hey, Alex the First ... you coming?'

Alex the First was just walking out of the shop after introducing Alex to Harriet a few minutes before. He was carrying a bag of crisps and a bottle of Coke. He was shorter than Alex, but stockier. Maybe he worked out. His hair was cut very short on the sides and longer at the top.

'Coming where?' he asked as he opened the bag of crisps and popped one in his mouth.

'Beaker Ravine.'

'Do you have a death wish or something? No one goes there, man. Didn't you read the article?'

Alex scoffed. 'Everyone knows most newspaper articles are written by journalists who just want to be famous. They'll make up any shit to write if they think people will read it.'

'I dunno, man. He looked pretty freaked when he came back from the ravine. His face was white, and he was sweating an awful lot. At the end of the article, he said he was never coming back.'

'And I bet that paper sold millions, right?'

Alex the First nodded. 'Yeah, the town was on the news for a while. Someone even wanted to make a documentary about it, but the council refused. I'm telling you, man, Beaker Ravine is not a place you want to be going.'

'All the more reason to go. Come on, it'll be fun.'

'Pass. You may be new around here, but you need to learn quickly about what you do and don't do in this town, and one of the things you definitely don't do is go to Beaker Ravine.'

Alex folded his arms across his chest and sighed. 'Are you scared or something?'

'I'm not scared ... I just don't want The Creature to come after me.'

He rolled his eyes. Alex looked over at Harriet, who had turned pale.

She nodded in agreement. 'You don't want The Creature after you. Trust me,' she said.

Alex threw his head back and laughed. 'Are you two for real? It's just some made-up shit to attract tourists.'

Alex the First chugged half the bottle of Coke and burped. 'Look, if you want to tempt fate then go ahead, but don't say I didn't warn you.'

'I dare you.'

'Excuse me?'

Alex shifted his weight from foot to foot and grinned. 'I dare both of you to come with me to the ravine. Come on, it'll be an adventure. Whatever The Creature is, it isn't real, and I'll prove it.'

Alex the First and Harriet swapped anxious looks before slowly turning their heads to focus on Alex.

'Fine,' said Alex the First, 'but if any of us die or jump to our deaths or whatever, or one of us goes crazy and pushes someone off the edge, then don't come back and haunt me, or I'll kill you.'

Alex rolled his eyes at the ludicrous sentence but then nodded. 'Fine. Whatever. I promise. Harriet ... you in?' He held out his hand.

Harriet hesitated for a second, but then her face lit up with a mischievous grin as she grabbed his hand and pulled him along the road.

'Let's go.'

Chapter Nine
JORDAN
Saturday 28 October 2023 – 06:11 a.m.

Jordan rolled over in bed, its creak echoing his own groan. He really needed a new bed, having adopted most of the furniture from his dad's house, so it was anyone's guess how old this double bed was.

After he'd attended to the leaking pipe at Linda's house and returned to his business, he'd worked for a few more hours and then went to the small gym in town to work off his frustration. He'd lifted weights until he couldn't lift anymore, then taken Morgan for his evening walk. The next morning he'd called Brooke, having been unable to sleep.

He understood her reasons for not wanting to come back to Cherry Hollow. He did. But, after speaking to her, he got the idea that maybe it wasn't the *real* reason she didn't want to come back. Brooke and Amber had been best friends; at least he thought they were. He had sensed some animosity between them towards the end, but, then again, Amber had been off with everyone. He had a feeling Brooke was hiding something from him. They'd become a lot closer over the six months since Amber had died, but he hadn't seen Brooke in the flesh since he and Amber had gone to visit her in London one time, not too long after she'd originally left to start her new career as a make-up artist. Had it really been almost four years since he'd seen her?

Jordan's body, especially his arms and shoulders, ached after the gym yesterday, which was a good thing because working out was the only thing in his life he felt he had any control over. Everything else – his business, his social life, his family, his friends – all seemed to be slipping away a little more each day. At least he was in control of his body. Unlike all those years when he'd wake up one morning to find his entire living room in disarray and be unable to remember how it had got that way. It was a time he didn't like to remember, back when he'd been a horrible human being.

A knock at the door caused Morgan to leap off the bed and start barking. Jordan glanced at his alarm clock. It was just past six in the morning. His alarm wasn't due to go off for another half an hour. What the hell?

Another knock rattled against the door.

He threw back the duvet, shuffled into a pair of grey tracksuit bottoms and jogged down the stairs of his family home to the front door. His dad had left him the house in his will, along with the business which was situated in the middle of town. This house, however, was near the outskirts. Jordan had thought about selling the house, but had instead sold the house he'd shared with his ex-wife, given her half the profits and moved back into the home he'd grown up in, hence he'd adopted almost all of the furniture.

Morgan was standing at the door, his nose pressed against the wood, wagging his tail so hard that his whole back end shifted side to side. It seemed he knew exactly who was on the other side. Jordan opened the door.

'Wow, that's a lot of naked flesh for first thing in the morning,' said Brooke as she shielded her eyes against Jordan's bare torso. 'Hey, baby!' She crouched down and accepted the overly enthusiastic welcome from Morgan by scratching his ears and ruffling his fur. 'You've grown so much!'

'Well, I wasn't exactly expecting company … Give me five minutes and I'll look as good as you. Seriously … do you wake up looking like that?' He had to admit that Brooke looked immaculate, from her perfectly applied make-up and tied-back hair to her tight-fitting jeans, t-shirt and leather jacket she was sporting. She looked the epitome of class and elegance, but in a casual way. It suited her.

'Well,' she said with a shrug, 'it beats how I used to look.'

Jordan silently agreed, thinking back to the day he and the gang had visited her in her bedroom, after not seeing her for twenty years. She'd looked pale, lifeless and empty. The difference now was quite staggering. She took his breath away …

Brooke straightened up and they stared at each other for a few seconds. 'Hi,' she said.

'Hi,' replied Jordan with a smile. They stepped towards each other at the same time and hugged. 'Been a long time.'

They disengaged from the hug and Jordan stepped aside as Brooke walked past him into the house, Morgan following closely behind.

'Can I assume by this unannounced visit that you've changed your mind about coming to help me, or did you drive all the way here for my amazing coffee?'

'Why is it amazing?'

'Because I make it myself.'

Brooke smirked. 'Well, if you're offering, I'd love to try some of this amazing coffee. And yes … I changed my mind. I spent all day yesterday telling myself I was a bad friend—'

'You're not a bad friend.'

'Aren't I? My first and immediate response to you asking for help was to say no because I was too afraid to come back to this town and face my past.'

'Well, you're here now. That's all that matters.'

Brooke nodded. 'Yes, I'm here, but you can't tell my parents that I'm here.'

Jordan leaned against the kitchen counter. 'You realise that word will get around eventually. It's a small town. Everyone loves to gossip. You may look a bit different than when you left, but people will still recognise you. You're going to have to go and see your parents. Your dad isn't well.'

Brooke sighed, as if acknowledging that she'd been beaten by his sound argument. 'I know he isn't, but I'm not going back to my old house.'

'Then don't. I'll invite your parents round here for a drink or something. Brooke … you must see your parents. I can't take another conversation with your mum where I have to explain why you haven't called or visited.'

Brooke bit her bottom lip. 'Fine. Since when have you been so convincing?'

'It's a talent, what can I say?' Jordan turned and switched the kettle on. 'What time were you up this morning if you're here before half six?'

'I left at one.'

'Couldn't sleep?'

'Something like that. After our chat on the phone, I started thinking about the last time I saw and spoke to Amber. I'm not sure if she told you, but we didn't leave on good terms.'

Jordan leaned against the kitchen counter again while he waited for the kettle to boil. 'No, she didn't, but towards the end she didn't exactly do a lot of talking, even to me. It felt as if she was pulling away from me.'

'Before you told me the other day about her possibly being murdered, I've always thought that I was the reason she took her own life.'

Jordan tutted. 'Don't be ridiculous. It had nothing to do with you. Amber loved you like a sister. Even if you did have heated words, she wouldn't have ended her life over them. Besides … now we know she didn't do it.'

Brooke sat down on one of the kitchen chairs. 'But she jumped into the ravine. That was the cause of death, right?'

'Right, but what if she was pushed?'

Brooke shuddered. 'This is horribly similar to what happened to Kieran, isn't it?'

'A bit too similar if you ask me.' Jordan turned and took two mugs from the cupboard above the kettle.

Brooke sat up straighter. 'Who would do something like this? Everyone loved Amber.'

Jordan didn't respond. This town was full of whisperings and musings. Amber had stirred things up towards the end and not everyone had liked it.

There were a few seconds of silence before Brooke spoke again. 'What about The Creature? The last time Amber and I spoke she said it was still hanging around and she told you the same thing, but I just can't get my head around it.'

Brooke stood up and stepped forwards. 'The Creature isn't real, Jordan. It isn't a real entity. It's something that Amber made up in her head, just like we made up The Fear and The Bad Man as a way of dealing with our guilt.'

'Maybe it started out that way, but when Amber brought Bethany into her delusion, it became real to her and now it's getting stronger. Bethany told people about it at school, right? Then those kids told their parents, then those parents told more parents, and they told more people. You might not know this because you've been away for so long, but The Creature is now a local legend and people believe it's real. The ravine has been cordoned off because everyone believes that if you go there, The Creature will call out to you and make you jump into it. There was even a newspaper article about it. The journalist got so freaked out that he drove out of here at top speed and hasn't been back since.'

'So maybe Amber did jump into the ravine because it was The Creature who killed her.'

'Or that's what someone hoped people would believe,' added Jordan. He finished pouring the hot water into the mugs and stirred the contents with a spoon. He handed a mug to Brooke, who took it without breaking his eye contact.

'You realise you sound crazy, right?'

Jordan shrugged. 'Wouldn't be the first time.'

Brooke stared at him for several long seconds and then took a small sip. 'This coffee tastes awful. Plus, it's instant. Don't you have a proper coffee machine?'

Jordan laughed. 'That's your opinion, Miss I'm-Only-Used-To-Drinking-Posh-London-Coffee.'

Brooke echoed his laugh and took another sip, grimacing. Her eyes turned serious. 'Okay, so how do we get rid of The Creature, which may or may not be real? How do we kill it?'

'You're asking me?'

'Well, don't you have at least some sort of an idea? What about a blood oath?'

Jordan scoffed. 'Oh hell no, I'm not going down that road again. It didn't exactly work last time. Plus … the whole blood oath thing was Tyler's crazy idea. I never believed all that crap.'

'Fine, then what do you suggest?'

Jordan thought for a moment. 'We could start by going back to where it all began … Beaker Ravine. Maybe something will jump out at us … figuratively speaking.'

Chapter Ten
LINDA
Saturday 28 October 2023 – 09:20 a.m.

Linda's plan for the day was to sort the lounge out because it resembled a dumping ground. Yes, the sofa, coffee table and bookcases were in their correct places, but dozens of moving boxes were piled high in the corners, and she wanted to have a relaxing and clean place to sit and unwind at the end of the day, so it was first on her agenda.

The television needed to be hung on the wall and the internet was being activated today, so she needed to ensure the router was set up and plugged in or risk the wrath of a teenage boy. Also, the walls were still bare. Pictures of the family when the kids were small and of Linda and Emma on their wedding day were ready to be hung in pride of place. She just needed to find a tape measure, the hammer and some nails.

It was Saturday, which meant the coffee morning was today and, despite Linda's apprehension about going, she knew it would be a good idea to get to know the local community and meet some new people. Plus, it would provide a break from sorting the house out. They'd only be away an hour at the most, but they needed to leave in half an hour.

Emma was upstairs sorting out one of the bedrooms. Linda could hear her moving around, dragging boxes across the floor. But then everything went quiet; too quiet, so after Linda had finished hanging the last of the pictures, one of Alex and Phoebe together three years ago (my God, Alex had changed so much!), she climbed the stairs to investigate the silence.

Emma wasn't in their bedroom or Alex's (he wasn't in there either). Phoebe's room was also empty, which left the spare room that she'd designated as the office. The door was closed. Linda furrowed her brows as she approached and as she opened it, she asked, 'Is everything okay in here?' and then gasped when she saw what was happening.

Emma was kneeling in the far-left corner of the room with her back to the door, but what had shocked Linda was the fact that the corner of the carpet had been ripped up and several of the floorboards removed and piled haphazardly to the right of Emma, who spun around when she heard Linda enter the room. Linda knew Emma had been caught doing something she shouldn't because her eyes widened and a flush crept up her neck as she started to speak.

'Linda, bloody hell, you scared me!'

'I scared you? What the hell are you doing in here? Why have you ripped up half the floor?' Linda stepped further into the room, assessing the damage. Granted, she hadn't ripped up half the floor, but it was still a mess. She saw Emma tuck something behind her back. 'What's that?'

'What? Oh. Nothing. I saw a mouse, so I thought I'd try and find its nest.'

Linda screwed her nose up. 'A mouse?'

'Yeah. It was a big one. Practically a rat. It ran to the corner and then disappeared underneath the carpet, so I pulled it up and removed the floorboards.'

'And?'

'And what?'

'Did you find the nest?'

'Oh, yeah … it's gone now. All gone.'

'Good. Well, I just came up to tell you that we have to leave soon to get to the coffee morning.'

Emma beamed a smile that Linda knew for a fact was fake. 'Great. I'll be down in a bit. I'll just finish replacing these boards.'

Linda frowned as she stepped back. 'Okay …'

As Linda closed the door, she realised two things.

One: Emma was lying to her.

Two: she'd found something under those floorboards … and it was no giant mouse.

As Linda entered the community centre, her wife at her side, every pair of eyes in the room swivelled in their direction. Emma tensed beside her, so Linda gave her hand a reassuring squeeze. Lucy and Trisha were over by the biscuit trays, and both immediately ran up to the new arrivals with huge smiles on their faces, clapping their hands together.

'I'm so glad you could make it!' exclaimed Trisha. 'This must be Emma.'

Emma nodded. 'Hi, yes, so lovely to meet you. I'm sorry I missed your visit yesterday. Thank you both for the lovely flowers and basket of food.'

'Think nothing of it,' replied Lucy. 'Here, have an oatmeal biscuit. They're homemade by Pam. She's over there. I'll introduce you to everyone. Come!'

Both women were dressed in casual yet sophisticated clothing. Linda's cheeks heated as she glanced down at her scruffy-looking top and jeans. At least she'd brushed her hair this morning, but she was cursing herself for not throwing on something a bit more appropriate.

Emma stuttered slightly as she said, 'My daughter, Phoebe, caught sight of the play area when she came in. Will she be all right out there?'

Lucy gasped with joy. 'Oh, you have a daughter too. How lovely. How old is she? And yes, she'll be perfectly safe. A few of the other women will be in there with their smaller ones, so they can keep an eye.'

'Thank you, and Phoebe is seven.'

'Such a lovely age.'

Linda glanced over her shoulder at the play area they'd passed on the way in, but before she could dwell any more on it, Trisha grabbed her shoulder and pulled her over to a group of women. Emma appeared to have been abducted by Lucy who was introducing her to another gaggle of women by the coffee station. It seemed they were the highlight of the morning.

'Everyone, this is Linda. She's just moved in to ... well, you know which house I mean. Linda, this is Pam, Sharon and Olivia.'

Linda smiled and nodded at each lady in turn, knowing she wouldn't remember any of their names later, but it was one woman in particular who caught her eye.

Olivia.

She was an older attractive lady, or at least she had been attractive once, but there was a deep sadness behind her eyes that Linda picked up on and, when Trisha had spoken about the house, Olivia had flinched. She'd tried to cover it up by taking a sip of coffee, but not before Linda had noticed.

'Lovely to meet you all,' said Linda.

'How are you settling in?' asked Pam, or it could have been Sharon. She'd forgotten already.

Linda smiled, fairly used to the mundane questions every new resident was bound to ask. 'Oh, you know, it's still a bit chaotic, but slowly the boxes are being unpacked. I'd like to get everything done before I start work in a few days.'

'You're going to be working at The Bean Café, is that right?'

'Yes, that's right.' It seemed gossip really did spread fast here.

'And what is it your wife does?' asked Trisha.

Linda gulped back the dry lump in her throat, knowing that this topic would have come up eventually, but she hadn't expected it this soon. 'Um, Emma doesn't work at the moment. She's taking some time off to ... recover, but she used to work in HR.'

Three of the ladies gasped in unison, their eyes wide with anticipation of some new gossip. But Olivia remained quiet and drank her coffee.

'My goodness,' said Trisha. 'I hope she's not recovering from anything serious.'

Linda shook her head. 'No, um ... nothing like that. She's just taking a career break.' Linda couldn't help but notice the disappointing frowns.

'Ah, lovely. It's always good to start fresh. Olivia's daughter did something similar a few years ago after she recovered. Isn't that right, Olivia?' asked Trisha.

All eyes descended upon poor Olivia, who looked as if she wanted to be swallowed by the floor.

'Y-Yes, that's right. My daughter suffered from a severe mental health condition, but miraculously recovered and is now living in London, working as a make-up artist.'

'I'm so sorry to hear she was unwell, but that's amazing that she's better now,' replied Linda.

'Thank you. Yes, when Brooke was unwell, she never left the house, not in nearly twenty years. I was her carer, you see. It was difficult to see her so unwell, and even more difficult when she left. I've barely seen her since. She's never come back home to visit.'

'I'm so sorry.' Linda felt a pang of empathy for the woman, who merely smiled her acknowledgement.

Trisha cleared her throat, breaking the somewhat awkward tension hovering in the air. 'Yes, well,' she said, 'maybe it's for the best that Brooke stays away.'

'What is that supposed to mean?' asked Olivia, her tone of voice rising an octave.

Trisha laughed, as if it were no big deal that she had insulted Olivia. 'Oh, you know, just that what with everything that happened, maybe it's best those involved stay away so as not to … corrupt anyone else.'

Linda sucked in a breath.

Clearly, the group of women had encroached upon a difficult topic. She was silently hoping Trisha would shut the hell up because it looked as if Olivia was about to burst into floods of tears at any second, but she didn't. Instead, she gritted her teeth and narrowed her eyes at Trisha.

'My daughter would never *corrupt* anyone.'

'No, of course not, I didn't mean—'

'And another thing, from what you're saying, you make it sound as if you're glad Amber is dead too. Next, you'll be passing around a petition to get Jordan Evans to leave! What happened to those children twenty-five years ago was tragic and they shouldn't be punished for it.'

Trisha's mouth dropped open, and Pam and Sharon took a step back. Linda didn't know what to do. Olivia turned to her and straightened her top.

'It was lovely to meet you, Linda. I'm sorry I've caused a scene, but when it comes to my daughter, I'm very protective. Good day, ladies.' Olivia glared at Trisha, who still had her mouth wide open, and then stormed towards the exit, leaving the group of women speechless.

Chapter Eleven
EMMA
Saturday 28 October 2023 – 10:25 a.m.

She didn't want to be here. She didn't want to be meeting all these new people, chatting about how lovely their new house was, or talking about things they may or may not have in common. She didn't want to listen as the women listed the various clubs they were a part of in the town or where the best place to buy free-range eggs was (Peter's farm, on the outskirts of the village – a bit of a drive, but worth it).

No, Emma wanted to be back at home, searching through the box of items she'd found under the floorboards. She hadn't even had a chance to read the letter she'd found before Linda had stormed in and disturbed her. There was no way Linda had believed her bullshit story of seeing a giant mouse and finding its nest. She knew her wife better than that, which meant that Linda knew she was lying and hiding something. No doubt she'd ask Emma about it soon when they were alone, or maybe she wouldn't and there'd be a strange awkwardness between them until Emma caved and admitted that she hadn't seen a giant mouse. Emma had hidden things from Linda before and that hadn't turned out well for anyone, but this was different … She was doing it for Linda's own good, wasn't she?

Emma's heart sank as she was dragged away from Linda towards a corner of the room by Lucy, who seemed hell-bent on introducing her to her gaggle of friends. Linda had been pulled in the opposite direction by Trisha. Did these ladies mean to keep them apart? It seemed a strange thing to do when the easiest thing would have been to introduce them both at the same time, but almost the second they'd stepped into the room, they'd been targeted and separated.

'Ladies, this is Emma!' exclaimed Lucy as if she were showing off a new shiny toy.

A woman with jet-black hair and big, silver hoop earrings reached out and shook her hand by grasping it with both of hers: a slightly too eager welcome, perhaps?

'So nice to meet you. I'm Penelope and this is Francesca.' She tilted her head to the left where an attractive, blonde middle-aged woman stood stirring sugar into a cup of black coffee. Emma noticed that all the cups had The Bean Café imprinted on them, so guessed that this coffee morning was run by the café, or maybe they supplied the coffee and biscuits. Emma didn't care enough to ask.

'Delighted.' It seemed Francesca wasn't one for over-exaggerated displays of kindness.

'Hi, nice to meet you all. I'm sorry I'm such a mess. We're still unpacking and sorting everything out.' All at once, three pairs of eyes scanned her shabby outfit and she wished she hadn't said anything.

Just keep digging yourself a hole, Emma.

'Oh, don't mention it. Moving house is one of the most stressful life experiences you can go through. Well, other than getting married and getting divorced. I should know, I've been through all of them.' Penelope laughed and Lucy followed with a fake cackle, but Francesca's face was deadpan.

Emma attempted to smile, but it didn't reach her eyes. She frantically searched her brain for something intelligent to say, but Lucy beat her to it and dove straight into some local gossip. Whilst not exactly intelligent, it did the job and took the focus off her.

'Oh, ladies, you'll never guess who I saw today heading towards Jordan Evans's place in the early hours of the morning. Brooke Willows!' Lucy flicked her eyes over towards where Linda was standing. There seemed to be some raised voices coming from that side of the room. 'I can't believe it.'

'Really, Brooke's in town? That is strange. Does Olivia know?' asked Penelope, keeping her voice low.

'No, I don't think she does, otherwise she would have told all of us herself this morning. It is strange isn't it, that her own daughter, who she spent nearly two decades looking after, runs away the first chance she gets and then never comes home to visit her parents. Frank isn't well, you know, and poor Olivia is looking after him at home, but does Brooke care that her father is sick?'

Emma was only half listening. She didn't know who Olivia was (she guessed she was one of the women over where Linda was standing), but the name *Brooke* ignited a spark of recognition from somewhere. Hadn't Alex mentioned her name the other night when he'd told the story of that boy's tragic death? Did Brooke have something to do with it?

'I wonder why she's here?' asked Francesca. 'What's made her come back?'

'Well, it's obvious, isn't it? She was going to see Jordan. I think there's something going on there.'

'No, there can't be. Jordan was deeply in love with Amber.'

'Yes, and then Amber tragically dies and leaves him open for—'

Francesca gasped. 'No! You don't think—'

Lucy shrugged and raised her eyebrows. 'I'm not saying anything or accusing anyone of anything, but the fact that Brooke is in town and—' Lucy was cut off by a woman storming past them, who had clearly caught the tail end of the conversation. She stopped and squared up to Lucy.

'Did you say my Brooke is in town?'

Lucy opened her mouth and turned bright red. 'I … I'm not sure, Olivia. It might have been her. She looks very different compared to the last time I saw her.'

Olivia's face fell and tears filled her dark brown eyes, but then she seemed to collect herself, sniffed loudly and titled her chin upwards.

'Well, if you aren't sure, then maybe you shouldn't be spreading gossip.'

And with that, she stormed out of the room, leaving the entire congregation of women, including the ones on the other side of the room, open-mouthed and speechless. Emma wished she could have applauded the woman for standing up to Lucy the way that she had. She hated gossip and hated the people who spread it even more.

Emma made eye contact with Linda across the room, who raised her eyebrows ever so slightly. Emma smiled back. Olivia hadn't been gone more than ten seconds before Lucy and Francesca started up again.

'I feel sorry for Olivia, you know,' said Lucy, refilling her coffee cup. 'She's always so stressed and busy. I'm surprised she even has time to leave her sick husband to come to these coffee mornings.'

A switch flicked on in Emma's head. 'Maybe if you stopped gossiping about her and started helping her instead, she wouldn't be so stressed.'

Emma walked away before anyone could retort. She headed into the corridor towards the play area in search of her daughter, but her mind had already drifted away from Lucy and her big mouth. She was thinking back to this morning when she'd decided to search under the floorboards.

The desire to look under the floorboards was too strong to ignore. Emma had done her best, and fought it as hard as she could, but it was inevitable that she'd land up on her hands and knees, clawing at the carpet and ripping it up like a woman possessed. She had no idea which room was the right one, but she decided to start in the office space.

As quietly as she could, she pulled the carpet up and checked the front left corner of the room. Using a hammer she'd found in the garage, she yanked at the nails in the boards.

Nothing in that corner.

Next, she moved to the front right corner and repeated the process. She didn't waste time by returning the boards and carpet. She'd do that later.

Nothing in that one either.

Emma could hear Linda moving around downstairs and banging nails into the walls, so she used the opportunity and moved swiftly onto the third corner, the one in the far left. Her heart hammered so hard in her chest that she could barely take a breath as she removed the final board.

There …

There was something wedged in the dark hole.

It was difficult to make out exactly what it was, but as she grabbed it with her hand, she realised it was a small box. All the moisture in her mouth seemed to disappear at once as she lifted the lid. Inside was a piece of paper and a few other small items, which appeared to be worthless: a pebble, a shell, a tiny plastic toy horse and a dried-up flower petal.

Emma picked up the paper and turned it over.

And that was the moment Linda had interrupted her. She hadn't had time to read it after that. She returned the box to the hole and replaced the floorboards, but she kept hold of the piece of paper, which she stuffed into her pocket.

That same piece of paper was still in her jacket pocket now. It was practically burning a hole through the fabric.

Emma dipped her hand into the pocket and felt the paper between her fingers. She found a seat near the play area and watched Phoebe as she played with some toys on the floor. All the other children were on the younger side, which was why she wasn't playing with them, but Phoebe had always been perfectly happy to play by herself. Once she started school, no doubt she would make many friends her own age. Emma couldn't wait to take her to play dates and birthday parties and, with Halloween coming up, she knew her daughter would want to go shopping for decorations and new costumes soon. As if she didn't have enough already.

Emma pulled the piece of paper out of her pocket without looking at it. She took a deep breath, attempting to quell the nausea that was rising, and then began to read.

The Creature

It's always with me; it's always near
I can't help but live in fear
It visits me in my dreams and stands beside my bed
Or silently hovers above my head

It's scary and large and it has sharp claws
It has evil red eyes and many flaws
Sometimes I'm afraid and sometimes I'm not
But I know for sure that it'll never stop

It hides in the shadows and in the dark
We are never very far apart
Mummy said that she is afraid for me
That she must tell the truth to be set free

Sometimes I think that it has gone
But then it appears again and proves me wrong
I wish it would leave me alone to live my life
And stop all the worry and suffering and strife

It is my enemy, it is my friend
It always follows me around every bend
I know that one day it will be out of my head
But that will only be ... when I am dead

By Bethany Walker
Age 11

Chapter Twelve
BROOKE
Saturday 28 October 2023 – 08:45 a.m.

Brooke and Jordan left for the ravine as soon as the sun was up and once Jordan had downed two further cups of strong coffee. Brooke had surreptitiously poured the remainder of hers down the kitchen sink. Bless Jordan, he may have looked good with his top off, but he couldn't make a decent cup of coffee to save his life. They decided to walk to the ravine as it was a dry day and Morgan needed his daily walk. He pulled at the lead at first, but then settled into a happy trot beside Jordan, stopping every few paces to sniff the bushes.

Jordan and Brooke chatted about random things while they strolled along the outskirts of the town, happily catching up with each other's lives. Brooke told him about an awful date she'd been on a few weeks ago where the man wouldn't stop mentioning how much money he made as an investment banker. Jordan explained how things were quite stressful with his business, but that he was glad he was keeping it afloat to honour his dad's legacy.

As they walked, Brooke couldn't help but notice several people glancing over at them and then leaning over to each other and whispering. It wouldn't take long for the news to get back to her mum, but the thought of calling her filled her with a sinking dread. Didn't people in this town have anything better to do than gossip and spread rumours? Brooke tried her best to ignore their stares, keeping her head down until they were far enough out of town not to be seen by anyone.

Jordan let Morgan off the lead when they reached the wide-open fields. It wasn't until Brooke and Jordan had crossed a large field and come to a barbed wire fence with a tiny gate that they stopped walking. The old, mouldy sign was still there, even more weather-beaten, which read *DANGER – Beaker Ravine Ahead. KEEP OUT.* The words were so faded that they were barely legible, but Brooke knew exactly what was on that sign. Everyone knew.

As Brooke absorbed the words again, her mouth turned dry and she coughed at the scratch in her throat. 'I haven't been back here since ...'

'Since the last time we were all together, looking for Kieran's body,' added Jordan.

'Which wasn't even there because Tyler had moved it when it first happened.' Brooke remembered it well. She'd never been so scared, but Amber had squeezed her hand the entire time and the four of them had stumbled through the dark and down to the bottom of the ravine. It didn't feel like it was only five years ago. It felt like yesterday.

Jordan sighed as he ran his fingers over the sign. 'Do you ever wonder how the hell we all wound up like this?'

'You still blame Tyler, don't you?'

'A part of me does, yes.'

'He was our friend.'

'A friend who forced us to help cover up the fact he murdered Kieran so he could keep his own family secret hidden.'

Brooke took a deep breath. 'What he did was wrong, but none of us knew what he was going through. His mother used to rape him while his father watched. That would mess up any kid.'

'Yeah, well … if he'd come to us about it in the first place …' Jordan tailed off and called Morgan over, who'd been busy sniffing in the long grass nearby. Jordan clipped Morgan to his lead and pushed open the rickety gate.

Brooke understood Jordan's issue with Tyler and what he'd forced them all to do, but that was in the past. There was nothing they could do about it now, except … Then again, Amber had needed her help and she'd ignored her pleas and only thought about herself. Why had she forgiven Tyler, but hadn't been willing to help Amber? The thing Brooke couldn't wrap her head around was why people seemed obsessed with bringing up the past. Why couldn't they just leave things alone?

Brooke swallowed back the rising bile in her throat and blinked away the tears that threatened to spill. She pressed further ahead, along the narrow path. The area was so familiar to her that a memory from the past played out before her eyes.

'Hey, remember when Amber dared you to climb that tree to get a leaf from as far up as possible?' she asked.

Jordan laughed. 'Yeah, I was so determined to impress her, I'd have done anything. I was scared shitless. I hate heights.' They shared a laugh.

'You loved her from the start, didn't you?'

Jordan didn't respond straight away, but kept his head down, dipping under a low-hanging branch. He then turned back to Brooke who was following behind him. 'Yes, always.'

Brooke tripped over a fallen branch, managing to right herself before she fell. 'She was totally into you too. She always was.'

Jordan smiled faintly. 'I guess I was worried that we'd ruin our friendship group or something if we got together. Plus, we were teenagers. Not many teenage relationships make it very long. She would have found someone better.'

'You don't know that.'

'True. She found Sean Walker, a fucking waste of space.'

Brooke raised her eyebrows at his stern words. She hadn't heard Jordan say a proper swear word for a long time. As a young man, before Kieran died, Jordan had been the kindest, most gentle and mild-mannered of the whole group. He'd been polite, funny and had cared more about the others than himself, but once his guilt had taken over, he'd been warped and twisted into The Bad Man, a vile, angry and abusive man who'd beaten his wife and hated everyone, most of all himself. Now, however, he was almost back to being the old Jordan, although maybe he was slightly rougher around the edges. But that was okay because Brooke liked the new Jordan.

Jordan reached the thick trees first, the ones that had practically made the old path invisible. Everything was overgrown, but there were some broken branches ahead.

'Someone's been through here recently,' said Jordan, touching a bent twig. He looked down at the ground. 'There are some footprints in the dirt here … look.'

Brooke followed his pointed finger and nodded. 'You're right. I thought the ravine was off limits.'

'It is, but when has that ever stopped anyone? We knew the dangers back then and still went searching for trouble, so what's to say the local kids around here wouldn't do the same?'

Brooke didn't respond, but she silently agreed with him. She just hoped whoever had been through here and visited the ravine hadn't done it for the wrong reasons. It was true, the place was fascinating to a lot of people, but three people had died there. It was a place that should be respected, not abused.

Jordan, Brooke and Morgan emerged through the trees on the other side after battling the thick undergrowth. The steep edge of the ravine was merely a few feet away from the edge of the woods, which made it perilous for anyone who didn't know the area. A person could easily step straight off the edge if they weren't keeping an eye on their surroundings.

Brooke's eyes landed on the fallen tree that bridged one side of the expanse to the other; the tree from which Kieran had lost his balance and fallen twenty-five years ago. Brooke closed her eyes against the vivid memory as Kieran's piercing scream echoed through her mind, and that ghastly thud as he'd hit the bottom with enough force to disintegrate his fragile body. Nausea flooded her senses, and she swallowed the bile that had risen in her throat again.

'You okay?' asked Jordan. He was staring at the tree too. His eyes were locked onto it, not blinking, until Morgan pulled at his lead, craning to get to the edge. Jordan pulled the dog back.

'Yeah, I'm okay,' said Brooke, taking a deep breath it. Her heart rate had increased, and she was struggling to catch her breath. She peered over the edge, spying the snaking river one hundred feet below, which looked almost dried up now. She raised her eyes, following the riverbed as far as she could see into the distance. A few miles down the ravine was Lake Peace, a scenic spot for tourists and the local community. In the summer, it was usually heaving with half-naked bodies swimming in its black depths, but Brooke hadn't visited the lake since she was a child, before everything happened.

'I forgot how steep it was,' said Jordan, keeping his eyes anywhere but at the drop-off.

Brooke shuddered, stepping back from the edge. 'There have been a lot of landslides by the looks of it. What exactly are we searching for?'

'Something … Anything. The truth is, I don't know, but I'll know it when I see it.'

Brooke rubbed her neck and peered over the side again. The almost vertical path down to the bottom had all but worn away now. 'I don't think there's a way down anymore. The only way to get to the bottom now would be to come at it from where the lake is and walk the few miles upstream.'

'I think you're right, and I can't risk taking Morgan down there anyway. I don't know what I was thinking coming here. This was a bad idea.'

'No, it wasn't.' Brooke held her hand up to stop him from speaking any further. 'Let's think about this for a minute. Amber was found at the bottom just underneath the fallen tree. She supposedly fell from the middle of the tree; the same place from which Kieran fell and Tyler jumped. Why?'

'What do you mean, why?'

'Why would she do that?'

Jordan stared at her for a moment. The way his eyes seemed to see straight through her made the tiny hairs on the back of her neck stand on end. Eventually, he shook his head.

'She wouldn't. If she truly did want to end her life then she'd have wanted to go out quietly, not draw attention to herself. By jumping from the exact same spot as where the others did, she'd have drawn huge attention to herself, which was never her intention.'

'Exactly. Amber liked to remain quiet and inconspicuous. She suffered in silence. She wouldn't have liked to cause a huge scene.'

'So ... if someone killed her, it means she was pushed.'

Brooke nodded. 'Right, but who in their right mind would follow Amber out onto the fallen tree? What were they both doing out there and why? I find it hard to believe that they were just hanging out and having a casual chat on a fallen tree above the ravine.'

'Yeah, you're right. That makes no sense.'

'Who else, besides you, Bethany and Sean, did Amber speak to regularly?'

Jordan shrugged. 'She didn't. Not really. She didn't have any friends, not that I knew of anyway. She worked with Hayley at the coffee place, but other than that ... I have no idea.' Jordan kicked a small stone into the ravine where it bounced all the way down to the bottom. 'Why the hell didn't I pay more attention to her? Why didn't I listen to her?' Brooke could tell, by the way his voice rattled, that he was furious at himself.

She was about to tell him that she was angry with herself too, but then he said, 'What's that?'

Jordan turned his head and stared across the vast chasm to the other side. Brooke followed his line of sight and, as she did, something glistened on the ground next to where the top of the fallen tree rested. Jordan took a few steps to the side to get a better look, but as he did, he lost his footing on the loose stones.

It all happened so fast.

Jordan's feet slipped out from underneath him.

Morgan broke free from his grasp and lunged forwards.

Brooke screamed, 'Morgan, no!'

And the dog bolted across the tree like a streak of black lightning, his lead dragging behind him.

Jordan scrambled to his feet, but Brooke had already jumped up on the tree roots ready to chase after the dog. A yelp made them both freeze, their hearts thumping.

Morgan's lead had caught on a small branch halfway across the trunk and he was unable to move any further, forwards or backwards. One wrong step and he could easily plummet off the edge, and either his weight would snap the branch that was holding him and he'd fall to his death, or he'd dangle from the end of his lead and hang himself.

'Morgan! Stay!' shouted Jordan. Brooke took a step, but Jordan yanked her back from the edge. 'No, I'll go. Stay here.'

'But I'm lighter. You don't know how much weight this tree will take. It's almost completely rotten through.'

'I don't care. You're not going out there. It will be fine.' Jordan turned to look out across the expanse and took a deep breath, his eyes looking anywhere but down. 'Morgan, be a good dog and do as you're told for once. Stay.'

Brooke sucked in a breath and held it as she watched Jordan inch his way across the tree. An image of Kieran, at nearly thirteen years of age, doing the same thing flashed across her vision. The same thing wouldn't happen again, would it? This place was out to get all of them. Were they all doomed to suffer the same fate as each other because of what they'd done?

Brooke closed her eyes, hoping that by the time she opened them, Jordan would have reached his dog, but something made her turn around on the spot.

A rush of wind.

A rattling noise, like a deep, husky breath of air.

She turned, but there was nothing behind her.

Heart pounding, she looked back towards Jordan and let out a sigh of relief when she saw that he'd made it to where Morgan was standing. She could just about make out the dog's legs, which were trembling, his claws gripping the trunk like his life depended on it.

Jordan grasped the lead and unwound it from the branch. He held tight to Morgan's collar so he was easier to control, but the tree was too narrow for them both to turn around safely.

'I'm going to have to go all the way across,' he shouted back to Brooke. 'Do you know if there's another way back to town from the other side?'

'I don't know,' she shouted back, 'I don't think anyone's ever been on the other side of the ravine.'

Jordan and Morgan shuffled awkwardly along the tree and finally jumped down on the solid ground. Brooke jumped up and down with joy and clapped. Morgan, hearing her cheers, wagged his tail and pulled at the lead to go back the way he'd come.

'Oh no you don't, you stupid dog,' said Jordan, pulling him away from the edge. 'What the hell made you run over here in the first place, huh?'

That was when Morgan started barking. It wasn't his usual playful bark, but a deep, vicious sound that made his hackles rise and saliva fly from his mouth. Jordan grasped the lead tighter, turning to search for the cause of Morgan's aggression.

'What is it, boy? What can you see?'

He scanned the surrounding area, but there was nothing out of the ordinary other than a rustle in a nearby bush, which could easily have been a rabbit or just the wind.

'What's the matter?' he asked the dog again. Morgan whined and stopped barking, backing up a few paces. Jordan stroked the dog's head and scratched behind his left ear. 'It's okay. Come on, let's go back then. We don't have to go that way.'

'Jordan, what's that thing glistening over there? I saw it earlier, just before Morgan ran across the tree.' Brooke's voice was clear across the void. He looked in the rough direction of where she was pointing and saw something caught underneath a stone. He bent down and picked it up.

'What is it?' asked Brooke. She stood on her tiptoes but was too far away to see anything.

'It's a keychain,' he shouted back. 'It looks new and clean. I don't think it's been here very long.'

'How the hell did it get there?'

Jordan turned it over and saw a name engraved in the metal. At first, he didn't recognise it, but then a slither of a memory popped into his head and clicked into place. He pocketed the keychain and pulled Morgan closer to him.

'We're coming back across!'

He picked up Morgan, which was somewhat difficult due to the dog's weight and cumbersome size, and made his way back over the tree. He didn't want to risk Morgan walking across himself again, even if he was on the lead. They'd been lucky last time that he hadn't slipped. Morgan seemed to sense the danger and remained perfectly still in Jordan's arms until they reached the other side. Morgan jumped down, ran straight up to the nearest tree and peed on it.

Jordan sighed. 'Honestly, that dog is like a cat. He has nine lives.'

Brooke threw her arms around Jordan's neck. 'Oh my God, I haven't been that scared since ...'

Jordan squeezed her back. 'I know. I'm sorry. We're okay. But look ... this keychain ... it's been dropped very recently by someone.'

'Who?'

He paused for a few seconds before replying, 'Alex Smithson.'

Chapter Thirteen
ALEX
Saturday 28 October 2023 – 09:45 a.m.

When Alex woke up late on Saturday morning, the first thing he heard was banging. He groaned and pulled the duvet over his head, but it was about as useful as blocking out the noise as a chocolate teapot was at holding boiling water. Then his brain clicked into gear, and he flung the covers back and grabbed his phone, a tingle of excitement flooding his body as he read a message from the girl he couldn't stop thinking about.

Harriet: *Hey, I'm sorry about what happened yesterday with Alex the First. Fancy meeting me later to hang out?*

Alex: *Sure. Meet me at the bench we walked past yesterday in an hour.*

Harriet: *Cool.*

Alex's heart lurched as he stared at the ceiling, listening to the banging. It was causing the walls to shake. He guessed either his mum or Linda was putting up pictures somewhere. He was hoping to avoid them this morning as he knew they were planning on going to that coffee morning in town. Alex checked his phone for a Wi-Fi signal. Nope. It was still off. At least there was a weak data signal in his bedroom. Did his mum intend to keep the Wi-Fi off on purpose to punish him for something? He wouldn't put it past her. It wasn't like she cared how having no access to the internet affected him.

Alex listened as his mum and Linda talked. It sounded as if they were in the spare room just down the hall. Due to the thick walls, he couldn't make out any solid words, until there was a knock at the door and Linda spoke through it.

'Alex, your mum and I are going to the coffee morning. The internet will be up later today. We'll see you later.'

'Yep,' was his response.

While he was waiting for them to leave, he cast his mind back to yesterday, mulling over the reason why Harriet had sent an apology this morning.

The trio reached the dilapidated sign at the barbed-wire fence and stopped. Alex went to push the gate open, but as he did, Harriet let out a whimper.

'What?' he asked, looking over his shoulder at her.

'N-Nothing … it's just … I have a really bad feeling about this.'

Alex laughed as he shoved the gate open. 'Trust me, it'll be fine.'

The teenagers walked for a little way, staying silent while Alex trampled the hanging branches and made a path for the other two.

'You don't know what it's like, man,' said Alex the First. He was at the end of the line, with Harriet in the middle.

'I don't know what what's like?'

'You don't know what it's like to have something terrible happen. Three deaths all in the same place. It's not right. People in this town are afraid.'

Alex scoffed, keeping up his pace. 'Trust me, I know what it's like.'

'Oh yeah? What's happened to you that's so terrible?'

But Alex didn't answer. He kept pushing forwards, kicking and stamping on the overgrown branches so Harriet could get through without being scratched.

'No one has been down this way for so long,' whispered Harriet. 'Everything's so overgrown as if the trees themselves are trying to stop us from getting any closer.'

Alex rolled his eyes. She may have been cute to look at, but Harriet didn't seem to have an adventurous bone in her body. What was wrong with this town? Why were they all so afraid of a made-up creature and a few tragic deaths? Surely it wasn't merely because of that newspaper article from some unknown chicken-shit journalist? Then again, he'd often found that words had a profound effect on people in more ways than one.

Alex grabbed a heavy branch and pushed it aside, but as he did a sharp twig sliced his left hand. He winced and yanked his hand away, splattering a few drops of blood on the ground. Grinding his teeth, he continued forwards.

Everyone remained silent until they reached the end of the woods. The sharp edge of the ravine had come out of nowhere. Alex took a deep breath as he leaned forwards to look down. It was at least a hundred feet to the bottom and the sides were almost vertical. There did appear to be a faint path, but even he didn't think it looked safe enough to attempt. One slip and he'd tumble all the way down. There was a small river at the bottom, but it didn't look very deep and was dry in places, so would likely offer little to no protection from a fall.

Alex whistled as he picked up a stone and dropped it into the ravine. 'Wow, this place is awesome! Is this the tree they all fell from?'

Alex the First and Harriet were standing as far away from the edge as possible, huddled close together.

Harriet nodded. 'Yes, that's right.'

'Okay man, you came, you saw, you conquered, now let's head back, yeah?' Alex the First reached out to grab Alex's arm, but Alex jumped away and stepped towards the fallen tree. He hopped up onto the roots, which creaked and groaned under his weight. Harriet sucked in a breath and held it.

'Bet you don't think I can make it all the way across?'

'Come on, man, this isn't funny anymore. Don't you know how dangerous this is? This is how it all started. It was just a silly game.' Alex the First's voice rattled as he spoke.

Alex stretched out his arms to the side for balance and began taking small steps along the tree. 'You guys suck. You're no fun.'

'Alex, please ... get off the tree ... please.' Harriet's voice told him she was close to losing it. Her eyes were glistening and her hands were shaking. 'I don't want you to get hurt. You don't know the power of this place.'

'This place has no power!' shouted Alex. 'It's just a load of fucking—' He stopped, having just heard a sound that couldn't possibly have been real. Alex glanced around, turning slowly on the spot. His left foot slipped, but he barely flinched as he righted himself. 'Did you guys hear that?'

'Hear what?' asked Alex the First.

Alex didn't reply as he turned to look out across the expanse, wobbling slightly on the rotten tree. What he saw on the other side made his blood run cold.

Phoebe was standing at the end of the tree, on the other side, smiling at him and waving.

Alex tapped his foot against the side of the wooden bench while he waited for Harriet. He was early, but after his mum and Linda had left for the coffee morning, he hadn't wanted to hang around the house any longer, so he'd chucked a piece of bread in the toaster and eaten it while he walked into town. He was wearing his favourite hoodie. It smelled a bit ripe, and the cuffs were torn and brown from overuse, but he refused to allow his mum to wash it. It was his good luck charm.

The bench he was sitting on was right next to a large rhododendron bush, but the flowers had all turned by now, merely shrivelled-up brown petals that were dropping off one by one. As he waited, he hummed a tune in his head, attempting to dispel the memory of yesterday's events at the ravine. He had been adamant that his little sister was standing on the other side of the expanse, smiling and waving at him as if it were no big deal, but that was impossible because when he'd returned home last night, his mum had been singing her to sleep and hadn't mentioned anything about her running away. So why had he seen her standing there?

'Hey.' Harriet's soothing voice made him look up. She sat down next to him, her leg brushing his ever so slightly. She was wearing tight jeans and a long-sleeved baggy top, but the vivid white colour really brought out the brightness of her hair.

'Hey,' replied Alex.

'Thanks for meeting me.'

Alex shrugged in response. 'Nothing else to do.'

Harriet frowned. 'Right … well, um … I just wanted to say I'm sorry for running away yesterday, and Alex the First is too. We just got freaked out after you crossed the tree.'

'Nice to know that when my life is on the line you'll turn and run away instead of helping me.'

Harriet hung her head and stared at the floor. 'I'm sorry, but we did warn you about the ravine. It does stuff to people.'

'Define *stuff*.'

'Makes them see things that aren't really there.'

Alex's heart thumped hard in his chest. 'Why would it make me see my little sister?'

Harriet gasped. 'Is that who you saw?'

'Yeah.'

'And you're sure she wasn't out for a walk with your mum or something?'

'Quite sure.'

'Maybe it wanted you to run across the tree and slip and fall. What happened when you reached the other side?'

Alex frowned. 'When you say *it*, you mean The Creature, right?'

Harried nodded slowly in response.

Alex sighed, still frustrated that she thought The Creature was real. It made no sense. 'I ran across the tree without thinking because I thought she was in danger. I slipped and nearly fell, but then when I reached the other side she'd run off and I couldn't find her. Then I heard … something … It called my name.'

Harriet's hands gripped the bench so hard her fingers turned white. 'What did?'

'I don't know. The wind, I guess. I know I heard my name, and it was so close that it was like someone was whispering in my ear, so I spun around, thinking it was Alex the First messing around with me and I saw … I saw …' Alex leaned forwards and buried his face in his hands. Harriet placed a hand on his back and he felt the warmth from her palm through his shirt.

'What did you see?' she asked softly.

Alex stood up and flinched at her touch as if it were burning him. 'Nothing. I saw nothing, okay? Now can we drop all this shit?'

'You saw it, didn't you?'

'I said I didn't see anything.'

'You saw The Creature.'

'No. I saw … It was just a dark shadow, that's all. It was nothing.'

Harriet bit her bottom lip as she stood up and took a step towards Alex. 'Please promise me that you won't go back there again. It's not safe.'

Alex narrowed his eyes at her. 'This town is ridiculous. Believing in creatures and seeing things that aren't real. This whole place is fucked up. Is there something dodgy in the water? Is that what it is? All of you are high on something?'

Harriet blinked as her eyes filled with tears and she looked away. Alex felt a punch to the gut. He hadn't meant to hurt her feelings, but he also couldn't believe the idea of The Creature being real. Bad things happened in life. It didn't mean some freaky entity was after you. It didn't mean you could use it as an excuse and blame every bad thing that ever happened on something else. It wasn't normal.

'Look,' he said, lowering his voice and gently touching her arm, hoping to reassure her he meant no disrespect, 'maybe I'm going about this all wrong. Maybe if I found out more about what happened twenty-five years ago, then I could start to understand it better.'

Harriet looked up at him and wiped her eyes. 'Digging into the past will only make things worse. No one talks about it because it was so painful. No one knows the truth except for two people.'

'Well, maybe it's about time this town started talking about it instead of spreading lies and rumours and causing everyone to become paranoid. Maybe I should speak to those two people. One of them is Jordan, right? The guy who works in town at the plumbing place. He's the only one left now of the five who lives around here, right?'

'No, Brooke Willows is still around. In fact, my mum said she saw her in town early this morning. It's the first time she's been back here since she left four years ago.'

'Right, then that's where I'll start. I'll go and speak to Jordan and Brooke. You coming with me?' Harriet flinched as Alex extended his hand towards her. She hesitated for a few seconds before placing her hand in his. He squeezed it. 'I promise I won't let anything happen to you.'

Harriet smiled weakly. 'Okay, and I promise I won't run away again if I get scared.'

'Deal.'

Chapter Fourteen
LINDA
Saturday 28 October 2023 – 11:05 a.m.

Linda turned to close the front door, but a strong gust of wind caught it and yanked it from her grasp, causing the whole house to shudder. The branches of the large tree at the end of the driveaway were still, not even a whisper of a breeze. She pushed the strange moment to the back of her mind and kicked off her shoes before placing them at the side of the hallway. She needed to set up the shoe rack so that everyone would have a place to keep their shoes. Alex tended to kick them off and leave them wherever they fell, and someone always tripped over them, usually her.

'I wonder if all the coffee mornings are full of as much drama as that one,' she said as she headed into the kitchen.

Emma followed behind her. Emma had been silent the whole walk home and had only spoken to stop Phoebe from running off or straying too close to the road. She seemed distracted by something. Linda wondered if it had anything to do with whatever it was she'd found under the floorboards. To be honest, Linda couldn't stop thinking about it either, not because she was curious as to what it was, but because it was clearly important enough for her wife to hide it from her and she wanted to know why.

'Emma, are you okay?' Linda decided to test the waters.

Emma looked up and smiled. 'Yes, fine. Just a bit shocked about what happened at the coffee morning. Do you really think that woman is in town? Brooke.'

Linda shook her head. 'I don't know, but it's none of our business. We only moved in two days ago. It's got nothing to do with us and, to be honest, I'd rather this family stay out of any drama. We moved away to start over, remember?'

Emma laughed, brushing off the seriousness of the situation as if it were a splash of water. 'Of course. You know me, I'm not one to pry ... I was just curious, that's all.'

'Are you sure it's just curiosity and nothing else?'

'What else would it be?'

Linda caught herself before she spoke the truth; despite her denying it, Emma loved drama and clearly wanted something to distract her. 'Nothing. It's just ... I can't help but think ...' *Nope, stop it, Linda.*

'Think what?' Emma's voice had taken a defensive tone. She stepped forwards. 'Wait ... you think I bought this house because I knew the history of the family who lived here?'

'I didn't say that. Why ... did you?'

'No! I had no idea. I had no idea about any of it, including the details of what happened here two decades ago.'

Linda squeezed her lips together. She didn't like it when she and Emma fought. It was usually because Emma never liked to talk about things. She preferred to bottle up her feelings and let them gnaw at her insides until she broke apart. And that was never a good thing.

'What did you find under the floorboards?'

Emma's body tensed. 'I told you. A mouse nest.'

'I saw you hide something behind your back.' Emma's face flushed and she opened her mouth but made no sound. Linda sighed. 'I thought we agreed we wouldn't keep secrets from each other anymore.'

'We did. I'm not keeping anything from you. What secrets?'

'Emma … if we're ever going to move forwards and deal with what happened then we have to work together. I need you with me. I need you on my side.'

Emma stepped closer to Linda and took both her hands in her own, squeezing them. Linda's body relaxed at her wife's touch. 'I promise you, I'm not keeping anything from you. I just found a dead mouse and I hid it from you because I know dead things freak you out, that's all.'

Linda looked into her wife's eyes and held her stare. She finally smiled and said, 'Okay, thank you.'

Emma took a deep breath. 'Now, let's finish putting these picture frames up in the lounge, shall we? I can't wait for this place to start looking like our home.'

'Great idea. I'll go and flick the kettle on.'

'You need more coffee even after this morning?'

'You can never drink too much coffee,' replied Linda with a laugh. She kissed Emma, gave her hands one last squeeze, and walked into the kitchen. She headed straight for the cupboard under the sink, pulled out her secret stash and downed what was left in the bottle, closing her eyes as she felt the burning liquid slide down her throat.

It hit the spot.

But it wasn't nearly enough …

The next hour was spent happily decorating the lounge. Linda accessed the radio via her phone, so they had some background noise while they worked. Emma seemed to have perked up after their chat and was humming a tune from *The Greatest Showman*, despite the radio playing the greatest hits from the 90s. Phoebe had, apparently, gone to play in her room. Linda had just finished hanging the last picture when there was a knock at the door.

'More nosey neighbours?' asked Emma, looking over her shoulder at Linda, who raised an eyebrow in return.

'God, I hope not. I'm not sure I can deal with having to fake-smile at anyone else today.' Linda left Emma in the lounge and headed for the door.

Jordan Evans was standing on her doorstep, looking a little dishevelled. A young woman stood next to him with beautiful blonde hair and a stylish outfit that Linda wouldn't have been able to pull off even in her wildest dreams. Jordan's dog was whining behind him in his work van, which was parked at the end of the driveway.

'Oh, hello, Jordan. What a lovely surprise. The pipe is working fine, thank you.'

'I'm glad to hear it, but actually I've come about something else.' He gestured at the woman standing next to him. 'This is Brooke Willows.'

'Ah, the infamous Brooke,' replied Linda with a small laugh.

'I take it someone has spotted me already and gossiped about me at the coffee morning?' At least Brooke seemed to be able to take a joke.

'Yes, I'm afraid so. Please, come in both of you. Will your dog be okay in the van?'

'He'll be fine,' replied Jordan. 'We won't be long.'

As Jordan and Brooke stepped into the hallway, Emma appeared from the lounge area with a frown on her face. 'What's going on? Is everything okay?'

'Yes, we're sorry to disturb you, but we were wondering if we could speak to your son, Alex.' Jordan shifted his weight from foot to foot as he spoke, a tell-tale sign of nervousness. Or maybe he just didn't like being in this house.

Linda attempted to hide her surprise. Her first thought was that Alex had already gotten himself into trouble. Maybe he'd been rude or stolen something. It wouldn't be the first time. Emma had no control over the boy, but it wasn't Linda's place to discipline him. He refused to call her Mum anymore, ever since …

'You want to speak to Alex?' asked Emma. 'Has he done something wrong?' It seemed Emma's first thought was the same as Linda's.

'No, nothing like that,' replied Jordan. 'I was just wondering if he'd be interested in a part-time job at the weekends. Just general stuff. Nothing fancy. Sorry, I should have asked you first …' He tailed off and bowed his head.

Linda raised her eyebrows. She couldn't help but wonder if that was the real reason Jordan was here. If it was, why was Brooke here too? Something didn't quite add up.

Chapter Fifteen
EMMA
Saturday 28 October 2023 – 11:15 a.m.

Emma's stomach clenched when Jordan said he wanted to speak to her son. Her mind sprang to the worst-case scenario; that he'd hurt someone. But of course, the idea of Alex hurting someone was crazy. He'd never do that, not intentionally. There was that time, right after it had happened, when he'd punched a boy at school who'd said the wrong thing in front of him. But Alex shouldn't have been punished for that because it wasn't his fault.

Once Jordan mentioned the part-time job, Emma's shoulders relaxed and her stomach unclenched, although it left a dull ache in its place.

'Oh,' she said, summoning as much enthusiasm as she could to cover up that she'd been flooded with dread only moments before, 'yes, I'm sure he'd love that. To be honest, it would be good for him to have something to do at weekends other than sit and play on his phone and Playstation all day.'

Jordan smiled. 'Great.'

'But I'm afraid he's not home. I don't know where he is. He met some new friends his own age the other day, so he may be with them.'

'Okay, no problem. Would you mind asking him to pop by the shop later? Then I can show him around and discuss things further.'

'Yes, of course. I'll tell him as soon as he's home. In fact, I'll text him, so he can maybe head straight there from wherever he is.'

Jordan nodded his thanks. 'Well, we won't take up any more of your time.'

Emma noticed that his eyes lingered on a family photo of the four of them on the side table for a few seconds. Then he and Brooke turned to leave.

'It was lovely seeing you again, Jordan. And nice to meet you, Brooke. We met your mother earlier this morning,' said Linda. As the final words left her mouth, Emma saw Linda wince, as if she knew she shouldn't have said it. Hadn't she just moments before they'd arrived told Emma that she hated drama and gossip?

Brooke smiled, but it didn't look like a happy smile. In fact, she looked as if she were about to burst into tears. 'Oh, yes, I'm going to visit her later today.'

Brooke and Jordan swapped a look, which told Emma there was some sort of awkwardness or issue going on. The urge to know everything was overwhelming. Okay, maybe she'd lied … Maybe she did crave drama and gossip. Anything to take her mind off …

Jordan and Brooke bade goodbye to Linda, who waved at them from where she was standing, but Emma followed them to the front door. As Jordan stepped outside, she reached forwards and tapped his arm.

'Wait … please … I need to speak to you about something.'

Jordan frowned. 'Are you okay, Mrs Smithson?'

'Um … yes, no … I … I found some things in the spare room this morning. Bethany, the little girl who used to live here, all but told me they were there. I shouldn't have looked, but I did and now I'm a bit freaked out.'

Brooke stepped forwards. 'Mrs Smithson, you look pale. Are you sure you're okay?'

Emma nodded vigorously and then crammed a screwed-up piece of paper into Jordan's hand. She stepped back and watched him as he read it. Brooke also leaned in to read and, as she did, her eyes widened.

They knew something about the poem. Emma could see it as clear as day in the way their eyes darkened. Jordan's hand, the one that was holding the paper, started shaking. He looked up and locked his stare with Emma's.

She kept her voice low as she asked, 'What is The Creature? My son mentioned it was just a made-up rumour, but Bethany seems to think it's a real thing.'

Jordan handed the paper back to her. 'I'm afraid Bethany used to have an overactive imagination. I think I remember her writing this for a school project and it freaked the whole class out for weeks. It's nothing to worry about, Mrs Smithson.'

Emma's mouth fell open. 'N-No, that's not true. You're lying. You know more about this.' She shook the paper as she glanced between each of them. Brooke took a step backwards, clearly not wanting to be involved with this conversation any longer.

'Try not to worry,' said Jordan again. He smiled one last time and turned to leave.

'I've seen it!' The words tumbled out before she could stop them, and her voice rose several octaves and decibels. She realised her mistake and lowered it again as she continued. 'It was standing over my daughter's bed last night.' Jordan's jaw clenched and his left eye twitched. 'Please, you have to tell me if it's real or not. Is my daughter in danger? Is what they're saying around here true? That you and your friends were involved in covering up a boy's death twenty-five years ago and that Tyler took his life because he couldn't handle the guilt anymore? I'm sorry, I'm aware this is all extremely personal, and I don't know either of you well enough to bring this up, but I'm telling you, I've seen The Creature, and if you don't help me, I'm going to search for the truth myself.'

Jordan stared at her for several seconds, which felt like hours. Eventually, he exhaled slowly and shook his head. 'Rumours spread like wildfire in this town, Mrs Smithson. The Creature is nothing more than a story a little girl made up while her parents were going through a divorce. It was her coping mechanism.'

Emma flicked her eyes over to Brooke, who was standing behind Jordan, looking down at the ground. 'If something happens to my daughter and I find out you're lying to me ...' Emma left the end of the sentence hanging and stepped backwards. 'Keep an eye on Alex for me. God knows he never listens to a word I say, but maybe he'll listen to you.'

Jordan nodded. 'I will, Mrs Smithson. You have my word.'

Emma closed the door and shut her eyes, fighting the urge to scream out loud.

'Is everything okay?' Linda's voice caused Emma to jump and clutch her chest.

'Fucking hell, Linda. Will you stop eavesdropping on conversations that have nothing to do with you?'

Linda held up her hands. 'I wasn't eavesdropping! Why'd you just bite my head off? What's the matter with you?'

'Nothing … Nothing, I'm sorry. I just …' Emma scratched the back of her neck. It felt like a cold clammy hand was stroking her skin and it was setting her teeth on edge. 'I think I'm ready to see a therapist again.'

Linda's eyes widened. 'Are you sure?'

'Yes.'

'Has something happened?'

'No. Well, yes, but it's nothing to worry about. I'm going to register with the local surgery today and see if I can get the ball rolling.'

Linda nodded as she walked forwards and gave her trembling wife a hug. Emma breathed in her scent, relieved as the tense muscles in her shoulders relaxed. It was all going to be okay now. The Creature wasn't real. There was nothing to be concerned about. It was all in her head.

'If you need me to come with you, then just let me know. You don't have to go through this alone.'

'Thank you. I love you.'

'I love you too.'

Emma hugged her wife and blinked away the tears that threatened to overwhelm her. 'Will you look after Phoebe while I head into town to the surgery?'

Linda nodded. 'Yes, of course. Where is she now?'

'Upstairs in her room.'

Linda pulled away from her and held her shoulders. 'Emma … look at me. I'm proud of you. You know that, right?'

Emma forced a smile but couldn't bring herself to say anything further. She grabbed her bag, slipped on her comfortable black shoes and headed out the door. As she reached the end of the driveway, she paused and looked back at the house. It was only the third day of living here, and already she felt as if her world was falling apart again, just like it had done two years ago.

Emma was annoyed she'd been called into work and made it blatantly obvious as she stormed into the office, flinging her coat on her chair and chucking her bag on the desk, which promptly fell off and landed in the wastepaper bin. She huffed as she fished it out and placed it on the desk with a thud.

'What's got you all in a hump?' asked Stewart, one of her co-workers who sat opposite her. She wouldn't have called him a friend exactly because they didn't hang out anywhere except at work, but he was her closest work colleague and she'd been able to confide in him when everything had kicked off with her divorce.

'Um, how about the fact that it's my day off and I'm not supposed to be here?'

'Who called you in?'

'Who do you think?' Emma lifted her chin in the direction of the closed office door at the end of the hall. 'Mr I-Think-All-Lesbians-And-Bisexuals-Are-Secretly-Straight.' It wasn't the cleverest of nicknames, but it was very apt for her manager. When she'd come out as a bisexual, he'd raised his eyebrows at her and said, 'But you have a husband and a kid,

so you can't like women too.' His real name was Darren Lower. He was twenty kilos overweight and had recently had a hair implant that didn't seem to have taken, yet he refused to acknowledge that fact.

'I'd better go and see what he wants,' she said with a sigh.

Stewart looked over his monitor at her. 'Good luck. He's in a bad mood.'

'When is he ever in a good mood?'

'I think he just needs to get laid.'

'His wife and his mistress not enough for him?'

'I think maybe his wife found out.'

'Ouch. Serves him right.' Emma steeled herself as she made the short walk down the corridor to the office door and knocked.

'Come in.'

Emma pushed open the door, slapped on a fake smile and entered. 'Hey, boss.'

'Ah, Emma, thanks again for coming in on short notice.'

'Sure, but Stewart wasn't aware I was coming in, so what's this about?'

Darren nodded at the door. 'Would you close that please?' Emma obliged and stood awkwardly until Darren gestured at the chair in front of his desk. 'Please,' he said. 'Listen ... um ... this is a little difficult, but I thought you should know before it becomes official. I know you put in an application for the Assistant Office Manager position, but I'm afraid we've decided to give it to someone else.'

Emma's heart sank like a stone for a split second, but then her heart rate increased as she realised what this meant. 'Wait … you're giving it to Stephanie, aren't you?'

Stephanie had been at the company for two years less than Emma, was nine years younger, twenty pounds lighter and had larger breasts and blonde hair. She was also the woman Darren was having an affair with, but no one was supposed to know that, and he didn't know that she and Stewart knew.

'Yes, I'm sorry, but she has more experience in—'

'Bullshit!' said Emma with a fake cough.

Darren narrowed his eyes. 'Look, there's no need for things to get nasty around here. There will be future opportunities to be promoted and you're more than welcome to apply for those as well.'

'Couldn't this have waited until tomorrow?'

'It's being announced in an hour. I thought it best you hear it from me directly and face to face.'

'Great. Thank you. I'll be going now.' She tried but failed to hide the aggravation in her voice as she turned on her heels and left the office. Once she'd shut the door, she headed straight for Stewart's desk. 'He's giving the job to Stephanie.'

Stewart sighed. 'Tough break.'

'Gee, thanks.'

'Hey, at least that means you get to work with me for a bit longer.'

'This is true. You do keep me supplied with chocolate when I need a pick-me-up.'

Stewart rummaged around in a desk drawer and pulled out a chocolate bar. 'Speaking of which …' He threw it and Emma caught it with one hand.

'Thanks. I better head home and—' Emma was interrupted by her phone vibrating in her bag. She picked it up and answered while grabbing her coat and waving bye to Stewart. 'Hey, babe, I'm just heading home now and—'

As Emma listened to Linda's voice on the end of the line, her legs buckled underneath her and she stumbled against the desk, clutching it for dear life as she felt her whole body go numb.

Chapter Sixteen
JORDAN
Saturday 28 October 2023 – 11:25 a.m.

As soon as he and Brooke reached the van, Brooke rounded on him. 'Why the hell did you just lie to that poor woman?'

Jordan ran his hands through his hair. 'I panicked, okay? Plus, it's probably better she doesn't know the truth, and if I told her there was some truth to what she saw, it could put her and her daughter in even more danger. Besides, I'm hoping we can sort this out before anything else happens. Trust me. We just need to speak to her son and find out why and when he was at the ravine.'

'But Alex Smithson doesn't have anything to do with The Creature. He's only just moved here.'

'Yes, but he is clearly digging around in the past. Why else would he have gone to the ravine? Everyone in town knows to stay away from that place. Maybe those kids he's made friends with know something.'

Brooke opened the door to the van and got in while trying to keep Morgan inside, who was bouncing around as if he'd been left on his own for hours, not minutes. Once they were both buckled up and Jordan had pulled out onto the road, she said, 'That poem that Emma found ... it proves Bethany saw The Creature. We should speak to her.'

'Absolutely not. She's free of this place now. There's no way I'm letting her get involved in this ever again.'

'I wish there was a way we could speak to Amber.'

'Maybe there is.'

Brooke raised her eyebrows. 'Oh, please don't tell me you believe in ghosts now?'

'No,' replied Jordan, shaking his head. 'But maybe Amber left us some clues, or maybe Bethany did. Emma found that poem under the floorboards in the spare room, right? Maybe she found more things under there too.'

'Like what?'

'I don't know.'

'So why don't we ask Emma herself?'

'Because something tells me she's close to breaking point as it is.'

Brooke sighed. 'I'm not breaking into anyone's house.'

'That wasn't what I was thinking. If we find Alex … maybe he can look around for us. He does live there, after all.'

'I don't like this. You're asking a kid we don't even know to snoop around in his own house behind his mother's back.'

'I don't like it either, but it's all we've got at the moment, and I reckon that—' Jordan stopped the van in front of his shop and smiled when he saw two young people standing outside it, looking a bit sheepish.

'That's Harriet Forrester,' said Brooke. 'She's grown up a bit since I last saw her. Who's that next to her?'

'Alex Smithson. I recognise him from the family picture I saw earlier at his house.'

Jordan got out of the van, allowing Morgan to jump down after him, and then closed the door. He approached the teenagers. 'Can I help you? Something tells me you two don't need plumbing supplies.'

Alex stepped forwards. 'You Jordan Evans?'

'That's me. Hey, Harriet.' Jordan nodded at the girl who smiled shyly. She looked as if she didn't want to be there.

'Hello, Mr Evans.'

'Call me Jordan, please. You remember Brooke?'

Harriet waved at Brooke who smiled back. 'Hey, Harriet, how's school going?'

'You know, it's school. It's okay, I guess.'

Jordan turned to Alex. 'I've actually been looking for you. We've just been to your house and spoken to your mother.'

Alex raised his eyebrows. 'Oh yeah? Why are you looking for me?'

Jordan slipped his hand into his trouser pocket and pulled out the silver keyring. 'I think you might have lost something.'

Chapter Seventeen
BROOKE
Saturday 28 October 2023 – 11:35 a.m.

Brooke watched Alex attempting to hide his surprise as Jordan held out the keychain. Harriet still looked as if she was trying to make herself turn invisible. In fact, she whimpered when she saw the keyring. Alex stepped up and grabbed it from Jordan.

'Where'd you find this?'

'Beaker Ravine.'

Alex put the keyring in his pocket. 'It must have fallen out of my pocket.'

'What were you even doing there?' asked Jordan. He sidestepped Alex and unlocked the front door to the shop, then held out his hand, allowing Brooke and Harriet to enter first.

'We tried to stop him,' said Harriet, her voice rising an octave as she spoke. 'B-But he wouldn't listen.'

Alex rolled his eyes. 'Gee, thanks, Harriet.' He rounded on Jordan. 'Look, I was just curious, okay? I didn't see the harm in going to have a look at the place. It's just a stupid ravine.'

'Let me get this straight then, Alex.' Jordan threw his keys onto the counter and turned around. Brooke knew what he was doing. He was trying to assert his dominance over the younger man, who was doing his best to look and seem tough, but she was almost certain it was an act. She'd seen it many times before, especially when she was a child, back before the incident at the ravine. 'You heard a story of how a boy was killed there, and then two more people died, and you thought, "I know what would be fun, visiting the place where three people lost their lives." Tell me, what exactly did you expect to find there?'

Alex appeared to shrink in size at Jordan's stern voice. Brooke smirked as she imagined Jordan as a father. He'd make a great father but had never had the chance. Although, back when he'd been controlled by The Bad Man, he hadn't been father material.

The boy opened his mouth, but then glanced at Harriet as if asking for backup. 'I-I didn't mean any disrespect. I was just curious. Harriet and the other Alex told me some weird stuff happened there. I was bored. I wanted an adventure, that's all.'

Brooke stepped forwards. 'What weird stuff?'

Jordan looked at her and then back at Alex and raised his eyebrows. 'Well?'

Alex gulped. 'Something about a creature.' A flush crept up his neck.

Harriet whimpered again, which caused the other three to swivel their heads in her direction. She sniffed loudly. 'I'm sorry. I know what happened to you and Amber and everyone was horrible, but you know what this town is like. Rumours spread so quickly and when Bethany started that rumour, all the kids in the whole school started talking about it.'

'What exactly is it the people in this town think happened?' asked Jordan.

Harriet blinked rapidly and looked away. Brooke took the opportunity to place her hand on Harriet's arm. 'It's okay.

We're not angry or anything. We just want to know what's going on so we can try and fix it.'

Harriet nodded, looking like a nervous rabbit caught in headlights. 'Some people – I don't know who – are saying that … that you all killed Kieran and then you, Amber and Jordan forced Tyler to take the blame and then killed him. Amber then couldn't live with the guilt any longer.' Brooke locked eyes with Jordan, whose jaw tightened. He kept his anger at bay while Harriet continued speaking in a whisper. 'Basically, people think that The Creature is some sort of ghost who's terrorising everyone.'

Jordan snorted. 'A ghost, seriously?'

Harriet shrugged. 'Or some sort of bogeyman. The legend is that if you go to the ravine then The Creature will call you by name and make you jump to your death. That's why we tried to warn Alex, but he didn't believe us.'

Jordan cleared his throat. 'Hang on … there's a legend now? Why the hell is this the first I'm hearing of it?'

Harriet shuddered. 'I guess people don't want to make you angry in case … in case …'

Jordan cocked one eyebrow at the girl. 'In case I kill them too?'

'Something like that.'

'Fucking hell,' muttered Jordan. Brooke shot him a stern look to tell him to cool it. He nodded at her. 'Fine … whatever. Alex, what happened when you got to the ravine?' Jordan readjusted his foot position. Brooke could tell he was nervous by the way he kept biting his bottom lip and shifting his weight from side to side. She had the unmistakable feeling of dread too, creeping up from the base of her spine, like tiny cold pinpricks. Everyone turned to face Alex.

'Nothing happened,' he snapped.

There was a brief pause.

'He heard a voice,' said Harriet.

'What voice?' asked Jordan.

'Just a voice.' No one moved. No one even breathed as they waited for more. 'My sister was calling me from the other side of the ravine.'

Jordan frowned. 'Your sister?'

'Yes. It was her, as clear as I'm seeing you now.'

Jordan turned to Harriet. 'Did you see her?'

Harriet shook her head, clamping her lips shut. Her eyes were wide. 'No, I didn't see anything. I ran off soon after Alex ran across the log.'

'Wait … you ran across the log? Are you crazy or just stupid?' asked Jordan, his voice rising again. Brooke was going to have words with him later.

Alex threw up his hands. 'Look, I wasn't expecting to see her standing there, was I?'

'Okay, fine, you ran across a rotten log which, had it collapsed under your weight would have plummeted you to your death … then what?'

Alex froze and turned a sickly shade of white. He glanced from one person to the next. 'I saw something. I mean, my sister wasn't there, but I saw a dark shadow.'

'What did it look like?' asked Jordan.

'I don't know, it was a fucking dark shadow!'

Jordan rolled his eyes. 'Did it have any sort of shape, any long arms or red eyes?'

'What the fuck? No, nothing like that.'

Jordan let out a long breath and looked at Brooke, who shrugged her shoulders. 'What does this mean?' she asked.

'Beats the hell out of me.' Jordan faced Alex. 'Are you sure your sister wasn't there? Did you ask her about it later?'

'What?' Alex laughed. 'How the hell would I be able to ask her?'

Jordan stared at him, a blank expression across his face.

No one seemed to understand Alex's question.

But then he spoke, and his final five-word sentence made their blood run cold.

'I don't have a sister. Not anymore. She died two years ago.'

Chapter Eighteen
LINDA
Saturday 28 October 2023 – 11:40 a.m.

As Emma shut the door, leaving to head into town, Linda closed her eyes and allowed the tears to flow freely. Pure relief and utter devastation racked her body at the same time. Seeing her wife so upset, so damaged and broken because of what had happened, because of what she'd done …

For two years Linda had carried the guilt on her shoulders.

It was her fault.

Phoebe's death.

That's when the headaches had started.

That's when she'd started drinking every day.

Linda even had a name for it, a name for the gut-wrenching, heavy weight of guilt pressing down upon her every single day. It was silly really, the name she'd given it, almost as if she were trying to make light of the fact that she was the reason her wife's little girl was dead. As if there was an excuse good enough.

The Void.

That's what she called it.

Because it was the perfect explanation of how she felt.

Ever since that fateful day, The Void had crept up on her, slowly at first, but then it had completely consumed her, transforming her into someone she no longer recognised.

The headaches arrived. Tension headaches. That was the medical and technical term for them, but Linda knew the real reason behind their appearance. It wasn't because her job was stressful. Everyone had stressful jobs, or some form of stress in their lives, and she was no different. Her old doctors had given her some pills to manage them, but there was no pill that could stand up to The Void. She'd fallen into its depths a long time ago. The walls were so high she couldn't see the top anymore.

There was no way out. She spent her days huddled at the bottom of The Void, desperately trying to stay alive, to stay sane, to hide the truth from everyone.

Next came the drinking.

Again, at first, her dependence on alcohol had started off small, barely even a drop in the ocean compared to what it was like today. A quick glass of wine at the end of a long day. Everyone drank after a busy day, she used to tell herself. Everyone used a glass of wine to relax in the evening, especially since her wife was practically catatonic and never left her room.

Linda deserved that glass of wine.

But then it turned to two glasses, then a bottle, and it wasn't just a couple of times a week. It was every day and every night and two or three bottles at weekends. Then, after a few months, the wine wasn't strong enough, so she turned to vodka.

Just one or two of an evening again. Just a small glass, with a splash of lemon, but then those glasses got bigger, more frequent, and she realised she was even drinking before breakfast, before work, before she went to the gym. She'd discarded the mixers too, so now it was straight vodka, sometimes direct from the bottle; she often didn't have time to fetch a glass because Emma needed her, or Alex needed picking up from school after lashing out again and hitting another boy.

Then there was the police investigation into Phoebe's death.

Emma had all but stopped talking and refused to see anyone, so Linda was left to deal with everything. She was asked exactly what had happened, exactly what had made Phoebe run out into the road that Halloween day …

Linda shook her head violently from side to side and screamed as she sank to the floor, her legs unable to support her any longer. The sounds coming out of her were more like a dying animal than a grown woman, but there was no one in the house to hear her.

Because Emma was wrong.

Phoebe wasn't playing upstairs in her bedroom.

But someone was …

Linda clamped her mouth shut, covering it with her hand as she stared at the ceiling.

Thud … thud, thud … thud …

Linda's heart rate jumped as she listened to the sounds of heavy footsteps above her.

'No,' she whispered to herself. 'There's no one up there.'

The Void …

'*Linda* …' The voice wasn't human, wasn't distinguishable as a voice at all. It had no tone, no depth and no pitch, but it was there. She'd heard it as clear as day.

'Stop it,' she cried. 'Stop it!'

Linda scrambled to her feet and ran into the kitchen, yanking open the cupboard under the sink. She grabbed the bottle. Empty.

'No!'

She dropped the bottle on the floor as another loud thud echoed above her. The whole house trembled. Had something fallen over? It sounded as if someone had tipped over a wardrobe … but there were no wardrobes in the house because they were all inbuilt as part of the design.

The bottle disintegrated into a million shards as it spread across the floor of the kitchen. She had no choice but to walk across it. She was barefoot, but as she placed one foot slowly in front of the other, she didn't feel the sting of tiny shards of glass embedding themselves into her feet. All she could focus on was the voice that was calling her.

'Linda …'

Upstairs. She needed to go upstairs.

Linda reached the bottom of the stairs and looked up.

'Linda …'

The sunlight lit up the top landing as if a spotlight was beaming in through a window. She shielded her eyes as she ascended the stairs, one step at a time, pausing on each one, debating whether she should even proceed.

But the voice kept calling her.

With every step she took, however, the voice became quieter. By the time she reached the top step it had gone completely, and she was left standing in silence with only her heartbeat thudding so loudly that she could hear it, for company.

Her eyes scanned the hallway ahead and then landed on the door to Phoebe's room. Emma had appointed it as Phoebe's room the second they'd moved in. She'd even begun to decorate it with the child's belongings, had made the bed up with Phoebe's favourite duvet set and had unpacked her clothes, all of which fit a seven-year-old. If she'd been alive today, she would be nine and too big for any of them.

It had almost broken Linda to hear her wife talk about Phoebe as if she were alive. The first time it had happened, Linda had been unable to react, merely staring at her wife in disbelief as she conversed with her dead daughter, but the smile on Emma's face had been the reason why Linda had kept her mouth shut ever since. Emma made Phoebe her favourite dinners, bought her ice cream, and even read her stories and sang her to sleep.

But Phoebe wasn't there.

She'd never been there and yet ... there was someone in her room.

A sweet humming sound pierced the eerie silence. Linda recognised the tune at once.

'A Million Dreams' from *The Greatest Showman*; Phoebe's favourite film.

'P-Phoebe?' Linda's voice quivered. She was going crazy. There was no other explanation for it. She was hearing things that weren't there, like Emma did on a daily basis. Was it this house? No. It couldn't be the house because, if she was being honest with herself, she'd been seeing things long before she moved here. Black shadows. Strange voices.

The humming stopped as Linda pushed open the door to Phoebe's room. Sunlight illuminated the space from all directions and Linda had to shield her eyes again. They stung with the effort of keeping them open against the blinding white light.

After a few seconds, the light began to fade and she was able to scan the room.

There was no one there.

There was no little dead girl humming her favourite show tune.

And there was no dark shadow hovering in a corner.

But there was a black shape staring at her. It had red eyes and long, claw-like limbs and a skeletal body that appeared to be made of nothing but smoke.

Linda screamed and the shape disintegrated into thin air.

She dropped to her knees and wept into her hands, rocking backwards and forwards as her mind took her back to that day: the day Phoebe had died and The Void had first swallowed her whole.

Linda searched down every aisle in the store, keeping her eyes wide open, afraid that if she blinked, she might miss Phoebe. Her breath came in short gasps as she darted down the next aisle.

'Phoebe!' She couldn't breathe. She couldn't—

'Excuse me, ma'am. Are you okay?' A man with jet-black hair and a t-shirt with the store's logo on the front stopped stacking the nearby shelves and turned to her.

'M-My daughter ... Have you seen a little girl? She's seven. Brown hair. She's wearing a red jacket and black leggings. Oh God ... She ran off and I can't find her.'

The man nodded, his demeanour immediately switching to one of professionalism and concern.

'Okay, don't worry, ma'am. I'll put an alert out at the front desk and ask my colleagues to help look for her. Come and wait by the desk in case someone finds her and takes her there. She can't have gotten far.'

Linda followed the kind man towards the back of the store. She kept throwing glances in every direction as she walked, her eyes on high alert for a flash of red. She thought back to when Emma had told her about the time Phoebe had disappeared in a local Tesco store. She'd apparently only turned her back for a moment to pick up some bread, and when she'd turned around the girl was gone. Emma had explained that it had been the worst five minutes of her life until she'd been found safe and sound, staring up at the array of chocolate bars two aisles over, completely unaware of the commotion she'd caused.

Linda took a deep breath, telling herself that Phoebe had only run off to go and find something, and in a few minutes one of the store workers would find her and everything would be okay.

But ten minutes passed, and Phoebe hadn't turned up. That's when Linda reached into her bag and pulled out her phone. She didn't want to call Emma, but the more time passed, the more likely it was that Phoebe wouldn't turn up. She'd seen those real-life documentaries on television, those horrible news stories about children going missing, about a child being abducted in the blink of an eye, and what better place to take a child than a Halloween store ... The few minutes after a disappearance were always the most crucial.

Linda's finger hovered over the call button ...

'Ma'am ... she's been found.' The black-haired man appeared at Linda's side and touched her arm.

Linda dropped the phone and let out a garbled cry. 'Oh my God. Where is she?'

'She was found trying on costumes in the changing rooms. She's with the store manager now, waiting by the front door.'

Linda bent down and grabbed the phone, shoving it back into her bag. 'T-Thank you,' she said as she breathed a sigh of relief. Her heart rate had more than doubled now and she was sweating as she ran towards the front of the store.

A flash of red caught her eye, and she threw herself to her knees in front of the child and hugged her around the waist as tears streamed from her eyes.

'Phoebe!' she cried. 'Please don't ever do that again.'

'I was just trying on costumes.'

The store manager looked at Linda and smiled. 'Is everything okay now?' she asked.

'Yes, thank you. Thank you so much.' Linda stood up and brushed herself down. She grabbed Phoebe's wrist and pulled. 'Come on, we're going home.' Her voice was stern.

'But I haven't chosen what I want yet.'

Linda dragged her through the door and out onto the pavement. She waited until the door to the store closed and then grabbed Phoebe's shoulders and shook her.

'You ran off! Do you have any idea what I've been through in the past fifteen minutes? I thought you'd been kidnapped. I thought you had run off and got lost. What were you thinking?' Linda's voice was too loud. Too aggressive. She

knew that, but the adrenaline flooding her body was causing her to overreact and she couldn't control herself. Relief and anger and frustration were all clawing for attention.

'I-I'm sorry, I didn't think, I didn't—'

'No, you didn't think! I'm supposed to be looking after you. Do you have any idea what your mother would say if— God, it doesn't even bear thinking about. Never do that again!' Linda shook her a second time.

Phoebe's eyes filled with tears, and she wailed.

'I'm sorry!'

The next few moments happened in the blink of an eye.

Phoebe was there, standing in front of Linda. She was crying.

She pulled away and slipped out of Linda's grasp.

A car hurtled along the road, exceeding the speed limit.

Phoebe stepped backwards into the road.

Linda screamed and lurched forwards to yank her back.

The car braked but hit Phoebe at full speed.

And Linda's world broke apart before her eyes.

Chapter Nineteen
ALEX
Saturday 28 October 2023 – 11:45 a.m.

Jordan, Brooke and Harriet stared at him with frowns across their faces and unblinking eyes. Alex's face heated, not fully understanding why they looked as if he'd spoken a foreign language. He hadn't wanted to bring it up, hadn't wanted to talk about his dead sister or the fact that his mum was a complete lunatic who still tucked her dead child into bed at night and talked to her as if she were alive. But …

It was this place. This town. The people. Or was it?

Alex knew it had started long before they'd moved here. He'd changed the day Phoebe had died, just like his mum and Linda had. The whole family had been split apart by grief and his dad had then paid the ultimate price …

Alex gulped back the nausea that threatened to engulf him. No, this had nothing to do with his dad. There was a time and a place for that subject, and this wasn't it. His dad was a different matter entirely.

'Wait … Phoebe's dead?' Jordan ran his left hand through his hair.

Alex nodded. 'Yeah, and she has been for nearly two years. She died on Halloween in 2021. Got hit by a car. Died instantly.'

Jordan and Brooke swapped glances. They knew something: something they didn't want to share. Alex clenched his fists at his sides, fed up with being kept in the dark and treated like a child.

'What?' he snapped. 'What is it?'

Jordan turned to face him. 'You said you saw your sister at the ravine yesterday, right?'

'Yeah, briefly.'

'And your mothers … Do they both see her too?'

'No, only my real mum. Linda isn't my mum. They got married three years ago.'

'So, Linda doesn't see Phoebe, but acts as if she does?'

Alex shook his head slowly. 'Not exactly. We're basically just going along with what Mum says and does because we don't want her to have another nervous breakdown, so Linda and I play along and sometimes pretend that Phoebe's alive. Mum doesn't seem to notice that we don't actually talk or interact with Phoebe.' Alex shuffled his feet. 'It got awkward back in Bedford. Mum was going around talking as if Phoebe was alive and all her friends and colleagues eventually couldn't deal with it, so she ended up pushing everyone away because she couldn't deal with Phoebe's death. But Linda and I didn't have the luxury of walking away. We've had to deal with it ourselves. That's why we moved here … for a fresh start, but it seems we're doomed wherever we go. Mum is still acting crazy and, eventually, the people in this town will realise she's crazy and speaking to a dead girl.' Alex shrugged. 'Then again, this town seems like it's full of crazy people, so maybe we'll end up fitting right in.'

An awkward silence filled the void after Alex's speech, but Harriet filled it by gasping loudly and running up to Alex, throwing her arms around his neck.

'You poor thing, I'm so sorry.'

Alex saw red and shrugged her off. 'Hey, I don't need any sympathy. I'm fine. I just want to know what the hell's going on. My mum may have seen my dead sister before coming to this town, but I haven't, and I want to know why I now am.'

Harriet shied away from him and moved a little closer to Brooke, who gave her a small smile. 'S-Sorry, Alex. It's just … it must have been so difficult and everything when your sister died and having to deal with all that.'

Alex shrugged again. 'Everything changed that day.'

'In what way?' asked Jordan. 'I realise losing your sister like that must have been painful and devastating, but I need you to be very specific with your answers now. After Phoebe died, what changed?'

Alex glared at him for a few seconds, but then his shoulders relaxed as the tension dissipated. Jordan was only trying to help. It was more than anyone had done for him lately, so he decided to offload some of his thoughts and feelings to a total stranger, something he never did, even with his mum.

'It was Linda's fault. I mean … she was there when it happened. She said that Phoebe ran off in a store while they were shopping and disappeared. She must have run out into the road and been hit by a car. By the time Linda got there, it was too late. She died instantly.'

Everyone in the room flinched, imagining the scene before their eyes.

Alex took a deep breath and continued, 'After that, everything was a blur for a few days. Mum broke down and locked herself in her room. Linda handled everything, including the funeral and the police enquiry, and I … I started getting into trouble at school.'

'Were you like that before? I mean … did you get in trouble a lot before she died?'

'No … I got straight As in everything and had never been in trouble. It was just how I dealt with everything. Dad started drinking heavily. Mum had a breakdown. Linda was busy. And I started lashing out at school. It was weird. It was sort of like my whole personality changed and I became a different person to the one I was before.' Alex watched as Jordan and Brooke exchanged glances again. 'Okay, what is it? You keep looking at each other as if you know something that I don't. Spill it.'

Jordan inhaled and held his breath for a few seconds before releasing it calmly. 'What I'm about to tell you might sound crazy, but hear me out, okay?' He glanced at Brooke who nodded and then back to Alex who held his gaze, then dipped his head in acknowledgement.

'Twenty-five years ago, Brooke and I, and three of our friends, were at Beaker Ravine playing a game. There was an accident and Kieran fell to his death. Our friend, Tyler, convinced us to help him cover up Kieran's death, so we did. We hid the body and then made a blood oath to never speak a word of what we'd done to anyone as long as we lived.'

At this point, Alex snorted. 'A blood oath? Seriously?'

'Will you shut up and listen? Back then, we were barely teenagers and Tyler had this way of talking that made him sound invincible, like he was in control of everything, but that wasn't the case at all as we found out twenty years later. Anyway, the point is after that day, after we'd covered up

Kieran's death and come up with a cover story to tell everyone, we started drifting apart as friends. We barely spoke to one another, but that wasn't the worst of it.' Jordan glanced at Brooke, who had tears swimming in her eyes. She gave him a slight nod, urging him to keep going. 'Over the coming weeks and months and years, we all started ... *changing* ... in a bad way. A very bad way.'

Alex frowned at him. 'What do you mean by ... *changing*?'

'Our personalities changed, and it was almost like we were different people to who we were before.'

Alex's eyes widened as he recognised his own words parroted back at him. 'Wait ... are you saying that whatever happened to you is happening to me and my family?'

Jordan shook his head. 'No, not exactly in the same way. It was just the way we dealt with what happened. We all carried the heavy weight of guilt around with us and it warped and twisted us into these people that none of us recognised.' He cleared his throat. 'Tyler, who was once the life and soul of the party, became severely depressed and thought about dying every day. Brooke ...' Jordan nodded in her direction. '... was happy, beautiful, and always lived life to the fullest, but she was trapped in her own home by a crippling fear of going outside. I was like you ... I was the good kid, never said a bad word or showed any sort of aggression, but I eventually started hitting my wife. I lied, I cheated and I hated everyone around me. And Amber, who was always lively and beautiful and happy, developed severe insomnia and eventually started having vivid hallucinations of a dark entity who she called—'

'The Creature,' finished Alex.

Jordan nodded. 'The thing is, The Creature began to change as well and even Bethany, Amber's daughter, started seeing it, or at least knew of its presence.'

Harriet gulped loudly. 'So … so is it … I mean, is The Creature real, or isn't it? And why is it still here?'

'After hearing Alex's story, I don't think it is real, not in a physical sense. The Creature disappeared when Amber was killed. It was always her imagination. It was only Amber who ever saw it. The rest of us saw our own version of The Creature, and I think that's what's happening with you and your family.'

'Okay …' Alex frowned again. 'But I thought Amber ended her own life.'

'There's been some new evidence to suggest that isn't the case. The police around here aren't saying much or releasing any details, but Brooke and I need to find out for ourselves. We owe it to Amber.'

Alex held up his hands. 'Let me get this straight … You're saying The Creature isn't real … Then what the hell is it that's terrifying this fucking town into thinking it is?' Alex flicked his eyes over towards Harriet, who shuddered. 'And why the hell is my mum seeing hallucinations of my dead sister? Fuck … why am *I* seeing hallucinations of my dead sister? Are you saying it's all in our heads?'

Jordan's voice remained calm as he spoke. 'The Creature appears differently to all of us, but it's not the same thing. The Creature was a manifestation of Amber's guilt, like The Fear and The Bad Man were to me and Brooke.' At the mention of the other names, Jordan saw Alex cock his eyebrow, but he didn't question any further. 'Your mother is seeing Phoebe as still alive because she's overwhelmed with grief and possibly guilt. To your mother, Phoebe is her version of The Creature. I expect Linda is experiencing something similar too. Have you noticed anything that's changed with Linda since Phoebe died?'

Alex coughed and nodded. 'Yeah. She started getting these bad headaches, and she drinks a lot. She thinks I don't notice, but it's obvious. Mum is too preoccupied with her dead daughter to care about what Linda's doing behind her back. Are you saying these headaches and her dependence on alcohol is a form of guilt because of what happened?'

'I believe it could be, yes.'

'What about me? My so-called rage and change in attitude … What am I supposed to be guilty about?'

'You tell me.'

Alex stared back at Jordan. He wasn't about to lose this staring contest. No way. But then Jordan broke his stare and cleared his throat.

'Well, whatever it is … now you know how to handle it.'

'And how do I handle it?'

'You confess.'

'I've got nothing to confess.'

'Then maybe it's Linda and your mother you should be worried about.'

Alex had known that all along. He knew Linda was hiding something, but how could he get her to confess? Would that truly make everything better again? Would it all go back to how it used to be before Phoebe died? That's all he wanted. He just wanted his mum back.

Alex's mind flashed back to the day Phoebe died, to the moment he'd found out what had happened. It was a moment he'd never forget.

Halloween was always a fun day at school because it was an excuse to put on fancy-dress and act like a kid in a sweet shop. Even the teachers got into the spirit and donned some weird costumes or trickled fake blood from their mouths in a half-hearted attempt to fit in.

Alex had dressed as a classic vampire. Not the Twilight version or anything lame like that, but the old-school Dracula version with a black cape, slicked-back hair and dripping fangs. Like his sister, Halloween was his favourite time of year. It even beat Christmas. The main reason why he loved it was because Phoebe loved it. Seeing her bright eyes widen with glee at the sight of sweets in a bucket always filled him with happiness.

Alex sat in an English lesson and was going over verbs when the headmaster stuck his head around the door and asked if he could come to his office. The fact the headmaster himself had fetched him seemed unusual and Alex got a few murmurs of 'Good luck, mate' and 'rather you than me' from his friends as he picked up his books and left the room. He followed Headmaster Jackson down the hall and into his office.

'Is everything okay, sir? Am I in trouble?' It seemed unlikely to Alex that he was, but he couldn't think of any other reason why the headmaster had taken him out of class and into his office.

'No, nothing like that, Alex. Please, take a seat. Your father will be here in a moment to collect you.'

Alex frowned as he sat down. 'Collect me? It's ten o'clock in the morning, sir.'

Headmaster Jackson avoided eye contact as he sat down behind his desk. Alex could sense something wasn't right, that the headmaster wasn't telling him the whole truth, but before he could open his mouth to question him further, the door to the office opened and his father rushed in. He looked awful, as if he'd run a marathon and not had a chance to shower. His wispy hair was plastered to his face, which was a sickly shade of white.

'Dad?' Alex rose to his feet.

'A-Alex ... it's ... I've come to ... I'm sorry ...' His father glanced at the headmaster, who looked as if he wanted to use his own desk as a shield against what was happening.

But what was happening?

Alex's father turned to him and held both his shoulders. 'Son ... your sister's been in an accident.'

Alex dropped his shoulder bag on the floor, ignoring the fact that one of his books fell out. 'Is she okay? What happened?'

His father's eyes flooded with tears. 'I'm sorry.' He shook his head and looked away from his son.

'Dad? What's going on? Where is she? What's happened?'

But his father lost all control and sunk to the floor, clutching his face in his hands. He spoke through his fingers, but Alex couldn't understand any of the words coming out of his mouth. There was one word he did catch right at the very end.

'Dead.'

Alex joined his father on the floor and wrapped his arms around him, holding him close, the way he wished his father would hold him.

He didn't cry.

In fact, he never shed a single tear over the death of his sister ...

Chapter Twenty
EMMA
Saturday 28 October 2023 – 12:05 p.m.

Every step Emma took on her way into town felt like she was climbing a never-ending mountain, but her head had cleared somehow. A great weight had lifted from her shoulders, allowing her to be able to take a deep breath for the first time in a long time. Something in her had changed.

There was no such thing as The Creature, and it wasn't after her daughter.

She was safe.

It must have been the stress from moving that had caused such a vivid hallucination. This was a new town with new people. It was bound to take her a while to settle in. Everything would be fine once Emma started seeing a therapist again. The first one hadn't helped in the slightest. In fact, it had made things worse. Back then, after Phoebe had disappeared, the therapist had tried to convince Emma that it was normal and okay to feel grief and guilt over what had happened, and that she should accept it and allow the grief to come when it needed to.

But Phoebe was fine now, so why did she still feel so … so … Emma couldn't even come up with a suitable word for how she was feeling because none of them fitted quite right.

Stressed?

Yes, she may have been stressed from the move, but everything had gone smoothly, bar the leaking pipe and that was now fixed. It wasn't stress.

Worried?

Maybe, but what did she have to worry about now that Jordan had told her there was no strange, black creature after her daughter?

Uneasy?

Possibly. There was certainly a flicker of uneasiness in her stomach, which never seemed to disappear entirely. Maybe she was uneasy because of how Linda was acting. She'd noticed her wife's skin didn't glow like it used to, and her eyes didn't sparkle as bright anymore, but nothing could change how she felt about her. Emma loved Linda with all her heart.

Yes, she'd loved Chris, her ex-husband, and a part of her would always love him because without him, she wouldn't have had Alex and Phoebe and they were now her whole world. There had been a time when Chris had been her whole world, back when they'd first got married and before Alex had come along, but the moment those two red lines appeared on that pee-soaked stick, Chris had taken a back seat in her life.

That's when things started to change for Emma. Slowly at first, very slowly, but after Phoebe had been born, she knew in her heart that she didn't want to spend the rest of her life with Chris.

But then, two years ago, he'd died …

It had happened so suddenly.

One day he was there.

And the next he was gone.

The police had said it was a tragic accident. He'd been drunk and fallen off a bridge. The phrase 'death by suicide' had floated around for a while, but Emma didn't believe it. Why would Chris want to end his life? He'd been happy. He'd even found himself a girlfriend and had forgiven Emma for leaving him for Linda. It didn't make any sense.

There had been an empty space in Emma's heart for a long time. Linda had allowed her to grieve for her ex-husband, giving her the space she needed to come to terms with her loss.

Alex had taken it hard too. It was around the same time his moods had started to change, and he became bitter and angry. Emma could only imagine how hard it must have been for her son to lose his father at such an important time in his life, just when he was on the cusp of turning into a young man.

But Emma had no idea why her anxieties were returning now.

This was supposed to be their fresh start, after Chris's death, where the family could recover and start a new journey together. But it was plagued by strange creatures and rumours of local deaths and now Emma was seeing things.

There was no denying the fact she'd seen *something* hovering by her daughter's bed the other night. Jordan may have denied the existence of The Creature, but there was something going on around here. Or maybe she was going crazy … either way, she was going to find out with or without Jordan's help. But first things first, she had to make an appointment to see a therapist, mainly to keep Linda off her back.

As she entered the small doctor's surgery, a woman approached her with a smile. 'Emma, isn't it?'

'Um, yes … Olivia?'

The woman nodded. 'Yes. I'm so glad I ran into you. I wanted to apologise for my behaviour this morning. I'm not usually like that, I promise.'

Emma waved her hand. 'Think nothing of it. It must be difficult when your friends bring up such a traumatic subject. Believe me, I know what it's like.'

'You do?' Olivia touched Emma's arm.

Emma lowered her eyes to the floor. 'My ex-husband died almost two years ago.'

Olivia sucked in a small breath. 'I'm so sorry.' A few beats of silence passed. 'Listen, I'm sure you're busy, but would you like to come round my house for tea and cake tomorrow morning around ten?'

'I'd love to, but isn't your daughter in town? I actually saw her ...' Emma stopped, realising she'd probably said too much.

Olivia smiled, but it wasn't a smile of happiness. 'Yes, apparently, she is, but she won't come anywhere near the house. To be perfectly honest, I don't blame her after what happened.'

'Then I'd love to come.'

'What's your number? I'll text you the address.'

Emma rattled off her mobile number.

Olivia typed them into her phone. 'Thank you. And your wife, Linda, is also welcome to come along.'

'I'll be sure to ask her if she's free.'

Olivia touched Emma's arm again. 'See you tomorrow. Take care, Emma.'

'Goodbye, Olivia. Thank you.'

Emma watched her new friend walk down the path away from the surgery and get into her car. One thing was for certain: she wouldn't be telling Linda about the morning tea invite. Olivia might not know everything about what had happened twenty-odd years ago, but she might know *something*, and that was good enough for Emma.

Chapter Twenty-One
JORDAN
Saturday 28 October 2023 – 11:55 a.m.

As Jordan looked deep into Alex's eyes, he saw nothing but a frightened little boy attempting to stay strong. It was like seeing a younger version of himself in a mirror and Jordan wanted nothing more than to help him and save him from any further torment. He never wanted anyone to go through what he had, not even his worst enemy; not even Sean Walker deserved the hell Jordan had been through.

'Are you sure you don't have anything to feel guilty about, Alex?' he asked again.

'No, nothing.' The boy was persistent. Jordan shrugged. Maybe he wouldn't get it out of Alex today, but one day he would. He reckoned, if things got a bit dicey, Alex would be spilling his guts as quickly as he could.

'Okay, fine, I believe you.'

Alex rolled his eyes. 'And while this has been great and everything and you've enlightened me on the fact that you and your friends had some mental health issues in the past and covered up a murder, it doesn't change the fact that *something* is happening in this town.'

'Why do you care so much? You've only just got here.'

'I just want my mum to get better, okay? She spends all her fucking time talking and playing with her dead daughter and barely even knows I'm alive and breathing. I want my mum back. That's all I've wanted.'

Jordan swapped glances with Brooke, who had been keeping Harriet company the whole time. She had her arm around the girl's trembling shoulders. Jordan had known Harriet for a long time. He knew her parents well and had nothing against them, despite her mother being a notorious gossip. They often came into the shop, and he was their go-to handyman. But there was something in Harriet's eyes that told Jordan she wasn't quite telling them the truth either. It seemed that keeping secrets was in this town's blood.

'Okay, if you want to help your mum, then I need you to do something for me,' said Jordan.

'Fine. What?'

'Brooke and I spoke to your mum earlier today. She said she found something underneath the floorboards in the spare room at your house. She found a poem about The Creature, but when she told us about it, she mentioned that she'd found *things* under the boards, which means she found more than just the poem under there. I need you to find out what else she found.'

Alex shook his head. 'She won't tell me directly. She never tells me anything anymore. She barely even speaks to me.'

'So, find another way. Maybe your mum didn't find everything, so it's worth double-checking to make sure. Meet us here tomorrow morning once you've had a look.'

'What is it you expect me to find?'

Jordan shrugged again. 'I have no idea, but Amber didn't die by suicide, and I think there may be clues in that house.'

'You realise that none of this shit makes any sense, right? All this talk of creatures and ghosts and suicide cover-ups … This town is fucking weird.'

Jordan smirked. 'Trust me, kid. You have no idea.'

Once Alex and Harriet had left, Jordan switched the sign on the front door to open. He could feel Brooke's eyes on him as he unlocked the till and booted up the computer system.

'What?'

Brooke placed both her hands on the countertop. 'You're becoming obsessed.'

Jordan raised one eyebrow. 'Obsessed with what?'

'Finding out the truth.'

'What's wrong with that? What I don't get is why *you* aren't more obsessed with finding out what happened to your best friend. You said you feel guilty about how you left things with her, right?'

'Yeah, but—'

'So, once we find out who killed her you can stop feeling guilty. You don't want The Fear creeping up on you again.' Brooke shuddered at the name. 'You know, in a way, it still controls you,' continued Jordan. He refused to meet her gaze in case he crumbled completely.

'What do you mean?'

Jordan typed his password into the keyboard. 'You've been away from this town for years and you refuse to go back to your mum's house to see her and your dad. The Fear is stopping you from going back there so, in a way, it still controls you.'

Brooke stared at him, and Jordan had no choice but to look up. He could tell by the way her eyes started to water that he had hit a sore spot.

'You're right,' she whispered. 'How did I not see that before? The Fear trapped me in that house and now it's trying to keep me away from my family.'

'What are you going to do about it then?'

Brooke smiled. 'I'm going to go and visit my parents tomorrow morning.' Jordan nodded, satisfied that he'd done the right thing. 'Thanks, Jordan,' she added.

'Any time.'

'Can I offer you some advice in return?'

'Depends on what it is.'

'You've told me I shouldn't feel guilty over Amber's death. Maybe you should take your own advice.'

Jordan stopped typing and snapped his head up. 'What? I don't feel guilty about what happened to Amber.'

'We both missed the signs that something was wrong. Or maybe we didn't. Maybe we didn't want to listen in the first place. Amber tried to warn us that something was wrong, and we did nothing.'

'Don't ...' Jordan turned his back on Brooke, unwilling to let her watch as his eyes filled with tears. 'I can't do this right now, Brooke.'

'Fine. I understand. I'll leave you to work and head back to yours for a bit.'

Jordan didn't reply. He waited until he heard the door click closed before dropping to the floor, his back up against the counter. He pulled his knees up to his chest and cried as his mind drifted back to the day he'd been summoned to identify Amber's broken body.

A day when another part of his soul died.

Words didn't make sense in his head. They were nothing but empty sounds and syllables.

'We've found the remains of a body.' They'd been spoken by Detective Chief Inspector Williams over the phone, only an hour ago.

What body?

What remains?

What was happening?

Jordan had been at work, sorting inventory, when he'd received the call. He'd driven on autopilot to the police station, parked his car and walked inside, his body and mind numb with icy dread.

Now he was here, standing over a body covered in a white cloth up to her neck, lying on a metal table. Parts of the white cloth were spattered in blood. Nothing made sense. Why was he here?

But he knew why.

As soon as the word 'body' had echoed through the phone, Jordan knew.

He'd failed her ... again.

The detective was standing behind him. 'She was found at—'

'Beaker Ravine.'

'Yes. We believe she fell from the fallen tree.'

'Why is her body not more ... damaged?' Jordan closed his eyes against the vivid memory of seeing his friend, Kieran,

practically blown apart by the impact of the fall. Amber's body appeared more intact. There was some blood and broken bones, but nothing as bad as what he and his other friends had found when they'd trekked to the bottom of the ravine that day twenty-five years ago.

'The river cushioned her fall slightly, but it wasn't deep enough to prevent fatal damage,' came the reply.

Jordan stared at the body of the woman he'd loved his whole life. Her skin was grey, her hair matted and wet, clinging to her face like a web. He wanted nothing more than to reach over, move the hair away from her eyes and kiss her on the forehead, like he used to do. But he had been told not to touch the body. It was killing him because, looking down at Amber on the cold, metal table, he knew she still needed him. She needed him to find out the truth.

'Are you sure she jumped?' Jordan looked up at the detective.

'There was only one set of footprints around the edge of the ravine. As far as I'm aware, no one goes out there anymore, ever since ... well, ever since Tyler jumped. They say the place is haunted. The question is, why was Amber there, and if she did jump, why?'

Jordan looked away. There were a lot of things Detective Williams didn't know about the case. Tyler had delivered a solid alibi and a believable story five years ago, and the police had bought it, just like he'd planned. Now that Amber was gone, only two people knew the truth now ... or so he thought.

Had someone else found out the truth? Was that why Amber was dead?

Jordan's mind raced with endless possibilities and scenarios, but nothing quite added up. Whatever the answer was, it was avoiding him, constantly dancing just out of reach.

'I don't know,' replied Jordan, bowing his head. 'Do you have any leads?'

Detective Williams coughed. 'Leads? You make it sound like it's a murder enquiry. There's nothing to investigate, Jordan. I'm sorry. I know this is going to be hard for you to accept, but Amber took her own life. I'm guessing she may have left a note somewhere, so if you find it, maybe that will give you the answers you seek. I'm sorry.' The detective placed a firm hand on Jordan's shoulder. 'There's nothing else I can do.'

Jordan nodded, accepting that the detective was just doing his job. But he didn't know Amber, not like Jordan did … or had. The detective didn't know she'd preferred to drink her coffee cold rather than hot. He didn't know that when she finally started recovering from her insomnia, she'd set an alarm in the middle of the night, just to be certain that she'd wake up. He didn't know that when she'd laugh, her nose would twitch, which made her look like a mouse.

But Jordan did.

He knew everything about Amber …

At least, he thought he had.

Chapter Twenty-Two
LINDA
Saturday 28 October 2023 – 17:20 p.m.

Her eyelids fluttered violently as she thrashed her head from side to side.

Something was constricting her breathing.

Her chest was tight; too tight.

A great weight was sitting on top of her, pushing her down, down, down.

Linda opened her mouth, gasping for precious air as she sat bolt upright.

Where was she?

Something wasn't right.

As Linda scanned the room around her, she realised it had been a dream. She'd fallen asleep in Phoebe's bed. She took a deep breath, feeling the pink duvet between her fingers and the soft mattress under her bottom. It was much later in the day now. The sun had disappeared, and dusk had set in. The room was no longer brightly lit, but dull and grey, lifeless … empty.

Linda licked her lips, attempting to draw moisture to her mouth. She needed a drink, and not the hydrating kind. She gingerly got to her feet and headed into the hallway. Her exhausted body screamed at her to relax. The pain in her head and neck not only hurt but was causing her to lose balance and all sense of direction.

The Void was punishing her again.

A scraping noise stopped her as she reached the top of the stairs, just as she was about to take the first step down.

The noise was coming from the spare room.

Was Emma rummaging under the floorboards again?

Linda huffed as she headed to the spare room door, which was ajar, but as she peered through the gap, she didn't see her wife crouched on the floor. She saw Alex.

Linda pushed the door all the way open. 'Alex? What are you doing in here?'

Alex froze as he snapped his head around to face her, his eyes wide. 'Nothing. I was just fixing the floor for Mum.'

'Did she ask you to do that?'

'No, but … I just thought … I'd do it anyway.'

Linda's mouth twitched. It wasn't like Alex to do something nice for his mum, not in the past two years anyway. Maybe before, when he'd been pleasant to be around, but not now.

'Okay,' she said, attempting to hide the suspicion from her voice, 'did you get rid of the mouse nest?'

'Um … yeah, totally. It's all gone.'

That confirmed it.

Now both Emma and Alex were lying to her. Then again, she was one to talk. She wasn't exactly sharing the truth with them either. Sometimes she thought that this family could do with a restart button. That was what this move to Cherry Hollow was supposed to have been about, yet they'd only been here a few days and already there were more lies and more secrets piling on top of one another.

'Did you have a good day?' she asked.

Alex nodded as he replaced one of the boards. 'Yeah, it was okay.'

'Care to expand?'

'I met my friends.'

Linda raised her eyebrows. 'And?'

Alex shrugged. 'And one of them is pretty cute.'

'What's her name?'

'Harriet.'

Linda smiled. Well, it wasn't much, but the fact Alex had shared the snippet of information was a huge step in the right direction. 'Once you've finished up here, why don't you come down and chat with us?'

'And by *us* you mean?'

Linda frowned. 'Your mother and me.'

'Phoebe won't be joining us?'

Linda sighed and lowered her voice as she spoke. 'I know it's hard to pretend sometimes, Alex, but I think your mum is improving. Today, she told me she was going into town to make an appointment to see a therapist.'

Alex scoffed. 'Yeah, and we all know how well that turned out last time. How much longer do we have to keep pretending that Phoebe is alive? It's sick and wrong and fucking creepy.'

Linda winced at his vile language, but she couldn't scold him for it because he was right. It was fucking creepy. It had to end sometime, but Linda had always been too scared to approach the subject with Emma. If Emma knew the truth about what happened that day ... Linda shuddered at the thought. Emma would leave her. There was no doubt in her mind about that.

No … Emma would *kill* her.

'Just a little longer, Alex, I promise.'

Alex stood up, dusting his trousers with his hands. He'd replaced all the boards and the carpet. It still stuck up a bit in the corner, but at least it wasn't noticeable. 'Fine,' he said.

'Thanks for fixing the floor.' Alex walked up to Linda. He towered over her, but she still placed a hand on his shoulder. 'Thank you,' she said in a whisper. 'Let's go and see what smells so good downstairs.'

'It smells like Mum's special Thai curry.'

'It certainly does.'

Linda watched as Alex walked down the corridor and descended the stairs. She turned back to the spare room, flicking her eyes around, checking for any dark shadows. Then she reached for the door handle and pulled the door closed before joining her family downstairs.

Emma looked up from stirring a saucepan on the hob as Linda entered the kitchen. Alex had taken a seat at the table and was typing on his phone, his eyes barely moving.

'Something smells good,' said Linda, inhaling. She kissed Emma on the cheek. 'Sorry, I fell asleep upstairs. How did everything go in town?'

Emma nodded as she switched the hob off. 'Good. I have my first therapy appointment next week. I'll put it on the wall calendar once I find the thing.'

'I think it was in one of the miscellaneous boxes.'

'Ah,' replied Emma with a nod. 'Would you like some wine?'

'God, yes,' gasped Linda.

Alex snorted without lifting his eyes from the screen.

Linda chose to ignore him as she slid into the seat opposite. The chair that was normally reserved for Phoebe was next to Alex, but there was something different about it. Linda blinked several times, in case her eyes were deceiving her, but they weren't.

A place hadn't been set for Phoebe. There was no placemat, no special pink cutlery, or her favourite pink glass. There were only three places set at the table for the first time in nearly two years. Linda's heart sank a little, which surprised her. For the first time, it truly felt like Phoebe was gone and she struggled to hold back a sob.

'So,' she said, clearing her throat, determined not to draw attention to this monumental moment. Was this the first stepping stone to Emma's recovery? Had a switch been flicked somewhere in her mind? But why? 'Alex has met a girl called Harriet who lives around here.'

Emma squealed. 'Oooh! Tell me about her.' She placed a full glass of wine in front of Linda and then went back to dishing up the dinner.

Alex rolled his eyes as he placed his phone down on the table. Maybe he'd sensed the shift in dynamics too and had noticed the fact Phoebe's presence wasn't being acknowledged by his mum. For once, she was actively engaging in conversation and not fussing over Phoebe. Linda knew Alex missed her attention.

'Yes, her name's Harriet and yes, she's a girl. Can we please try and be cool about it?'

'Of course! What's her mother's name?'

'How should I know?'

'Well, what's Harriet's last name?'

'Um … she didn't say.'

Emma placed a clean plate in front of Alex and Linda and then one in front of her own chair. She set the pot of curry and rice in the middle of the table.

'Well, dig in everyone.'

Linda's and Alex's eyes swivelled to Phoebe's usual seat, but then settled on the dinner. The conversation flowed easier than it had done in years. There were no awkward quiet moments as Emma asked her daughter a question, only to be met with silence, and then carried on talking to her as if she were there while Linda and Alex sat with their heads bowed, pretending everything was normal. Linda and Emma drank their wine and laughed and even Alex joined in from time to time, his phone left lying on the table next to him, momentarily forgotten.

The evening was close to being perfect, but no matter what Linda said or did, nothing could quell the anxiety that was rising in her throat and building with every passing second.

The truth was, this family may have looked perfect from the outside, but on the inside, they were barely surviving and every single member at this table was hiding a secret.

And Linda didn't know how much longer they could play make-believe.

Sooner or later, the truth was going to come out.

Chapter Twenty-Three
BROOKE
Sunday 29 October 2023 – 06:05 a.m.

She'd set her alarm for six and had, as usual, woken up five minutes before it was due to go off. As she grabbed her trainers and tied her hair back, she heard Jordan's gentle snores coming from down the hall. Things had been a bit tense between them when he'd come home after closing the shop yesterday, but the awkwardness had eventually eased and they'd put aside their differences of opinion and enjoyed a quiet night in, watching some crappy soap opera while sharing a bottle of wine. They'd been through too much to quarrel over things and she was relieved that their friendship was remaining strong. He'd also said last night that it was okay to take Morgan out with her on her run this morning.

Brooke attached the lead to the dog's collar and off they went, along the narrow paths through town and down the country lanes. Her feet pounded the ground effortlessly, through every twist and turn.

Morgan, as it turned out, wasn't naturally gifted at running for long periods of time. He preferred to stop and sniff every blade of grass and chew sticks the entire way. Nevertheless, Brooke enjoyed their time outside together and they returned to Jordan's house forty-five minutes later, tired, sweaty, but happy.

Jordan greeted Brooke with a cool glass of water as she strolled into the kitchen, which she took and downed in one. Morgan sprinted for his water bowl and consumed its contents, making an exceptionally loud slurping noise as he did so and splashing some over the sides.

'Good run?'

She couldn't help but notice Jordan's eyes linger on her sweaty top. She inwardly cringed, never usually caring that she looked like a red tomato after her runs, but knowing his eyes were on her made her feel … She couldn't quite put her finger on it.

'Yeah, not bad. I didn't realise there were so many good running trails around here.'

'I sometimes go for runs myself.'

'Oh yeah? When was the last time you ran?'

Jordan eyed her with a grin. 'A year ago. I prefer the gym, okay?'

Brooke laughed as she set the empty pint glass by the sink. 'Please don't tell me you're one of those grunting, gasping meatheads who spend more time looking at themselves in the gym mirror than lifting weights?'

Jordan scoffed. 'I hate those guys.'

'Good. Right. I'm going to have a quick shower and then … I guess I'm off to Mum's.'

'You want me to come with you?'

'Thank you, but no. I think this is something I have to do myself.'

'Okay, but text me if you need any support or need me to come and rescue you, and I'll call you once I've heard from Alex.'

Brooke nodded as she headed for the stairs, glad to get out of sight of Jordan's gaze. 'Thanks,' she called out. Her face was still burning, but not from her run.

She showered, dressed, and grabbed her bag, slinging it over her shoulder. When she came down the stairs, Jordan and Morgan had already left for work. He'd left a spare key on the side table, which she scooped up and used to lock the front door behind her.

Brooke decided she wasn't going to drive to her mum's house. More fresh air would do her good and maybe help focus her mind some more, but her stomach performed flips as she turned in the direction of her family home. Her feet knew the way without having to engage her brain, which was doing its best to tell her to run in the opposite direction. With every step, she found it harder and harder to breathe. Her body fought against her the whole way.

Her parents' house was at the top of a long hill leading out of town, and by the time she was standing at the bottom of the front garden by the rickety old gate, Brooke was hyperventilating. Not from the exertion of the walk, but because her fear and anxiety were mounting and clawing their way up her throat, squeezing, cutting off her air supply. She wished she hadn't turned down Jordan's invitation of coming with her. She needed someone to push her the rest of the way, needed that guiding, supportive hand on her shoulder.

The pink roses that adorned the wooden archway over the garden gate had grown a considerable amount since she'd last been here. The sweet scent filled her nostrils, and for a split second, it helped calm the rising anxiety within …

And then it happened.

Brooke took a breath and closed her eyes.

She breathed in.

She breathed out.

And someone gently clasped her left hand and squeezed it. Brooke smiled as she opened her eyes, expecting to see Jordan standing next to her.

But there was no one there.

Her heart rate calmed as she focussed on breathing in through her nose and out through her mouth, the way she'd been taught to help control her panic attacks. Back then, nothing had helped calm her down. Nothing. But now … now Brooke could feel her body responding to the extra oxygen she was providing it, and something was still squeezing her hand.

'Amber?' she whispered into the wind.

The pressure on her hand released itself and a strong gust of wind whipped around her, blowing open the gate and practically shoving her through it. She stumbled on the uneven stone path.

'Brooke!' Her mum's high-pitch squeal boomed from the front door and down the garden path.

Brooke snapped her head up, momentarily forgetting about the wind that had pushed her. 'Mum,' she said, jogging towards her.

Olivia ran down the steps and threw her arms around her daughter. Brooke squeezed her mum back harder than she intended, but Olivia didn't seem to care. Tears flowed from Brooke's eyes. Olivia started laughing and crying at the same time, clawing at her daughter's back, attempting to hug her as much as possible.

'I can't believe you're here. You look wonderful. Have you had your hair cut? You look so fit and well.' Olivia let Brooke go and stared into her eyes.

'Mum … I'm … I'm sorry—'

Olivia shook her head. 'No. Stop. No apologies. You're here. That's what matters. I don't care how long it's taken you to arrive, I'm just glad you're here. Come on. Come in. Your father will be beside himself.'

'How is he?'

Olivia smiled, but her eyes were sad. 'The doctors have told us he has about six months.'

'Why didn't you tell me how serious it was?'

'I told you enough. I didn't want you to feel guilty for not coming to see us or use your father's illness to drag you back here. Darling, I don't blame you for staying away for so long. You were trapped here for two decades, but you're here now and that's all that matters. Now come.' Olivia grabbed Brooke's hand and pulled her towards the house. She let go just as she reached the front door, allowing Brooke to linger on the front step.

Brooke looked up at her childhood home, her previous prison, took a deep breath and held it as she stepped over the threshold.

Nothing bad happened.

The door didn't slam shut behind her, trapping her inside.

The world didn't end.

And The Fear was ... somewhere in the background, but not overwhelming her.

The bright sunshine gently warmed the hallway, and nothing grabbed her and pinned her to the floor. Her breathing was stable and although her stomach did feel twisty and twirly, she didn't feel like she was about to die if she didn't get out of there.

Everything was going to be okay.

The next few hours flew by. Brooke settled into her favourite space on the sofa and was fed tea and biscuits by her mum as she told her parents everything about her life back in London. Her father listened quietly, every so often erupting into a coughing fit, which Olivia would help him through. She handed him his medication when he needed it and helped him out of his chair and walked him to the toilet. Brooke watched her mum in awe. The woman had tended to Brooke's every whim and need for twenty years, never complaining, and now she was a carer for her dying husband as well. It was at that point Brooke realised her mum was a prisoner in her own home, and she always had been.

Brooke stood as Olivia walked back into the room alone. 'I've put your father to bed for a morning nap. I have a friend visiting me soon, so I thought it would be too much for him to cope with more company.'

'Can I do anything to help?'

'Grab the empty cups and plates for me?'

Brooke nodded and began picking up the empty cups. 'Who's coming round to visit?'

'Emma Smithson. She's just moved into town.'

Brooke froze, almost dropping one of the plates. 'Oh, right, yes. She lives in Amber's old house now, right?' Brooke followed her mum into the kitchen.

'Yes, that's right. Darling, I'm so sorry about what happened to Amber. I know she was your best friend.'

Brooke blinked away the tears that were burning her eyes. 'It's okay.'

'Did you speak to her before … she died?'

'Um … yes, very briefly.'

'And did she seem … herself?'

Brooke gulped against the lump in her throat. She turned away from her mum and started washing the cups in the sink. 'Mum, please, I can't talk about Amber right now.'

'I'm so sorry. Of course. Would you like me to cancel the tea with Emma?'

'No, that's okay. I'll need to leave soon anyway. I promised Jordan I'd give him a hand later.'

'How is Jordan? I haven't seen him much lately. He always seems so busy.'

'Yeah, he's good. Business is booming and everyone loves him.'

'It's so lovely that he turned things around. I know he struggled a bit when his father died.'

Brooke swallowed her guilt once again. Yet another time a friend had needed her help and support and she'd hidden away in London and allowed Amber, who'd already been struggling enough, to deal with Jordan's grief at his father's passing. She couldn't help but wonder if she really was a good friend anymore, or even a good daughter. Family and friends had always gone out of their way to help her through her darkest times, yet as soon as they had needed her help, she'd pretended like nothing was wrong and had distracted herself by working overtime and going for long runs until the ache in her legs was greater than the ache in her heart.

As Brooke replaced the dry plates in the cupboard, the doorbell rang and Olivia scurried off to answer it. The butterflies in Brooke's stomach flapped at the thought of seeing Emma again. Yesterday morning, they hadn't exactly left on good terms.

Brooke checked her phone, hoping for a missed call from Jordan. Nothing.

Olivia and Emma entered the kitchen a few seconds later. Olivia had clearly mentioned to Emma that Brooke was there because Emma was smiling, and she nodded at her.

'Hello, Brooke. It's lovely to meet you.'

Brooke sighed, grateful Emma had decided to keep the fact they'd already met from her mum. 'Hi, Emma. How are you settling in?'

Emma was wearing a much brighter outfit today, a pink and yellow top with jeans, rather than the baggy tracksuit bottoms and black hoodie from yesterday. She seemed brighter in herself too. Maybe what Jordan said had sunk in and she truly believed that The Creature wasn't real … which it wasn't … But even so, it couldn't have been easy for Emma to hear. She clearly knew there was something going on, but Brooke reckoned she had no idea that her son was working with herself and Jordan to get to the bottom of everything.

'It's been fine so far,' replied Emma with a nod. 'Everyone has been so lovely and welcoming.'

Olivia started making a pot of tea. 'Take a seat, Emma. Was Linda not able to come?'

Emma flinched as she sat down on a chair at the kitchen table. Olivia didn't appear to notice it, but Brooke did. 'Oh … no … she said she was sorry, but she really needed to finish the decorating in the dining room.'

'Ah, yes, I don't blame her. When you get into the swing of things, it's better to keep powering through until you finish.'

Emma squeezed her lips tight together and her left eye twitched. Brooke had her eyes trained on her the whole time. The woman may have looked better on the outside, but Brooke could see the turmoil going on inside.

A loud chirping pierced the silence.

Brooke's phone.

'I'm sorry, I need to get this,' she said as she shuffled out of the room and into the bright conservatory that had views across the back garden. 'Hey, Jordan. Perfect timing, as always.'

'Wasn't interrupting anything important, I hope.'

'No, not really. Emma's here.'

'She is? Is she okay? Has she said anything?'

'No, nothing. She hasn't told my mum that we already met yesterday, and she seems much happier today, but she's just lied to my mum about her wife not being able to come over for tea. I have a feeling she didn't even tell her. I could be wrong of course.'

'That's strange. Anyway, I thought you should know that Alex has just texted me and he'll be here in about half an hour.'

'Did he say if he found anything?'

'No. He's a teenage boy. The whole of his text message was two words long. *Half hour.*'

Brooke smirked. 'Typical kid. Okay, I'll finish up here and head over. You at work?'

'Yeah.'

'Okay, see you soon.'

Jordan cleared his throat. 'Just don't mention to Emma that you're about to go and meet her son. I feel a bit sneaky about this, but I also feel like we might be on to something.'

Brooke laughed. 'Yeah, don't worry, I won't. Bye.'

'Bye.'

A split second before Brooke hung up, she heard Morgan's bark in the background. She put her phone in her pocket and took a breath as she stared across the large expanse of grass. The garden was in a state. She guessed it was due to her father not being well enough to tend to it and her mum not having the time either. Another pang of guilt stabbed her in the side.

'Hey, Mum,' she said as she re-entered the kitchen. Emma and her mum were sitting at the table sharing a pot of tea. 'I'm sorry, but I have to go now. Jordan needs my help at work.'

'Okay, darling. Thank you so much for coming. Will you and Jordan come round for dinner soon?'

'I'll ask him and give you a call.' She hugged her mum and nodded at Emma. 'Nice to meet you, Emma.'

'And you, Brooke.'

Brooke closed the front door behind her and headed in the direction of town, her mind racing with the possibilities of what Alex may or may not have found under the floorboards in Emma's house.

Maybe Emma had removed everything she'd found. Or maybe she hadn't.

Was she hiding something else?

She was certainly hiding things from her wife and child.

Chapter Twenty-Four
ALEX
Sunday 29 October 2023 – 09:40 a.m.

Alex flipped his phone over and over in his hand as he strolled out the front door of his house. He'd just messaged Jordan to say he'd be half an hour. Last night had been unexpected, to say the least. Not only regarding what he'd found under the floorboards, but the family dinner he'd had with his mum and Linda. Without Phoebe.

His mum would always fuss over her invisible daughter, cutting up her food or fetching her more juice, while Alex would sit and eat his dinner, invisible to her. But not last night. She'd engaged him in conversation, asked him about his day, made stupid mum jokes about him meeting a girl and had even given him the rest of the ice cream in the tub. It was normally Phoebe who'd get it all and then it would end up being thrown in the bin. For a few hours, it seemed he had his old mum back. How long it would last, he didn't know, but he was hoping that the things he'd found under the floorboards would be enough to help Jordan and Brooke with their investigation into Amber's death. He didn't know the woman. Had never known her, but it was clear she was a big part of what was going on, and finding the cause of her death would help put the demons to rest and perhaps help his mum in the process.

As Alex approached the front of the building to Fix It All, he heard his name being called from behind him. He turned and saw Alex the First jogging across the street. He looked as if he'd recently stepped out of the shower. His floppy hair was still damp and sticking to the sides of his face.

'Hey, man, I thought that was you,' he panted as he stopped next to Alex.

'Hey. What's up?'

'Not much. Why are you going into Fix It All?'

'My mum needs some stuff.'

'Gottcha. Hey, listen, about the other day ... I'm sorry I took off like that. It's just ... that ravine is kind of spooky, don't you think?'

Alex nodded. 'Yeah, sure.' He was having a hard time forcing the words he really wanted to say back down his throat, but there was no point in creating an enemy out of this boy. He seemed harmless enough, but Alex didn't trust him. Not even a little bit. And he'd always trusted his gut when it came to first impressions. 'Don't worry about it. It's forgotten.'

'Okay, great. Hey, listen, you've got my number, right? Text me if you want to hang out later.'

'Sure. Catch you later.'

Alex the First nodded and then turned and jogged back across the road, carrying on down the street. Alex watched him, narrowing his eyes.

Yep. He was definitely not trustworthy.

Alex was greeted by a thirty-five kilo Labrador running full pelt at him as soon as he opened the door, followed closely by a shout of, 'Morgan!' from Jordan who came bounding into the room after him. Alex grinned as he knelt on the floor and ruffled the dog's fur, receiving licks in return.

'I always wanted a dog,' he said, scratching behind Morgan's ear.

'Well, you're more than welcome to have him. He's a bloody menace.'

'Linda is allergic I think, or maybe she just says that as an excuse.'

'In that case, you can come and take Morgan for a walk or play in the park any time.'

'Thanks.' Alex stood up and brushed a load of dog hair off his top and jeans.

'Brooke's on her way over,' added Jordan.

'Cool.'

Jordan scratched his head. 'Listen, I told your mum that I was offering you a job the other day as an excuse for why I came to your house looking for you. But to be honest, I really could use the help at weekends. Are you interested?'

Alex stared at Jordan for a few seconds. 'Why me? Why not one of the other kids in this town?'

'Why not you?'

Alex shrugged. 'I dunno.'

'Okay, well, how about you have a think about it and talk it over with your mum. It would be minimum wage because you're under eighteen, but I could teach you how to make and send invoices, deal with customers and even give you some work experience if you want to come with me to customers' houses when I get callouts.'

'Yeah, sure, whatever. I'll think about it.'

Jordan nodded. Alex knew he was being difficult, but it was as if his brain was hardwired to be as awkward as possible. Maybe it was his natural teenage hormones, or maybe it was something more. Jordan seemed like a decent guy, but he was still a stranger to Alex and from what the town's people had said, he hadn't always been a decent guy so it was difficult to fully trust the man.

The doorbell pinged and Brooke walked in, which meant Morgan's attention went straight to the new arrival. Jordan sighed and threw up his hands.

'I give up,' he muttered as he watched his unruly dog jump all over Brooke. She didn't seem to mind because she was talking to the canine in a baby voice and planting kisses on his velvety nose. Once she finished, she stood up, repeating the brush-down procedure to remove the black dog hair.

'No Harriet today?' she asked.

Alex bit his lip and looked from Jordan to Brooke and then back to Jordan. 'No. I didn't message her to say I was coming here.'

'Okay … did you two have a fight or something?'

'No, not exactly. I just don't feel like including her. She's a bit clingy and I'm not sure if I fully trust her.'

Jordan stepped forwards. 'Fair enough. Did you find anything under the floorboards?'

'Yeah, you could say that. I found some random items, including a pebble, a shell, a plastic horse and a dried-up petal. I'm not sure what any of those mean, but I did find something else.' Alex reached into his jacket pocket and pulled out a piece of paper that had been folded several times. It was dirty and worn and jagged at the edges. He held it between his fingers and fiddled with it as he spoke. 'I think Mum must have missed this because it had slipped down between some joists. I barely noticed it myself. It's really old and worn too.'

'What is it?' asked Jordan.

'It's a letter written to Bethany from Amber.'

'What the hell? Are you sure?'

'Pretty sure, yeah. Here, read it for yourself.'

Alex handed the paper to Jordan, who took it with a shaking hand. Brooke moved into position beside him. They bowed their heads and read.

Chapter Twenty-Five
JORDAN
Sunday 29 October 2023 – 09:51 a.m.

I'm sorry to do this to you. I love you more than anything and this is the only way I know to keep you safe. I'm so sorry I wasn't there for you when I should have been. Your dad loves you. You'll be okay, baby. I love you.

Jordan's eyes absorbed the words on the paper. When he finished reading, he waited for Brooke to look at him and then screwed the paper into a ball and threw it in the bin.

'That's bullshit,' he said.

Alex raised his eyebrows, clearly expecting them both to have reacted differently to the letter. He looked at Brooke, who didn't appear that affected either. 'Am I missing something here?'

'Amber didn't write that note,' snapped Jordan.

'How do you know that?'

'I know her writing style. She dots her i's with dashes, not dots.'

Brooke turned to Jordan. 'What does this mean? The letter sounds as if she really was going to end it all.'

'It means that someone made it look like she killed herself and wrote this note to try and convince everyone that she did.'

Brooke held up her hand. 'Hang on. Alex, you said you didn't invite Harriet here today because you don't trust her and you didn't want to include her. What did you mean by that?'

'Yeah … so, the other day Harriet and Alex the First mentioned that some older kids from school had bullied Bethany over a poem she wrote.'

Jordan frowned at Alex. 'Who the hell is Alex the First?'

'I don't know his last name, but we decided that he would be Alex the First and I'd be Alex the Second.'

Brooke stepped forwards. 'It could be Alex Sharp. I remember him from a few years ago. He was a bit of a troublemaker back then. His mum is Trisha Sharp.'

'Ah, another of the local gossips. Like mother like son by the sounds of it.'

Alex shuffled his weight from one foot to the other. 'It didn't click into place until I read this letter, but I think maybe Harriet and Alex the First know more than they're letting on. They seem to know an awful lot about The Creature and everything that goes on in this town. The fact that Harriet was with us yesterday and said nothing while we were talking about The Creature and everything proves to me she might have something to hide. That note mentions Amber not being there for Bethany when she needed her the most … Maybe it was when Bethany was being bullied.'

'If that's true, no wonder she looked so nervous,' said Brooke, picking up the note from the bin. She straightened out the paper and scanned it again. 'Something about this note is wrong. It's really dirty and old.'

'It has been stored under the floorboards for several months,' replied Alex with a shrug.

Brooke scratched her head. 'Maybe … But the question remains … Who wrote this note? Because whoever did wanted Amber dead.'

Jordan ran his hands through his hair, a nervous habit he'd picked up recently. The thought that someone who lived in this town had killed the woman he loved was more than he could bear. He needed answers, but he didn't know where to start or who to ask.

Alex fiddled with the edges of some files that were on the side of the front desk. As he pulled his hand away from the files, he knocked them and the whole pile slid to the floor. 'Oops,' he muttered, bending down to pick them up.

Jordan sighed, knowing it would take him a few minutes to put the files back in order again, a task which had taken long enough before. 'Look, right now it doesn't matter who wrote the note, but what does matter is finding out what Harriet and that other Alex kid know. I also want to know what went on in that school and why it isn't more widely known. Who covered it up and why? And why didn't the school tell anyone?'

'Maybe they did, but since you don't have a child that goes to the school, you weren't informed,' pointed out Brooke. Jordan nodded in agreement. She'd made a good point. 'The only person who will know the answers is Bethany,' continued Brooke. 'Jordan, you can't just call her up. Sean will kill you.'

'I couldn't give a fuck.'

'Why don't we ask Harriet and Alex Sharp instead?'

Jordan screwed up his face. 'Fine, but if they refuse to talk then I'm calling Bethany. She'll want to talk to me.'

'I thought you said you wanted to keep her out of this now?'

Jordan glared at Brooke for a second, but then relaxed his tense jaw muscles and rubbed the back of his neck. 'Yeah, okay, you're right. I just want to know who the hell killed my girlfriend and why this town is covering it up.'

'We all do. But we have to remember … twenty-five years ago, we did exactly the same thing. We need to be careful about how we approach this. We can't go in all guns blazing and accuse two teenagers of killing a grown woman when we have no proof. We'll ask them if they ever spoke to Bethany and what happened the last time they saw her, something like that.' Brooke's voice remained calm as she spoke. Jordan was glad she was here, the level-headed counterweight to his explosive temper. Not that he'd exploded at anyone for a while, but the more they uncovered all the secrets and lies, the more his anger appeared to be growing, like fuel being added to a small flame a tiny bit at a time. He had it under control though. Yes, The Bad Man was under control. It didn't have power over him anymore. This wasn't about him. It was about Amber and bringing her killer to justice, putting an end to The Creature once and for all, no matter if it was real or not.

'No offence, but they aren't going to talk to you guys.' Alex stepped forwards after chucking the files back on the desk in a haphazard manner.

'What makes you think that?' asked Jordan.

'They're going to know we're on to them if we all approach them and start asking questions.'

'Okay, so what do you suggest?'

'Let me handle it.'

Jordan laughed. 'Absolutely not. You're a fifteen-year-old kid with a huffy attitude.'

'I'm sixteen.'

'Whatever. The point is, we don't know you. Yes, you found the letter under the floorboards for us, but this is important information we need, and I'm not about to put my trust in you when I have no idea what your true intentions are.'

Alex folded his arms. 'You should be grateful I'm even helping you out at all. I didn't know this Amber woman. I couldn't give a fuck about her. All I care about is helping my mum get back to her old self. We moved here to get away from a horrible situation, but it's even worse here. I'm not doing this for you, Amber, or anyone else. I'm doing this for my mum. That's it. I may be a bit arrogant and huffy, but by the sounds of it, you were once way worse than me.'

Brooke sucked in a breath as she looked from Jordan to Alex. Jordan was glaring at Alex, deliberating whether to retaliate or just accept the fact that the boy was spot on, thereby admitting he was wrong.

Jordan held up his hands, palms facing Alex. 'All right. You got me. I shouldn't judge you because I would have acted the exact same way at your age. In fact, you're right, I was worse.'

Brooke exhaled loudly.

'So, I can question Alex the First and Harriet on my own?'

Jordan nodded. 'Yes, but on one condition. The second you find out anything, you message me. And you need to do it today, not sit on it for a week, got it?'

'Got it.'

'Oh … and one more condition too.'

'What?'

'You come and work here at weekends.'

Alex rolled his eyes, but Jordan could have sworn he saw a hint of a smirk. 'Fine.' He slammed the front door when he left the building, leaving Jordan and Brooke in silence while they waited for the echo to subside.

'I'm proud of you,' said Brooke, patting Jordan on the shoulder.

'What for?'

'For looking out for his best interests.'

Jordan scoffed. 'He reminds me of Tyler before everything happened.'

'I know.'

'And Tyler was unpredictable and lied to us for years.'

'I know that too. Alex will come through for us. We must have a little faith.'

Chapter Twenty-Six
EMMA
Sunday 29 October 2023 – 10:05 a.m.

Emma spooned two sugars into her tea and stirred slowly, enjoying the high-pitched ting of the spoon as it knocked the side of the fine china teacup. Olivia had exquisite taste. Emma wondered how often she brought out the good china or if it was only reserved for special occasions, which led her to question why Olivia might consider her visit a special occasion.

She watched quietly while Olivia set the table with plates laden with cakes and biscuits. She'd offered to help, but Olivia had refused, saying she was glad to feed and host someone who wasn't her husband. Olivia's house was spotless. It was like a show home, not a single object out of place, and Emma knew Olivia hadn't just tidied up because she was coming for tea. She got the impression Olivia had nothing better to do with her days than clean her house and look after her husband. Was she trapped here too, as her daughter had been? Granted, she'd been present at the coffee morning yesterday, but was that all she was able to do outside of her home? Emma sipped her tea, her heart aching for the woman in front of her who was smiling, despite her troubles.

'I'm so glad you got to meet Brooke,' said Olivia, her face beaming as she mentioned her daughter. She tucked a stray piece of grey hair behind her ear. Emma applauded her for embracing her grey hair, although she'd heard in passing that she used to dye it blonde but had stopped once Brooke left home. 'I had such a shock this morning when I saw her standing at the end of the garden path. I thought I was hallucinating!'

'She's really never been back here since she left for London four years ago?'

Olivia shook her head as she finally sat down after putting everything on the table. 'No. I've been to see her in London and so has Frank before he started getting sick. And Brooke has visited Dorothy and her son Patrick, who also live in London. She lived with them very briefly at the start, but she's always so busy now. Dorothy is my youngest daughter and Patrick is my grandson. He's four now and such a handful.'

'They always are at that age. I didn't realise you have two daughters.' Was that a flicker of jealousy she could feel growing inside her?

Olivia smiled as she served Emma a delicately made slice of carrot cake. 'Yes. They haven't always seen eye to eye and gotten along, especially when Brooke was … sick and homebound. Dorothy just didn't understand it, that's all. She said Brooke was selfish, but it wasn't her fault. She wasn't well but seeing her today has been wonderful. She looks so well, don't you think?'

Emma nodded, taking the plate from Olivia. 'Yes, she looked wonderful. So beautiful.'

'She always was. Back before … it happened … she was the envy of every girl in town and the object of every boy's affection. She changed a lot over the years. I barely recognised her sometimes, but she looks like the old Brooke again now.'

'That's wonderful,' said Emma. She took a bite of the cake and sighed happily, relishing the delightful taste. 'I know you said you looked after Brooke, but did you work before that? Sorry, I don't mean to pry.'

Olivia waved her hand. 'No, it's completely okay. I used to be a school nurse, so looking after Brooke, and now my husband, has come naturally to me. It's not easy though … not easy …' Olivia's eyes dropped to the floor. 'But I suppose I'm paying my dues.'

Emma's face turned hot. She wished she hadn't said anything. But what had she meant by that last statement? Emma burned to question her further.

Olivia raised her eyes and stared past Emma towards the garden. She seemed lost in thought, so Emma let her be. A quiet sadness surrounded the woman and Emma wanted nothing more than to give her a hug, but seeing as she'd only recently met her, she thought it might be inappropriate.

'Anyway,' said Olivia, appearing to snap out of her trance as she picked up a fork, 'enough about me and my woes. How are you? How are your daughter and son settling into the area? Do they start school soon?'

'Yes, Alex starts next week. It will be good for him to make new friends around here.'

'And your daughter?'

Emma looked blankly at her. 'My daughter?'

'Yes, I'm sorry, I've forgotten her name. I'm sure you said you had a daughter …'

Emma set down her cup of tea before she spilt it down her front. Nausea was rising fast from within, and her face turned hot again. She fanned her face with her hand. 'I'm so sorry, but I'm having some sort of hot flush.'

Olivia leaped to her feet and rushed towards the set of double patio doors. 'You poor thing, I used to get such hot flushes. Awful things. Come and stand by the open door. The fresh air will help.'

Emma rose to her unsteady feet and walked slowly to the door, taking deep breaths. Olivia was right. The fresh air did help quell the hot flush, but it wasn't dispersing the nausea.

'Are you feeling well?' asked Olivia. 'Surely you're too young for menopause!'

'Yes, sorry, I'm not sure what came over me.'

'That's quite okay. Would you like something cool to drink instead of tea?'

'Water, please. Thank you.'

Olivia nodded and returned to the kitchen, leaving Emma standing by the open patio doors. She stared across the garden, relieved that Olivia had forgotten about Phoebe. She didn't want to talk about her. Maybe Emma could steer the conversation in a different direction so she could learn more about Amber and the house she was now living in. Not that she believed there were such things as ghosts or haunted houses, but it never hurt to ask.

Olivia returned with a glass of water and handed it to Emma. 'There you are.'

'Thank you. Your house is lovely by the way.'

'Thank you. When I looked after Brooke, I didn't have a lot of time to do housework, but Frank is a walk in the park compared to what she was like, so I try and make it as nice as I can. If only the same could be said about the garden,' replied Olivia with a laugh. 'But I'm afraid I'm not green-fingered at all.

That was always Frank's domain, but he can't do it anymore. He's had to stop a lot of things, even working.'

'What did Frank do?'

'You know the convenience store in the centre of town? He used to be the manager. Worked such long hours too, but he loved it. A couple of years ago, he was diagnosed with cancer, but it was Stage 1, so we were optimistic, but … nothing has worked. Nothing. It's almost as if …' Olivia stopped and bit her lip.

Emma studied the woman's face. There was a story buried deep. There were words that longed to be free, but Olivia held them back.

'Anyway,' she said, brushing off her sorrow, 'I guess it comes for all of us eventually.'

Emma held her breath as she asked, 'What comes?'

Olivia looked at her and held her gaze. 'The darkness.'

Emma exhaled. For a moment, she'd been expecting Olivia to say something else. 'Do you mean death?' she asked.

Olivia smiled and nodded. 'Yes, of course.'

'I'm so sorry,' said Emma. 'However … Linda loves gardening. I'm sure she'd love to come round and give you a hand sometimes. As would I.' She hoped it would be enough to change the subject.

'Oh, no, I couldn't ask you to do that—'

'I insist. You've been so kind to me, and I'd love to return the favour.'

Olivia blinked and turned away as a tiny hint of red sprang to her cheeks. 'You're very kind. Thank you.'

'Speaking of houses and whatnot,' said Emma before taking a quick sip of water, 'did Amber ever mention anything about her house?'

'What do you mean?'

'Nothing really, but I see a lot of ... shadows ... and was just wondering ...' Emma took another sip, frowning as she did so. It had been a silly idea to bring it up. Olivia probably thought she was crazy now that she'd implied there were dark spirits of some kind living in her house. Emma sensed Olivia's eyes on her. A few seconds of silence passed before Olivia spoke.

'I don't like to speak ill of the dead, and Amber was such a wonderful woman and an amazing friend to Brooke, but ... she was very troubled towards the end. Her poor daughter had nightmares. I don't know what exactly went on in that house behind closed doors, but ...' Olivia looked across the garden and sighed. 'I do know that Amber being dead is probably the best outcome for everyone.'

Emma failed to disguise her shock. Olivia seemed to suddenly realise what she'd said. 'Oh, please don't think that I wished her dead. No, that's not what I'm saying, but she was trying to stir up the past, and when that happens it doesn't always work out for the best, does it?'

Emma gulped back the lump in her throat. 'No, I guess not.'

The vibe coming from Olivia wasn't one of friendliness or concern, but something more sinister. Emma couldn't put her finger on it. Had Amber and Olivia fallen out before she died? If so, what about? Maybe it had something to do with Brooke. Olivia seemed like the type of mother who would do anything for their child. Emma could tell because she was the same. Emma would die to protect her children. She'd kill to protect them.

'Well, anyway,' said Olivia brightly, 'let's not do the same and dwell on the past. More tea?'

Emma smiled. 'Yes, perfect. I'm feeling better now.'

Chapter Twenty-Seven
LINDA
Sunday 29 October 2023 – 10:45 a.m.

Emma had left for the morning, saying she had some errands to run. The clothes she'd decided to wear today, however, told a different story. She looked like she'd put in some effort when getting dressed this morning. Was she trying to impress someone? Did this have anything to do with their lovely family dinner last night; the one without the invisible daughter? Maybe Emma had finally turned a corner in her recovery. Linda didn't expect her to ever get over the loss of her daughter, but it couldn't be healthy to keep pretending she was alive, could it? There would have to come a point in the future when Emma would have to accept it and attempt to move on, so was this it? Had the moment arrived? Maybe moving here had kick-started her recovery after all.

Linda thought maybe she should follow her, but then decided against it, telling herself she needed to start trusting her wife again and not make up strange scenarios in her head about what she might be up to. The house was quiet, and she'd just finished arranging the furniture in the hallway after unpacking the numerous boxes that had been piled high. The coat rack was screwed into the wall, the side table had a pot plant on it (which needed watering) and the picture frames of various holiday destinations they'd visited were arranged by size order above it. Now at least people could enter the house and not immediately be met by boxes and mess.

It was beginning to look like a happy family home … at least on the outside.

The second item on her list of things to do today was to head into town and introduce herself to her new boss at The Bean Café. She'd only met Hayley via a Zoom chat when she had her interview. Hayley had texted her earlier this morning to ask if she could pop in this week to sign some paperwork, so today seemed as good a day as any now that the house didn't resemble a dumping ground.

After locking the front door, Linda walked into town. It was nice not to have to drive the car everywhere. They'd only need it for the big weekly food shop and if they wanted to explore the surrounding countryside, which she was sure they would once they'd been here a few weeks and settled in. The Lake District was renowned for its beauty, wide-open spaces and, of course, its numerous and vast lakes. There was also The World of Beatrix Potter located at Windermere, which she secretly wanted to visit, having been a huge fan of Peter Rabbit as a child. Phoebe would have loved going there too …

Linda shook away the negative thoughts as she walked. When she reached the café, she stopped and looked up at the building. It appeared recently renovated due to the fresh coat of paint. The sign gleamed bright pink in the sun above the red-painted door and the windows sparkled.

Pushing open the door, the bell chimed above her head as she scanned the area, and she was surprised to see a line of customers waiting at the tills and almost every set of tables and chairs occupied. The place was immaculate. No used coffee cups and plates on tables, no crumbs on the floor and no spilled drinks in sight.

'Hi, Linda!'

Linda turned and came face to face with Hayley, who was at least ten years her junior. Her long black hair was startling against her tanned skin, but what really made her stand out was the copious amount of jewellery she had on. Earrings, bracelets, necklaces and even a nose stud. It made Linda feel older than her thirty-five years. Had she ever been that cool?

'Thanks so much for coming in. I know you don't start till next week, but while you're here, I thought I could show you around, maybe?'

'Yes, that would be great, thanks. This place looks amazing.' Linda took another look at the café and recognised a couple of the women who had been at the coffee morning the previous day. She nodded hello and then smiled and waved back.

'Thank you. Yes, it used to be very rundown, but when I took over as manager, I thought I'd spruce it up a bit and, as you can see, business is doing well now.'

Linda nodded. 'For a small town, this certainly is the place to be.'

'We also supply the local coffee morning with drinks and cakes. Have you been yet? It's held on a Saturday morning at the community centre.'

'Yes, my wife and I attended yesterday and met a few of the locals.'

Hayley leaned in close to Linda's ear. 'Just watch out for Trisha and Lucy ... a couple of troublemakers, if you ask me.'

Linda held back a laugh, already agreeing with her as she followed Hayley through to the back of the shop and into a small and exceptionally tidy office. Her boss may have been young and had a cool dress sense, but the woman was certainly organised and appeared to take her role as manager very seriously. Her desk was laid out to perfection, everything having its own place. However, Linda's eyebrows raised as she scanned a few items on the shelves; pink bunnies, fake succulents, and a collection of miniature figurines of skulls dressed up in cute outfits.

Linda took a seat while she watched Hayley unlock the grey filing cabinet and fish out a folder. 'How long have you been working here?' she asked.

'About ten years,' replied Hayley. She pulled out a few sheets of paper and put them in front of Linda, along with a pen which she picked from a selection in a pink pot on her desk.

'Oh, wow.'

'Yeah, I actually started working here when I was like, sixteen I think, and I've never done anything else.'

Linda took the pen and scanned the document. It was her work contract. She couldn't imagine it was anything complicated. 'Ah, here's my passport.' She handed the passport to Hayley.

'Thanks. I won't be a minute. I'll just go and scan this and you can have it right back.'

'No problem, I'll stay here.'

Hayley smiled and left the room, leaving the door ajar so Linda could still hear the murmur of conversation from the café in the next room. She signed the form and replaced the pen in the pot.

With nothing better to do while she waited for Hayley to return, she stood and approached the shelves, smirking at the figurines. There were a few framed pictures too, mostly of Hayley in her work uniform with her arm around a work colleague or two. It appeared to be a fun and friendly place to work.

As she scanned the pictures, a familiar face caught her eye. The young woman standing next to Hayley had dark hair, which was limp and lifeless. Her lips were curved into a smile, but her eyes told a different story; they were dark and empty, as if nothing was going on behind them. But the one thing Linda noticed about this woman, more than anything else, was the way she held herself. Her body language told Linda she had all but given up on life. Her shoulders were hunched forwards in the photo, like she was carrying a tremendous weight on her back.

Linda heard the door creak behind her but didn't turn towards the sound. Instead, she picked up the photo to examine it more closely.

'Ah,' said Hayley, 'I always like to take pictures with all the people I've worked with here over the years. I've outlasted them all!' She chuckled vaguely and handed Linda her passport. 'All done.'

'Who is this woman?' asked Linda, although she already had an idea.

'Amber Walker. She's quite hard to miss, isn't she? That was taken when she first started working here … ooh, gosh … many years ago now.'

'Was she unwell?'

'Oh, no, nothing like that. She always looked like that. As if she'd never slept a wink in her life. She never really looked after herself either, as if everything was an effort.'

'Do you believe what they say about her, that she took her own life?'

Hayley raised her manicured eyebrows. 'Oh, so you've heard of Amber then. I guess that makes sense, considering you now live in her old house.'

Linda replaced the photo on the shelf and tucked her passport into her jeans pocket. 'Yes, her name has come up quite a lot. It seems her death has caused quite a stir in the town.'

'You could say that, but yes, I believe she took her own life, as tragic as it is to think. She had a lovely daughter and an attractive husband and yet she threw it all away. Clearly, she wasn't quite right in the head if you know what I mean.'

'She was mentally ill?'

Hayley scoffed. 'I wouldn't say that, but she certainly had a dark aura about her. To be honest … and this is an awful thing to say, I know, but … it's been much easier at work since she *left*. She brought the entire place down. Towards the end, everyone was on tenterhooks around her, too afraid to speak to her in case they set her off on one of her crazy spiels.'

'What did she use to say?'

Hayley looked towards the door leading to the café and took a step closer to Linda. 'Well, you didn't hear this from me, but … a few days before she died, she told me that her own husband wanted to kill her.'

Linda flinched as if she'd been burned. 'What?'

Hayley nodded enthusiastically. 'Yeah, I know. Crazy, right? I mean, Sean wouldn't hurt a fly. Sure, he'd been cheating on her for years, but who could blame him when she made no effort whatsoever.' Hayley laughed. 'She even started telling everyone that something was after her.'

'The Creature,' said Linda. Hayley sucked in a breath and held it. 'What?' Linda asked.

'We don't say that name out loud around here.'

'Why not?'

'It's like, bad luck or something. Anyway! Enough talk of doom and gloom. Let me introduce you to the rest of the team. They're all dying to meet you.' Hayley waltzed out of the room, oblivious to the fact that Linda was rooted to the spot, trying her best to absorb the amount of information she'd received.

Could it be true? Could Sean Walker have murdered his wife? The thought didn't bear thinking about, but as Linda followed her new boss out into the café to meet her fellow colleagues, she couldn't help but imagine the horrors Amber Walker must have endured in the days leading up to her death. She didn't know the woman, but someone had been out to get her.

The question remained ... who?

And why?

Half an hour later, Linda emerged into the sunshine after meeting three of her new co-workers; David, Lisa and Penny, all of whom were barely out of their teenage years but had been more than welcoming. Linda felt like the mum of the group already. She stretched her arms above her head and clicked her neck side to side, feeling the taut muscles creak and groan.

The headaches were back, travelling up from the base of her neck, over the top of her head and down around her eyes. It felt like a creepy hand was clawing its way into her skull. Even her shoulders ached. She fished around in her bag, found a half-empty packet of painkillers, popped three in her mouth and washed them down with the dregs of vodka from a miniature bottle she hid in a secret compartment in her bag.

As she put the bottle away, she heard a familiar voice and turned in the direction of the sound. It was Alex. She knew he wouldn't want to run into her, especially as it appeared he was with his new friends. Linda ducked down the nearest alley and waited while the trio of teenagers walked past on the other side of the street. Alex was holding hands with a girl, who looked as if she was hanging on his every word. She stroked his arm up and down as they walked.

Linda watched them until they turned the corner and disappeared. She stepped out of the alley and headed in the direction of the shop. She needed to buy more vodka because she was dangerously close to running out.

Once she'd bought a large one-litre bottle (she almost bought more, but hadn't wanted to draw attention to herself) she walked home, but as she did her mind drifted back to what Hayley had said about Amber and her husband. Granted, it had been Emma who had met him when he and his daughter had said goodbye to the house, so she didn't have any sort of read on him at all, but the idea he would kill his wife was odd. Hadn't they been in the middle of a divorce? And he'd been cheating on her, so it wasn't as if he'd been a jealous husband.

Linda rubbed her eyes.

No, she would not get involved. It was none of her business.

Sean and Amber Walker were just the old owners of her house. She didn't owe either of them anything. She had her own family to think about, her own wife to look after and her own demons to deal with.

Chapter Twenty-Eight
ALEX
Sunday 29 October 2023 – 11:35 a.m.

Alex had texted Harriet and Alex the First to meet him fifteen minutes ago and, as he rounded the corner, he could see them loitering at their agreed meeting place: the small circular patch of grass in the town centre. He had already learned it was the place where most of the teenagers hung out because it was within walking distance to all the shops and, as it was located on a small hill, it was the perfect vantage point to people-watch. Also, there was a wooden bench there in memory of Kieran Jones, the boy who had died twenty-five years ago. Sometimes, the townspeople would leave bouquets of flowers by the bench.

Harriet spotted him first and waved. Her smile lit up her whole face and the sun accentuated her freckles on her nose even more. Alex found it hard to believe that she was capable of anything sordid. Surely, she had nothing to do with Amber and whatever it was that had happened to Bethany? Alex the First on the other hand, he wasn't so sure about.

'Hey!' Harriet jogged down the slight hill and greeted him at the bottom. 'I'm so glad you messaged me. What happened last night? Did you find anything under the floorboards?' She threw a glance over her shoulder at Alex the First who was making his way towards them.

'No, nothing. It's a dead end,' replied Alex with a shrug.

Harriet frowned at him.

Alex the First arrived. 'Hey, man, what's up?'

'Hey. Look, I think we got off on the wrong foot. I wanted to apologise to both of you personally. My family is fucked up. My own mum talks to my sister as if she's still alive—'

'Wait … what?' Alex the First held up his hand as if he was halting a parade. 'You *don't* have a sister?'

'I did, but not anymore.'

'And your mums are pretending she's still alive?'

'Just my real mum. Linda is playing along to keep her happy. Look, the point is, I'm sure we all have our own skeletons we keep in the closet. You guys are the only people my own age I've met here so far, so, I dunno … thanks … I guess.'

Alex the First and Harriet swapped looks with each other. Harriet beamed as she threw herself at Alex and hugged him, her arms draping around his neck. She almost knocked him off balance. Alex caught Alex the First's eye and they smirked. Once Harriet released Alex from her tight embrace, she turned to the boys.

'Trust me, everyone in this town has skeletons in their closets. Your family isn't the first to have them and they won't be the last.'

'Yeah, man, I mean, there's stuff we know about people that, if it got out, would seriously fuck this town up even more.' Alex the First grinned at Harriet, who winked back at him.

Alex tilted his head. 'Oh, yeah? Well, let's hear it. I told you my mum is nuts and speaks to my dead sister. Let's see you top that.'

Alex the First exaggerated clearing his throat. 'Okay, so you remember we told you that Amber and her daughter, Bethany, kept saying they were seeing The Creature? Well … Bethany wrote a poem about it and handed it in as homework. I overheard the teachers talking about it. They were concerned about her mental stability, or whatever. The teachers had a word with her and her mum about it, but me and Harriet got hold of the poem, photocopied it and hung it up all over the school. The teachers weren't going to show it to anyone in the class, but we got there first.'

Alex looked from one person to the other. 'Wait … so *you* were the ones who started the rumours about The Creature?'

Alex the First laughed. 'Hell, yeah! Well, technically, Amber and Bethany started it, but we … expanded upon it, as it were.'

Harriet giggled beside him. She sidled up to him and took hold of his hand, resting her head against his shoulder. Alex did his best not to flinch away. She didn't appear so innocent now.

'Plus,' she added with a giggle, 'Alex crept into Bethany's room, dressed up as a creepy, black demon and freaked her the hell out.'

Alex swallowed back a gasp as he realised that his two new friends were deluded psychopaths. It was almost worse than killing someone. The fact they'd tortured a little girl into believing a demon creature was after her was unthinkable.

'Wow,' said Alex, attempting to keep his voice level.

Alex the First laughed again. 'Yeah, I mean, we didn't expect things to go so far. We only did it as a joke, but then everyone started freaking out over The Creature and the rumour just kept getting bigger and bigger.'

'What about the ravine? You guys were petrified when I suggested going there.'

'We were testing you,' replied Alex the First. 'We wanted to see if you really had the guts to do it. We tried our best to freak you out, but you're one of us now. You're cool.'

Alex nodded. 'Right, cool … thanks? I guess. But there's still one thing I'm confused about. What really happened to Amber Walker?'

Harriet and Alex the First shook their heads at once. 'Like we said, we didn't mean for things to go so far,' replied Harriet in a whisper.

'We didn't kill her, if that's what you're getting at,' snapped Alex the First.

'I wasn't suggesting that you did. I just want to know what happened to her.'

'Jordan and Brooke are sniffing around,' said Harriet to Alex the First. 'They want someone to blame for her death.'

'How about they blame her for her own death?' snapped Alex the First.

Harriet lowered her eyes to the ground. 'We may have bullied Bethany a bit, but it wasn't our fault Amber died.'

Alex squeezed her hand. 'I believe you.'

'I'll tell you who did have something to do with her death though,' added Alex the First. 'Her husband, or rather ex-husband. I can't remember his name, but it sure seems suspicious that two days after she's found dead, he puts the house on the market and makes plans to move away.'

'Really? Two days?'

'Yeah. He wasn't living with Amber and Bethany at the house. He was living at The Cherry Tree, the hotel in town where he worked. Plus, he hated Amber's new boyfriend, Jordan.'

Alex scratched his head with his free hand. 'Nothing seems to make sense.'

'Nothing ever does, man,' said Alex the First. 'Anyway, who fancies taking a few beers and heading to the ravine to drink them?'

'There are two things wrong with that plan.' Harriet held up one finger at a time as she spoke. 'First of all, we're underage and can't buy beer, and secondly, the ravine is creepy as hell and, all joking aside, I really don't want to hang out at a place where people died.'

Alex the First held up his backpack and shook it. The unmistakable sound of glass clanging brought a smile to Harriet's face. 'No way! You swiped them from your dad?'

'Yep. He drinks so many of them he can't remember how many he has left anyway. Alex the Second, you in?'

'Sure, but I'm not going to the ravine again. It's too far to walk.'

'Yeah, you're right about that. Okay, screw the ravine. Let's go to the graveyard. We'll show you the graves of three of the Fated Five.'

'The who?'

Alex the First laughed as he slapped Alex on the back. 'The Fated Five. That's what we call the five of them who started all this crap. Kieran, Tyler, Amber, Jordan and Brooke. Who knows, Jordan and Brooke might find themselves joining their friends in the graveyard soon.'

Alex the First and Harriet shared a laugh, which shook Alex to his core. Could it be true? Were Jordan and Brooke in danger?

Alex allowed Harriet to drag him through town. She clutched his hand as if she were afraid that he'd run away from her. He desperately needed to get a message to Jordan and Brooke, not only to pass on the information he'd received, but also to warn them.

Because it was possible that not everyone in this town liked them or wanted them here anymore.

Chapter Twenty-Nine
BROOKE
Sunday 29 October 2023 – 11:45 a.m.

Filing her nails as she sat on the stool behind the reception desk at Fix It All, Brooke watched Jordan as he stacked shelves with new items, mostly plumbing tubes and nuts and bolts, which Brooke had no idea about how to use. As she studied his movements, she felt her lips curve into a smile.

Jordan had always been an attractive man, but he was one of those men who didn't realise the effect he had on people. Brooke had never met his ex-wife, Eleanor, but she'd heard how badly he had treated her, that he used to sleep around back when he'd been under the control of The Bad Man. It seemed impossible to think of him like that now. He had his issues, and his idiosyncrasies, but he genuinely cared about people, especially his friends. He was maybe a bit rough around the edges, but he had a good heart under it all. Jordan was all Brooke had left of her childhood friendship group. One by one, they'd diminished in numbers and now she and Jordan were the only ones left standing, left to deal with the aftermath. Without him, she had no one whom she'd call a friend. Not anymore.

'Why are you smiling at me like that?'

Brooke jumped and almost dropped her nail file. 'I wasn't smiling at you.'

Jordan raised his eyebrows. 'How about instead of sitting there filing your nails, you give me a hand with stacking shelves?'

'Why'd you think I'm filing my nails in the first place? Because I tore one helping you move those boxes in the back half an hour ago.'

Jordan rolled his eyes. 'You're such a girl.'

Brooke stuck out her tongue, grinning as she returned to nail filing. She was not flirting with him. No, she was not …

Her face heated and her heart rate sped up.

Oh God … was she flirting with Jordan?

When they'd been growing up, before Kieran died, it had always been Jordan and Amber who'd been destined to end up together. Brooke had been able to have her pick of any of the boys in the entire town back then but had never once attempted to steal Jordan away from her best friend. Even now, she felt sick just thinking about betraying Amber by flirting with Jordan.

But no …

She wasn't flirting …

Brooke cleared her throat and put her nail file in her bag before hopping off the stool. She straightened her top and pulled it away from her neck. A hot flush was creeping up her chest.

'I'm going to go and get a coffee from across the road. Want one?' She avoided eye contact with Jordan as she headed for the door. The air had become stuffy, and she needed to breathe. She often had moments when her claustrophobia would attempt to come creeping back, but a quick breath of fresh air was usually enough to stomp it back down into the depths where it belonged. The Fear did not control her anymore.

'Yeah, a vanilla latte would be great, thanks.'

Brooke paused with her hand on the door handle. 'A vanilla latte? You're such a girl,' she said with a laugh. She turned and caught him looking at her with a smirk across his face. He stuck his tongue out at her. Brooke gulped and escaped through the door, slamming it a little louder than she intended. She took a calming breath. Something was weird between them. What the hell was going on?

Her heart still hammering, Brooke jogged across the road to The Bean Café, her eyes widening in surprise as she noticed it had received an incredible upgrade since the last time she'd seen it, which had been four years ago, the day before she'd left Cherry Hollow. She'd met Amber for coffee and they'd shared a chocolate muffin, although Brooke had ended up eating most of it since at the time she'd been hell-bent on putting on weight, having spent twenty years being exceptionally underweight.

She pushed open the door and headed for the counter, her mouth already watering from the smell of freshly brewed coffee and warm chocolate brownies. She placed her order with the young lady in the pink apron and then waited at the end of the line for her name to be called. That was when she noticed several customers pretending not to stare at her. She could see them out of the corner of her eye, swapping whispers and nudging each other. She prayed her order would be ready any second now …

'Brooke!' A shrill voice echoed across the café. 'Oh my God! It *is* you!'

Brooke, cursing herself for coming for coffee in the first place, slapped on a smile and turned just in time to see

Hayley, who flung her arms around her neck and squeezed her much tighter than was deemed necessary for a friendly hug.

'I'd heard rumours you were back in town, but I didn't believe it.'

'Yeah, thought it was time I came home for a while.' Brooke attempted to lower the volume of Hayley's voice by keeping her own voice quiet, but Hayley had always been a loudmouth. Amber had told her stories about how she was the type of person who often spoke out loud before thinking about her words and how they could be interpreted by others, but Brooke couldn't fault her for her effort at renovating this café. She clearly loved her job.

'It's so lovely to see you. How are you?' asked Hayley, flipping her long black hair over her shoulder, her multiple earrings jangling.

'I'm great, thanks. Hayley, this place looks amazing. You've done so much work. Honestly, it looks fantastic. When I left it was practically on its last legs.'

Hayley shrugged as if it were no big deal. 'Oh, you know, when I got promoted I thought, there is no way I am being the manager of a dump like this, so I asked my dad for a loan, and he gave it to me. I've even been able to hire some new help as the place is so busy. I just didn't have the staff to keep up. People love their coffee!' she exclaimed, gesturing at the bustling café and happy customers, who smiled at her as they raised their coffee cups in response. 'In fact, I've seen Linda just now. She's going to be starting work here soon. She seems ever so nice, although maybe a bit obsessed with Amber.'

'Order for Brooke!' came a shout from one of the baristas.

Brooke raised her hand and stepped forwards, picking up the two cups, both of which had lids on with steam still escaping out the top. 'I'm sorry,' she said, turning back to Hayley, 'did you say Linda? As in Linda Smithson, who's just moved into Amber's old house?'

'Yes, that's right. Have you met her yet?'

'Um, no, I mean, yes, sort of. Only very briefly. Why was she interested in Amber?'

'Who knows, but Amber's death is sort of a hot topic around here, what with her taking her own life and all. I guess, since you've been away and weren't here when it happened, you haven't realised.' Hayley's words dripped with condescension, but a smile was still plastered across her face.

Brooke narrowed her eyes, remembering what Amber had said not to do when it came to Hayley. Never react to her digs. Never bite back. But, then again, Amber had always been one to shy away from a fight or a confrontation. But Brooke wasn't Amber, and she wasn't about to let some stuck-up rich girl talk to her like that. Hayley probably assumed she'd be able to get away with it, but she didn't know the real Brooke. She only knew the Brooke who'd locked herself in her own home for twenty years and came out looking like a living skeleton.

'Actually, Hayley, Amber was my best friend, and she didn't take her own life, so I'll ask politely that you stop spreading that rubbish around town.'

Hayley's body language shifted ever so slightly. She tensed as if gearing up for a fight, but her smile stayed on her face, despite the fact her teeth were clenched as she spoke.

'And what would you know about Amber and how she died? You haven't even lived here for four years. Are you a cop? I haven't heard anything from the police about her being murdered.'

'I don't remember saying anything about her being murdered.'

The women locked eyes. Had Brooke just caught her out? Why would she have mentioned *that* word? Hayley stood her ground, not giving anything away. Brooke happened to glance sideways and saw several people at the nearby tables craning their necks and pausing midway through a sip of coffee to listen. Brooke took a breath, realising she'd already said too much in the presence of too many people.

She spoke slowly. 'The thing is, Hayley, I knew Amber a lot more than you did, and she'd never have ended her life and left Bethany without a mother. There's no way.'

Hayley laughed. 'I worked with Amber for many years. You knew her briefly as a child and then didn't speak to her for twenty years while you rotted away in your house.'

'Yes, but Amber never liked you. There's a difference.'

At this point, several heads turned in their direction and all eyes, apart from the baristas behind the counter who were still busy fulfilling orders, were on the two women who were now glaring at each other.

Hayley snorted. 'You're a piece of work, you know that, Brooke? You waltz back into town four years after leaving your poor mother to look after your sick father and expect everyone to love you and feel sorry for you.'

'Don't you dare brings my parents into this!'

'Why shouldn't I? I'm the one who visits your mother every week to make sure she's okay and not dead on the floor. I'm the one who has helped pick up the pieces in this town after Amber died. You should be thanking me.'

Brooke opened her mouth but found there were no words. She relaxed her body as she glanced around the café. Numerous pairs of eyes lowered to the floor to avoid her gaze.

Hayley had won this round. Amber had been right. It wasn't worth going up against her. Brooke was wrong and Hayley was right.

Brooke sighed as she nodded her head. 'You're right, Hayley. I should be thanking you.'

Hayley looked momentarily stunned, but then sniffed loudly and flipped her hair over her shoulder again. 'Yes, well … if you ask me, this place is better off without Amber and her dark demons dragging us all down. She's in a better place.'

Something inside Brooke snapped.

She turned to the nearest person, a young man who appeared to be sitting with his girlfriend and asked, 'Could you hold these a moment?' The man took both her coffee cups from her with his eyebrows raised and his mouth open. Brooke turned back to Hayley, pulled her fist back and punched her hard in the face.

An almighty gasp erupted in the café.

Chairs scrapped across the floor as people rose to their feet to get a better view. Brooke could have sworn she heard a cheer from across the room as Hayley stumbled against the nearest table, knocking over a customer's drink. Hushed whispers spread across the café like wildfire and several people fished out their mobiles and started filming, probably expecting a proper fight to start.

Brooke turned and took her coffee cups back from the bewildered-looking young man. 'Thank you,' she said before turning back to Hayley. She took a sip of her cinnamon cappuccino. 'Thanks for the coffee. You really do make the best in town.'

She turned and made a swift exit.

As the door to the café swung closed, she heard a round of applause from behind her and couldn't help but grin as she crossed the road back to Fix It All.

She'd probably pay for that later.

Chapter Thirty
JORDAN
Sunday 29 October 2023 – 12:10 p.m.

He flat-packed the final box and chucked it in the large recycling bin at the back of the shop. As he re-entered the main reception, Brooke came in, carrying a takeaway cup of coffee in each hand. Her face was flushed and her breathing seemed erratic.

'Are you okay? I was about to send a search party out to look for you.'

Brooke handed him one of the cups. 'I may have just punched Hayley in the face.'

Jordan frowned as he took a sip of the coffee. 'Bloody hell, Brooke, her coffee's not *that* bad.'

'Funny. No, she came and gave me a hug and was acting all nice and overly fake and then she started bad-mouthing Amber and then told me I was a piece of work for leaving my mum alone to look after my dad, so I punched her.'

Jordan lowered his cup. 'She said what?'

'To be fair to her, she's probably right about me.'

Jordan shook his head. 'Don't be ridiculous. What was it she said about Amber?'

'She said this town was better off without Amber's drama and that she was in a better place.'

Jordan clenched his teeth and slammed his cup down on the counter, causing the lid to pop off and coffee to splash over his hand, but he didn't flinch at the heat.

Brooke held her hand up to stop him from speaking his mind. 'I sorted it. I don't like her, nor do I trust her, but she did say something that sparked my attention.'

'Oh yeah?'

'Yeah. When I said I didn't think Amber ended her own life she said that she hadn't heard anything from the police about her being murdered. I didn't use that word at all, so why did she use it when she could have said something else like … Oh, I don't know … It just seemed odd to me. As I said, I don't trust her.'

'Hayley's always liked to be the centre of attention. I think she gets off on spreading gossip, like most of this fucking town.'

'Yeah, well, I had a few people on my side in there. Got a few claps and cheers.' Brooke smirked as she took a sip.

Jordan cleaned up the spilt coffee with a nearby cloth and continued drinking the rest. 'Did you at least punch her hard?'

'Yes, quite hard. I think I broke another nail.'

Jordan chuckled. 'I've got some ice in the back if you need some for your hand.'

'Thanks.'

'I'll go and grab you—' Jordan's phone rang. It was laying on the counter. He scooped it up when he saw the name on the screen. 'Alex? Are you okay?' Jordan put him on speakerphone. Brooke stepped closer and listened.

'Err, yeah, I'm okay, but I've found out some stuff. I can't talk long, but it's not good. Basically, Alex the First and Harriet are a couple of psychos. They're nuts. They're the ones who started and spread the rumour about The Creature at school. They stole that poem from Bethany and pinned it up for everyone to read. The fuckers even crept into her room at night dressed up as The Creature and scared her. Amber knew about it. Also … they said something about her husband being responsible for her death. I don't know the guy, and they could just be making more shit up, but I thought you should know. Also, most of the people in this town don't like you … either of you.' Despite Alex speaking quickly, Jordan had caught every word, and as the reality sunk in, his eyes grew wider and wider. Brooke watched him as his face turned red.

'Well, that's not surprising, I guess. Thanks, Alex. You've been a great help. Keep yourself out of trouble, yeah? And you start work at nine a.m. on Saturday.'

'Thanks, Jordan.'

'Oh … and ditch those new friends of yours.'

'Don't worry. I have a plan. See ya.'

'Bye.' Jordan dropped the phone on the counter and turned to Brooke.

'Uh oh. I don't like the look on your face. Jordan … whatever it is you're thinking about doing, stop and think first.'

'I'm going to fucking kill Sean.'

'What did I just say?'

'He might have had something to do with Amber's death.'

'Exactly. *Might*. I assume there's no solid proof. You can't go accusing the guy of murdering his ex-wife just because some teenagers said so.'

Jordan breathed in through his nose and out through his mouth, silencing the rage that was building inside. It was threatening to engulf him if he didn't quell it soon. 'If I find out he had anything to do with her death, I'm going to kill him.'

'And leave Bethany without a mum or a dad?'

'Better than having a fucking murderer as a parent.'

Brooke huffed and stood directly in front of him. She placed her hands on either side of his chest and looked him straight in the eyes.

'Jordan … look at me. We will find out the truth about who killed Amber, okay? But we must be patient, and collect the evidence and facts, not just dive straight in at the deep end. I know you've never liked Sean …' At this point, Jordan snorted. 'But that doesn't give you the right to accuse him of murder just because a couple of psycho kids said so. You heard what Alex said. They started the town's obsession with The Creature. They're the ones who are giving it power now.'

Jordan looked down at Brooke's hands touching his chest. He held her eye contact for several seconds once she'd finished her speech. Brooke wrenched her hands away from him as if touching him was burning her skin.

'What do you suggest we do next?' he asked in a calmer voice.

He hated to admit it but having her hands on him had soothed him more than he expected. In fact, he could have sworn he'd felt a spark ignite inside him, but that wasn't possible. Sure, he'd noticed how attractive she was. A man would have to be blind not to notice, but it had always been Amber he'd loved. There had never been anyone else … But Amber was gone. His ex-wife had taken off years ago and he hadn't heard from her since, not that he blamed her. Even his dad had left him. His mother was still around, and he saw her from time to time, but as for this town, there was no one he'd call a friend, but when Amber had been here, he hadn't needed anyone else. Brooke had moved to London, and he'd been happy for her, but with Amber now gone, Jordan realised the only person left in his life, the only person he cared about, bar Bethany, was Brooke. And for the first time, he was looking at her not as a friend, but possibly as something more. It scared the life out of him.

Brooke took a breath. 'Text Bethany. Ask her to get Sean to call you, or maybe to call me instead. Say it's urgent.'

Jordan nodded as he picked up his phone.

Brooke stepped away, her face and chest slightly flushed.

Jordan swallowed back the confusing feelings that were bubbling to the surface and typed out a message to Bethany.

Chapter Thirty-One
EMMA
Sunday 29 October 2023 – 12:20 p.m.

Her stomach continued to churn during the walk back home, but the fresh air was helping with the hot flushes. She was too young to be experiencing menopause … wasn't she? Of course she was. She was only thirty-five. Menopause at that age was ridiculous.

Emma wrestled with the front door keys, her fingers trembling so badly that she dropped them on the doorstep. Groaning, she bent down and retrieved them, only to be hit with another wave of nausea and heat as she stood up. She steadied herself against the side of the house and took a few deep breaths. Her conversation with Olivia kept repeating in her head, especially the part about what Olivia had said about Amber, that things were better around here now that she'd gone. What an awful thing to say about someone. Surely Amber hadn't been that bad. So, maybe she'd been a little eccentric and spoke of seeing creatures and whatnot, but it seemed as if the whole town had been against her in some way. Emma didn't blame her. If she started seeing demonic-type creatures and feared for her daughter's life, she'd have spoken up about it too … which she had, to Jordan and Brooke, and they'd dismissed her worries as nothing. Was that what the residents of the town had done to Amber? Had she been ignored too? Was she going to end up like Amber …

Another wave of nausea hit at the thought. No. She could never end her life like that. Not even if it meant she'd be reunited with Phoebe in the afterlife …

Phoebe …

Emma's gut wrenched again as the image of her perfect daughter at age seven popped into her mind. Because, of course, she'd always be seven. Emma would never see her grow up, never experience those troublesome teenage daughter years, never see her drive off to university, never help her pick out her wedding dress, never see her have a child of her own.

Emma collapsed to her knees and buried her face in her hands. She'd been living a lie for so long. She knew it had been difficult for Linda and Alex, but there had been no other way of dealing with it for Emma. Her daughter *couldn't* be dead because if she was dead then Emma had failed as a mother. She used to stay awake at night, rocking her baby girl to sleep in her arms, whispering over and over that she'd never let anything bad happen to her, that she'd always keep her safe from harm.

But that day … that day she'd been with Linda. She'd trusted another human being to look after her child. Emma loved Linda with all her heart. She didn't blame her. Phoebe had run away and gone outside onto the street. Linda had still been frantically searching inside the shop when she heard the shouts. It hadn't been her fault …

No, she didn't blame Linda.

After it happened, Emma had been so out of it that she'd barely heard what had happened. Linda had told her the bare minimum. She'd shielded Emma from the police investigation, the funeral plans, everything. But there was something that didn't quite add up in Emma's mind. Her mind was clearing for the first time in two years and she wanted to ask more and more questions, seek out those answers that were fuzzy and had been hiding behind her cloud of grief for so long.

Was Linda telling her the whole truth about what had happened that day? They didn't speak about it ... ever, but was that because Emma never brought it up or because Linda had something to hide? For the first time, Emma wanted answers. She wanted to know *exactly* what had happened. Every little seemingly insignificant detail, even if it crushed her soul to hear them.

Emma stood on shaky legs and relocked the front door. She was going back into town to look for Linda. This couldn't wait. Linda had told her earlier that she'd be popping into her new workplace to complete some paperwork, so she'd start there.

As she rounded the corner, she spied The Bean Café in the distance. There seemed to be a lot of people milling around the front. People were jostling for positions to peer through the windows. She couldn't see Linda anywhere, but when she peeked through a spare section of the window, she saw a young woman with a bloody nose holding a damp cloth to her face. A few customers were hovering around her, comforting her, while others were snapping photos.

Linda was nowhere to be seen.

Emma raised her eyebrows. Clearly, something had happened in the past few minutes, but she wasn't one to stick her nose into other people's business, unless it had something to do with her, so she turned and headed towards Fix It All instead, deciding to pay Jordan a visit to offer up an apology in the way of giving him the information she'd gleaned from Olivia earlier this morning. Not that she suspected Olivia of murdering Amber; it was ludicrous to even think of it, but the whole idea of the town being against Amber didn't sit right with Emma.

Pushing open the door, Emma saw Brooke standing by the counter. 'Oh! Hello, again.'

Brooke smiled timidly at her. 'Hi, Mrs Smithson.'

'Emma, please.'

'Emma.' Brooke nodded. 'Have you come for some plumbing supplies?'

'Oh, God no. Everything's fine. I came here to talk to Jordan, and well, you as well.' At that point, Jordan walked in from the back room.

'Everything okay in here?'

Emma took a brave step forward. 'I wanted to apologise to you both for … overreacting the other day over the poem I found in my house.'

'It's totally okay, Emma,' said Brooke. 'We understand how difficult things must be for you.'

'Well, yes, but … the thing is, I've not been very honest with myself lately and it's high time I stop hiding behind my own issues and face up to the truth. The Creature may not be real, but it's certainly shown me the error of my ways. There's no point in letting things get so out of control that they consume your life, is there?' Brooke and Jordan looked at each other, sharing a look that Emma assumed was laden with meaning, but she pressed on regardless. 'I also wanted to mention something that Olivia – your mother – mentioned earlier today.'

At the mention of her mother, Brooke sat up a little straighter. 'What did she say?'

Emma's face turned warm as she wondered whether she should mention it. Was she any better than those nosey neighbours of hers, spreading gossip and making drama when there more than likely was none?

'She said something about Amber … She said that maybe the town was better off without her now.'

Brooke sucked in a breath as if she'd been punched in the stomach. 'She said what?'

'I don't think she meant anything bad by it,' added Emma.

Brooke frowned at Jordan. 'I've never known my mum to say a bad word about anyone. I thought she always liked Amber.'

'I think … I think maybe she was worried about Amber dragging you down a dark path.' Emma gulped, knowing she was treading on thin ice here, but these things had to be said. She was fed up with keeping secrets. 'As a mother myself, I know where she's coming from. I'd do anything to protect my children …' She stopped, realising she'd spoken as if she had two. Brooke and Jordan noticed her slip-up, but they didn't mention it.

'You don't think … No, that's impossible. My mum wouldn't kill Amber.' Brooke shook her head vigorously, taking a step back.

Jordan stepped forwards. 'No one is saying that, Brooke, but what I am realising is that a lot of people in this town had an issue with Amber and we're only learning about it now.'

'What … because she tried to protect Bethany from those horrible kids?'

'I think we have to believe that, under the right circumstances, anyone is capable of murder.'

Chapter Thirty-Two
LINDA
Sunday 29 October 2023 – 12:30 p.m.

The strap of her heavy bag dug into her shoulder the whole walk home, so Linda was relieved when she was able to set it down on the kitchen counter with a thud. She opened the vodka straight away. She skipped the glass and swigged a gulp straight from the bottle, sighing with ecstasy as the liquid burned her throat. Her headache was getting worse too, so she popped a couple more pills, despite having taken three less than an hour ago.

Where the hell was Emma and Alex? Why was this house always so damn quiet?

The ground wobbled underneath her, and her head swam as she stumbled against the counter. The pain in her head was so bad she thought her head might explode; the pressure was building by the second. Linda closed her eyes, attempting to calm her thoughts and not think about The Void.

But The Void was opening again … and she could have sworn it was bigger than before …

A bath.

That was what she needed, and it was a perfect time to have one too because the house was quiet. Linda took her bottle upstairs, swaying as she staggered up the steps, which seemed to go on forever. Were they getting steeper too?

She entered the bathroom, put in the plug, turned on the taps and added a good measure of bubble bath, which promised to relax those tense muscles and help quiet the mind. She scoffed as the bath filled and she stripped out of her clothes, bundling them into the wash bin. She stood in front of the mirror, bottle in hand and stared at herself. Self-loathing flooded her senses as she took in her naked body, which was softer and more rounded than she cared to admit.

A black shadow darted across the mirror.

Linda shrieked and spun around to find nothing but the bare bathroom wall.

'Go away!' She drank another mouthful of vodka. 'Go away!' she shouted again. 'What do you want from me?'

She was going crazy. She had to be. There was no other explanation. Was this how Emma had felt? Or Amber, the woman she'd never even met? The Creature was tormenting her, driving her to the edge of sanity. She knew what she had to do to stop it. She knew what it was that was eating her alive.

The truth.

The truth would set her free, if only she would allow it to fly.

But she couldn't, could she? Because if she told the truth, Emma would be destroyed by it, and Linda didn't want to cause her any more suffering. Therefore, the only way through this was to suffer herself, or maybe … maybe there was one other option. She just wanted to not feel anything for a moment.

Linda sunk into the hot water, ignoring the fact it was practically scalding her. She drank more and more and more until the pain in her head sank into the abyss and her whole body turned numb. She kept her eyes closed because she didn't want to see the darkness floating around her.

The Void began to swallow her ...

The almost empty bottle of vodka slipped from her grasp as her head lolled to the side. The glass bobbed on the surface of the water for a few seconds before filling up with bath water and sinking to the bottom.

Linda sank too, sank lower and lower and lower ... down into the depths of The Void.

And then there was nothing but peace.

The Void had claimed its victim.

At last.

Chapter Thirty-Three
ALEX
Sunday 29 October 2023 – 12:48 p.m.

He opened the front door, slammed it behind him and kicked off his shoes into the hallway, ignoring the rack where he knew shoes were supposed to live when not in use.

'Mum, you home?' He waited several seconds. 'Linda? Anyone home?' Eerie silence greeted him, enough to set his teeth on edge as he realised he'd opened the door without having to unlock it first, so someone must be home. The lounge was empty and so was the kitchen diner, but Linda's bag was on the counter.

'Linda?' he called again.

Maybe she was out in the garden. Alex peered out the window, but there was no one there. The boiler whirred to life, gurgling away in the kitchen. A cold tingle crept up his spine.

Something was wrong.

Alex headed upstairs, calling Linda's name. As he reached the top step, he saw the bathroom door ajar and steam seeping out into the hallway through the crack.

She was taking a bath, but why wasn't she answering him? He stood outside and knocked on the door, pressing his ear close to listen for any noise. He couldn't hear any music or running water.

'Linda, I'm home. You good?'

No answer.

'Linda?' Alex gulped back the lump in his throat. 'I'm coming in … just … I have my eyes closed, okay?' He opened the bathroom door and was hit in the face by a waft of steam, but he kept his eyes tightly closed. 'Linda, if you don't answer me, I'm going to open my eyes and if I happen to see you naked, then it's your own damn fault.'

No answer.

Alex sighed and cracked one eye open.

Linda lay slouched in the bath with her eyes closed. She'd slipped so far down that her mouth was beneath the water. Her nose was barely breaking the surface, creating bubbles as she breathed. But her chest was barely moving. In fact, she looked …

'Fuck!'

Alex leaped forwards and yanked the plug out. Then, ignoring the fact he was seeing his stepmother naked, he pulled her head up and shook her.

'Linda! Linda, wake the fuck up. Shit!'

The water continued to drain from the bath, gurgling and spluttering as it disappeared down the plughole, but Linda remained unconscious.

His hands shook so violently that he dropped his phone as he fished it out of his trouser pocket. It clattered to the floor.

'Fuck!'

He scooped it up and dialled 999, taking a few deep breaths as the call engaged.

'Operator. Which emergency service do you require?'

'Hello? Yes, I need help. My mum, I mean, Linda, she's unconscious in the bath …'

'Transferring to the ambulance service now.'

Alex gripped the phone tighter. That was when his eyes landed on the bottle of vodka next to Linda. All the water had drained now, so he grabbed a nearby towel from the wall hook and draped it across Linda's body.

'You're through to the ambulance service. Is the patient breathing and awake?'

'Um … fuck … I mean … yes, she's breathing, but only barely, she's unconscious.'

'Okay, I need you to try and stay calm. The first thing I need you to do is tell me your name and your address and the number you are calling from.' The woman at the end of the line spoke with composure as if she'd done this a million times. Alex could hear her fingers tapping against a keyboard in the background.

'My name's Alex. My address … it's um … fuck, it's … 6 Baker Street, Cherry Hollow.' He rattled off his mobile number.

'Thank you, I'm sending an ambulance to your location now. You said that Linda is breathing, but only barely. Is her chest moving up and down?'

Alex took a step closer and peered at Linda's chest, which was rising and falling, but only slightly. He nodded as he spoke. 'Um, yes, I think so, but she's not conscious and … she's been drinking. I found her in the bath.'

'Okay, you've done a great job. She may have inhaled some water, but that's okay, the ambulance will be there soon to take over. I need you to remain calm and try and keep her warm until the paramedics get there. They are ten minutes away.'

'Should I try and get her out of the bath?'

'Does she look hurt? Is she bleeding?'

'N-No, I don't think so.'

'Then, yes, if you're able to lift her out of the bath it will be easier to get her warm and dry.'

'I've drained the water.'

'That's good. Now, put me on speaker and let me know when you've done it. If you slip or think it's going to be too dangerous to move her or you're unable to lift her, then stop and wait for the paramedics to arrive.'

Alex nodded as his shaking hands fumbled with the phone. He pressed the speaker button and set the phone down on the side. He readjusted the towel so it was covering her modesty and manoeuvred himself over the bath, sliding both arms under her body, one beneath her legs and the other around her back. She was heavy, but he knew he had to get her out of the bath. He was surprised by his own strength as he picked her up and placed her down on the soft bathmat.

'Okay, she's out,' he shouted.

'Well done, Alex. The paramedics are minutes away. Do you know how to put someone in the recovery position?'

'Um, no, I don't.'

'That's okay. I'll walk you through it step by step. It's just to ensure she is comfortable and her airway is clear, okay?'

Alex nodded and listened as the caller provided him with instructions. He did exactly as he was told and by the time he'd finished, there was a loud knock on the door.

'They're here.'

'Okay, I'm going to hang up now, Alex. You did a great job. They will take it from here. If you need to call anyone else, I suggest you do so now.'

'Thanks, bye.'

'Goodbye, Alex.'

Alex jumped down the stairs two at a time and yanked open the door.

'She's upstairs in the bathroom.'

The two paramedics sprang into action as they stepped past Alex and rushed up the stairs.

Alex leaned against the nearest wall and took a breath.

It had felt like he hadn't taken one for the past ten minutes.

He looked down at the phone in his hand, scrolled to his mum's number and pressed dial.

Chapter Thirty-Four
BROOKE
Sunday 29 October 2023 – 12:58 p.m.

'I think we have to believe that, under the right circumstances, anyone is capable of murder.'

Jordan's words echoed around the room, leaving Brooke with a bad taste at the back of her throat. It couldn't possibly be true. Was her mum involved in Amber's death? There was no way. But, then again, her mum had been through enough turmoil to last a lifetime. People changed when catastrophic things happened to them; she was walking proof of that. She'd once been a happy, bubbly young girl, the life and soul of any party, and when she'd witnessed one of her best friends killing one of her other best friends, and then helped cover it up, she'd changed almost overnight. They all had. But it'd had nothing to do with them being cursed or haunted or any other strange phenomenon. They were the cause of their own suffering.

'Brooke, are you okay?' Jordan had been speaking to her, but Brooke hadn't heard a word. She shook her head, snapping herself out of her downward spiral.

'There must be another explanation. I'll go and talk to my mum and find out.'

Before Jordan could answer her, a phone started ringing.

'Ooh, sorry, that's my son. I should get this,' said Emma, stepping away from the group.

Brooke and Jordan held eye contact while Emma answered the phone. They turned to look at her when she let out a gasp and a shriek. Her body shook and her hands grasped the phone tighter as she spoke.

'I'm on my way. I'll meet you at the hospital.' She hung up. 'I'm sorry, I have to go. My wife … she … she's been taken to hospital. Alex found her unconscious in the bath and called an ambulance. Oh God …' Tears filled her eyes as her body shook so violently it was a wonder her legs were still able to hold her up. Brooke ran to her side and steadied her.

'I'll drive you. You're in no state to drive yourself.'

Emma opened her mouth to protest, but Brooke was already ushering her out the door.

'Don't do anything stupid while I'm gone,' she shouted over her shoulder at Jordan, who mumbled something she didn't quite hear.

Brooke's mind cast back to a decade ago when she was still possessed and controlled by The Fear; a day that caused her insides, even now, to clench. She knew the repercussions of not responding in an emergency all too well.

Brooke was in her room. The same place she'd been yesterday, and the day before, and the day before and the day before. Usually, she was able to come downstairs and take up residence on the sofa, as long as the curtains were drawn, but for the past four days, she'd locked herself in her room, only leaving to use the bathroom which she restricted herself to using only once per day. Therefore, she only drank and ate small amounts. Her weight had plummeted until she was now at least a stone underweight for someone of her height and age. The anxiety and build-up of leaving the safety of her prison were too exhausting to cope with, so that was another reason why she stayed in her room day in and day out.

She sat in the corner with her back up against the wall and her knees pulled up to her chest. She studied her fingers, counting them over and over ...

'Brooke!' Her mum's scream echoed throughout the house. Brooke lifted her head and looked at her closed bedroom door, which had numerous bolts across it.

'Brooke! Help me!'

Again, the screams of agony came from her mum, but Brooke didn't move. Her dad was at work and wouldn't be home for several hours.

Brooke stayed where she was and listened as her mum's screams turned to quiet whimpers and eventually to silence. Tears streamed down her face at the reality of what she was doing. The fact she couldn't even leave her room to tend to her mum who'd had an accident was unforgivable, but what else could she do?

The Fear was real.

Her mum would understand ...

Several hours later, her dad returned home and called an ambulance. Brooke listened at the door and learned that her mum had fallen down the last few stairs and bumped her head, which had eventually led to unconsciousness. She was alive, but her ankle was also broken.

Brooke remained at home while her dad went with her mum to the hospital. Neither of them spoke of the incident when they came home. No one asked any questions as to why Brooke hadn't responded to her mum's call; her mum told the hospital staff she'd been unconscious the whole time, that she hadn't shouted for help and that she hadn't called out to Brooke.

Brooke had never thought or spoken about it since.
And her mum had never brought it up.

Chapter Thirty-Five
EMMA
Sunday 29 October 2023 – 13:15 p.m.

By the time Brooke pulled up outside the double doors of the emergency drop-off point, Emma had calmed down enough to form coherent sentences. She thanked Brooke for the lift, they swapped numbers so she could keep Brooke updated on Linda's condition and then Emma hopped out of the car and sprinted to the hospital reception.

Her eyes scanned the corridors as she followed the receptionist's directions, hoping for a glimpse of her son so she could throw her arms around him. Because not only was she scared for Linda, but she was petrified for Alex too. No teenager should have to find a parent in such a terrible condition …

As she rounded the corner, almost slipping on the polished floor, she spotted Alex slouched on a plastic chair, his head bowed, staring at his feet, for once not at his phone.

'Alex!' His head snapped up at the sound of her voice and she ran to him, wrapping her arms around him and squeezing tight. 'Are you okay?'

He nodded while still hugging her. She soaked up the moment as best as she could, given the circumstances. It wasn't every day Alex let her hug him.

'I'm fine, Mum.'

'What happened?'

They sat on the bright blue chairs, Emma still grasping Alex's hands as he explained how he'd found Linda in the bath and called 999 before putting her into the recovery position. The paramedics had allowed him to travel in the back of the ambulance with her.

'I've been told she's unconscious, but she's stable. They've had to pump her stomach. Mum … she'd drunk almost a whole litre of vodka in the bath and taken too many pills. She could have drowned herself or overdosed.'

Emma flinched at his words. 'Are they treating this as a suspected …' She stopped, unable to physically manipulate her tongue into saying the word.

'I don't know, but yeah, I guess,' replied Alex.

Emma looked away from her son for a moment, unable to cope with the judgement in his eyes. 'I … I didn't realise things had gotten so bad,' she whispered, still ignoring Alex's firm stare.

'Oh, Mum, you don't realise a lot of things about this family.' His sharp words pierced her like a dagger to the heart.

'Alex, I … I've been trying—'

'You haven't been trying at all. You've been hiding and running away from everything. That's why we moved here, isn't it? Because you wanted to run away and not deal with anything back in Bedford. Phoebe died. Dad died. And you just ignored everything, including me. You took me away from my friends and uprooted our lives just to come here and do the same as you always do.' Alex's eyes filled with tears, but he didn't turn away from her, not like he normally did. Now he wasn't ashamed of his tears.

Emma reached out her hand to touch his arm, but he flinched and scooted further away in his seat. 'Mum, Linda has an alcohol use disorder.'

Emma stared at her son. 'She … *what?* I don't understand.'

'Linda has been drinking more and more every day since it happened.'

Emma's mouth fell open, but her words became tangled in her throat. 'A-After Phoebe …' Emma stopped, her daughter's name fading on her tongue. She couldn't bring herself to say anymore. The ache was back, deep down in her soul.

Alex blinked back tears, but his face was contorted and his jaw clenched. His fists grasped the edge of his seat, as if he was afraid that he'd fall off. 'Yeah, after Phoebe died, but it wasn't because she was sad that she died, it was because she was the *reason* she died.'

Emma looked at her son, searching his face for signs that he was lying. He'd lied to her before, on many occasions, and she'd always been able to tell. Like the time, when he was ten, he told her Phoebe had broken her expensive crystal vase. His right eye would twitch and he'd lick his lips. Those were his tells, but right now there was no eye twitch, and his jaw was firm.

'W-What do you mean? Phoebe ran out of the shop on her own and straight into the road without looking.'

'No, Mum, she didn't. That's what Linda told you happened.'

Emma stared blankly ahead at the wall, studying a poster of cervical cancer and the signs and symptoms to look out for, but the writing zoomed in and out of focus. She swayed to the side, feeling as if she were on a boat in choppy waters.

'Linda I-lied to me? Why?'

'To protect you from the truth. Actually, no, to protect herself. Why'd you think I've been so off with her since Phoebe died?'

'B-But why would she lie!'

Alex stood up and looked down at Emma. 'Because Linda killed Phoebe. Maybe not on purpose, but she killed her. Phoebe ran away in the store and when Linda found her, she got angry and took her outside. She grabbed her shoulders and shouted at her. Then Phoebe turned and ran because she was scared and ran straight into the road.' His words echoed around the almost empty corridor. Each one cut Emma so deep that by the end she was gasping for breath.

'N-No …' Emma stood up and faced Alex. 'She would have told me.'

'And what would have happened if she had?'

Emma didn't have to search for the answer because it was right there as soon as the question left his mouth; she would have left Linda. There was no doubt about that. If she'd known the truth from the start, whether it was an accident or not, Emma would have divorced Linda. The only reason she hadn't blamed her these past two years was because Linda had told her Phoebe had run away and not been anywhere near her when she'd been hit by the car. There had been no way of saving her, but now Emma knew Linda had been within arm's reach of her little girl as she'd stepped out into the road, that she'd shouted at her, causing her to run in the opposite direction, it changed everything.

Linda had killed her daughter.

And she'd been lying ever since.

And she'd been forcing Alex to hide the truth from his own mother.

'How did you find out?'

Alex sighed. 'A few days after it happened, Linda told me. I don't know why she did. Maybe she had her reasons.'

'Why didn't *you* tell me then?' asked Emma, her voice quivering.

'Because, Mum, you were a mess. I only had to take one look at you to know that if you knew the truth, you'd never come back from it. You could have done something stupid, like end your own life to be with Phoebe and I didn't want to lose my mum too. I couldn't save Phoebe … or Dad, but I could try and save you.'

Emma erupted into hysterical sobs as she watched her son cry. Her ex-husband had started drinking himself into practical comas a couple of weeks after Phoebe's death and then had stepped off a bridge, plunging into the freezing river below. His body had been found two days later. Death by suicide or accident, no one really knew. But Emma had been too numb, too out of it to even notice her ex-husband was dead, let alone that her wife had started being dependant on alcohol. All she'd cared about was Phoebe …

Again, she reached for Alex, wanting to wrap her arms tight around him and never let go, but again he flinched from her touch and took several steps backwards.

'No, don't,' he said between tears. 'I've told you the truth now, so you can deal with it however you like, but I'm done keeping secrets from everyone in this family. Linda's been suffering too and by telling you the truth, I've saved her from herself. Now I just need to save myself. I'm done.'

'What do you mean by—'

But Alex had already turned and run down the corridor and disappeared. Emma wanted to chase after him, but her legs were so weak and jelly-like that she couldn't take a single step. She merely stood there, unable to move as the reality of what Alex had just unleashed on her sunk in. How could she possibly face Linda now? Her wife had possibly attempted to end her life over the fact she'd been keeping such a devastating secret …

'Mrs Smithson?'

Emma heard the polite voice of a man behind her but couldn't seem to summon the correct muscles to move her body. A hand rested on her shoulder. Emma screamed as her whole body switched into fight mode.

'I'm so sorry, Mrs Smithson. I didn't mean to scare you. You looked miles away.'

Emma gasped for air, placing a hand over her heart. It thudded erratically as she looked at the doctor in front of her. There was nothing remarkable about him at all, other than the fact he had a slight scar on his left cheek. He had a solemn look on his face that all doctors wore when delivering serious news.

'Is she? I mean … is Linda, okay?'

'Your wife is stable for the time being. We had to pump her stomach due to the amount of alcohol she'd ingested, and she'd also inhaled some bath water. If your son hadn't found her when he did, we'd be having a very different conversation.'

Emma nodded to show that she'd heard him, but inside she was screaming because part of her was flooded with relief that her wife was alive, but another part was angry she'd survived and Phoebe hadn't. How was that fair? Phoebe had died. Chris had died. But Linda had got to live when it was her fault and she'd started the whole awful chain of events in the first place.

'T-Thank you,' she managed to say. 'Can I see her?'

'Yes, but she's still unconscious. She should wake up soon, so I think it's best you're there when she does.'

'Do you think she did it on purpose?'

'On the outside, yes, it does look that way, but only she can tell us what really happened.'

Emma squeezed her lips together to stop from mumbling, *Yeah, right*.

'This way. I'll take you to her.' The doctor turned and walked away and Emma followed him, her head bowed low, dreading whatever was about to come.

As she entered the hospital room, she lifted her eyes to the bed in front of her where her wife was lying. Numerous wires snaked across her body, hooking her up to several machines by the side of the bed. She was breathing on her own without a respirator and her heartbeat was at a steady rhythm; a lot steadier than Emma's was right now as she slid into the uncomfortable chair beside the bed.

Emma couldn't bear to look at Linda looking so vulnerable, so she looked up at the ceiling. It was only when she noticed the room growing darker that she pulled her eyes away and glanced at her wife.

A large, looming shadow was crawling across Linda's body. It appeared to have long, gangly arms which ended with sharp, claw-like fingers. The claws surrounded her face and clamped down on her wife's mouth.

Emma screamed and scrambled to her feet just as a nurse rushed in.

'What's wrong?'

Emma pointed to Linda, who now appeared perfectly normal.

There was no dark shadow-like creature suffocating her or attempting to squeeze the life from her fragile body.

'Nothing. I'm sorry, it must have been a bad dream,' replied Emma, sinking back down into the chair.

The nurse smiled. 'Can I get you anything? Some water or a cup of tea?'

'Thank you. Yes, some water please.'

The nurse left the room.

Emma closed her eyes and squeezed the bridge of her nose between her fingers.

'E-Emma?' The weak voice of her wife made her eyes spring open.

'Linda!' Emma rushed to her bedside and grabbed her hand. 'Welcome back.'

Linda's eyes flooded with tears as they stared at each other.

It was time to get the truth out of Linda …

Chapter Thirty-Six
LINDA
Sunday 29 October 2023 — 13:40 p.m.

Her throat burned as if she'd swallowed a ball of fire or a piece of barbed wire. Her head didn't feel much better. It felt like all the moisture in her body had been sucked out. She licked her lips, attempting to moisten them, but she ended up coughing when she swallowed. Panic overwhelmed her as she struggled to breathe. Warm, gentle hands stroked her arm as alarm bells sprang to life, jolting her fully into consciousness.

'It's okay, I'm here, Linda. I'm here.'

Linda would have recognised her voice anywhere; even in a sea of voices, she knew the tone and pitch of her wife's words like the back of her hand. Linda looked into Emma's eyes, which were flooded with tears.

'Thank God you're awake,' she said, as a nurse came rushing in.

'Water,' squeaked Linda.

'I'll get her some,' said the nurse. 'All your vitals look stable, but now you're awake the doctor will want to talk with you.' The nurse backed out of the room, leaving Linda and Emma alone.

Emma grabbed Linda's hand and squeezed it hard, harder than normal. 'I was so worried.'

'I'm sorry,' said Linda, shaking her head and closing her eyes as the tears threatened to consume her again. 'I don't know what happened. I don't remember anything.'

'Alex found you unconscious in the bath.'

'Oh, God. Is he okay?'

'He's fine. He panicked, but he saved your life by calling the ambulance.'

Linda closed her eyes and took a deep breath. 'I'm so sorry.'

There was a long pause and then Emma said, in a stern, emotionless voice, 'What *exactly* are you sorry for, Linda?'

Linda flicked her eyes open, caught unaware by the direct question. 'W-What do you mean?'

'I think you know very well what I mean.' Emma's voice changed. No longer was it soothing and full of empathy. It was now laden with anger and unanswered questions. She'd also increased the pressure on her hand, digging her nails into the thin skin on the back of Linda's hand so hard that Linda had to fight the urge to flinch and pull away. She relished the pain because she knew she deserved it.

'I ... I don't—' But she did.

Emma's grip increased further. Now she was pushing her hand and wrist down against the bed. Linda's eyes filled with tears. 'S-Stop, you're hurting me. What are you doing?'

'I want you to say it.'

Linda gulped back the saliva that swam in her mouth. Only moments ago, her mouth had been dry, but now her stomach rumbled as she desperately fought the urge to be sick.

'I ... I ... Emma, it all happened so fast.'

'Say it.' Emma's voice cracked. Linda knew she was on the verge of losing her composure. 'Stop lying to me.'

'It was my fault. I shouted at her … I scared her … She ran away and—'

Emma lunged forwards, stopping merely inches away from Linda, whose eyes widened as the aggressive threat spilled from Emma's mouth.

'You know what upsets me the most? The fact that you told my son to lie to me for the past two years. I will never forgive you for this. *Never.*' Emma released Linda's hand and stormed from the room, leaving it cold with the echo of her words dancing in the air.

Linda wept, not because the back of her hand was oozing blood caused by Emma's nails, but because she knew she'd lost her wife forever.

There was no coming back from this, but at least she no longer felt the unbearable tension in her head and shoulders.

There was no longer a never-ending void of nothingness inside.

The Void was truly gone …

But in its place was something much worse.

Chapter Thirty-Seven
JORDAN
Monday 30 October 2023 – 07:35 a.m.

Jordan had gone to sleep with a foggy head, and it had nothing to do with alcohol. He'd only had one beer and had struggled to finish it. The taste had been bland, and it had unsettled his stomach. He woke up on the sofa with a blanket half draped across him. He was only wearing a pair of grey tracksuit bottoms. Brooke had taken the bed again (and because he no longer had the spare room set up as a room, but as a dumping ground for various objects which he had no use for), but not before giving him a weird look that had caused Jordan's mind to wander and go around in circles. Something in their relationship had shifted and he knew they needed to talk about it like adults, but it made him feel like he was a young boy again, too nervous to talk to girls and express his feelings.

Wait … No … He didn't have any *feelings* for Brooke, only the friendship kind …

Right?

Then why was his heart palpitating at the thought of talking to her?

Jordan let out a low groan as he sat up and ran his hands through his hair. Morgan came bounding in from the kitchen and jumped all four feet off the ground, springing up and down as if he were on a trampoline.

'Okay, I get it. It's breakfast time.'

Jordan pushed himself to his feet and padded into the kitchen. He prepared Morgan's breakfast and turned the kettle on in a robotic fashion. He then slid a couple of pieces of bread into the toaster. His mind drifted to Brooke upstairs, wondering how she'd slept.

A loud buzzing interrupted his thoughts.

'Phone,' he said groggily. 'Where's my phone?'

Jordan followed the sound back into the lounge and scooped his phone up from the floor where it had fallen last night after he'd drifted off to sleep. He didn't even look at the name on the screen as he answered, 'Yeah. Hello?'

'Who the fuck do you think you are texting my daughter after I specifically told you not to? You're not her father. I am. You're nobody. The next time you text her, I'm going to report you for—'

'Hold it right there, Sean. I texted Bethany because I was worried about her, and I've found out some stuff I need to clear up. Besides, it's you I really need to speak to.'

'Oh yeah? Why's that? What sort of *stuff*?'

'Did you know about Alex and Harriet bullying Bethany at school and spreading rumours about The Creature?'

'What the hell are you talking about? Who are Alex and Harriet?'

'They are older kids at Bethany's old school. She was being tormented by them. They made fun of her because of the poem she wrote about The Creature.'

There was a long pause on the other end of the line and then, 'The Creature was nothing more than Amber's vivid imagination and her way of trying to get sympathy from me. The fact she kept her hallucinations from me for so long is mind-boggling. In the end, she even had Bethany believing it was real and I've struggled to forgive her for that. She suffered for twenty years from sleep deprivation. I knew it was bad, but she never told me just how bad until … well, until Tyler went and jumped off the bloody cliff and all that shit came up about him killing Kieran.'

'It doesn't matter whether The Creature was real or not. The point is that Bethany believed it was real, and she was being bullied because of it.'

'Okay, well … I didn't know anything about that. Amber didn't tell me … Fuck …' Another long pause. 'What's this got to do with anything anyway? Why do you want to speak to Bethany now?'

Jordan blew out a breath. 'Look, there's no easy way to say this, but there's another rumour going around now.'

'Of course there is because Cherry Hollow is the fucking gossip mill of the Lake District.'

'Detective Williams told me several days ago they're now suspecting Amber didn't take her own life.'

'I know. He called me too. What, you think you're special, Jordan? You think he only called you?'

'No, I didn't say that.'

Another long pause. 'Let me guess … You think I killed my wife, don't you?' Jordan didn't answer. 'I'm right, aren't I? That's what you think, isn't it?'

Jordan bit his tongue. The truth was that yes, when he'd first heard the rumour, his mind had jumped to the conclusion that Sean must have been involved, but now he'd had a chance to think about it and slept on it, it didn't seem likely anymore.

'No,' he finally said, 'I don't think you did. You wouldn't do that to Bethany.'

'Thank you.'

'Huh?'

'I said *thank you*. Don't make me repeat myself, you arrogant twat.'

Jordan smirked. 'You're welcome. Did Detective Williams give you any more details?'

'No. He remained as tight-lipped as ever. He just said he was looking into it, which God only knows what that means. I don't even know whether to believe him, but it's almost easier to accept that she was murdered than she took her own life and left her child without a mother.' Sean paused again and sighed. 'Will you do something for me? When you find out who's responsible … make them pay for taking my daughter's mother away from her.'

Jordan nodded. 'I will. You have my word. How's she doing now that you've moved away?'

'It's too soon to tell, but I'm just glad she's out of that town.'

'Right.' Jordan paused, realising that they'd come to the end of their conversation, and he didn't have anything else to say to the man he'd hated for years. 'Well, I'd better go—'

'Jordan … you can call Bethany on Fridays after school … if you want. And keep me updated with whatever's going on in that town, but don't tell Bethany. I've finally got her away from all that and she needs to recover and be a normal kid again.'

'Of course. And thanks, Sean. I really appreciate that. Actually, one more thing … Has Bethany ever mentioned anything about a note that Amber left her?'

'A note? No, Amber didn't leave a note.'

'Okay, thanks.'

Sean grunted his response.

Jordan smiled as he disconnected. He looked up to see Brooke staring at him from the entrance of the lounge. She was leaning against the doorframe, dressed in her usual morning getup of running trainers, leggings and sports top. Jordan could see a hint of her midriff and it made his heart flutter.

'Was that Sean you were talking to?'

Jordan nodded. He quickly remembered he was still topless as he watched Brooke's eye flick over his torso. It was only a minuscule movement, but he noticed, and it made his heart speed up even more. 'Yeah. I believe him. He didn't kill Amber.'

Brooke took a deep breath. 'I know.'

Jordan cleared his throat, hoping to dispel the awkwardness that was rising like a tide. 'Coffee?'

'Run.'

'Right. Have fun.'

'Fancy coming with me?'

'And make myself look like an idiot when I can't keep pace with you? No … but thanks.'

Brooke grinned as she twirled a loose strand of hair around her fingers. 'Fair enough. I'm going to call Emma later to check on Linda and go and see my mum again. I need to find out what she meant about the town being better off without Amber around.'

'Want me to come with?'

'No, thank you. I think I need to speak to her alone.'

'Okay.' Jordan frowned as the tension filled the air once again. 'Brooke … I think … we should talk soon about … you and me.' As soon as the words left his mouth, he wished he could take them back. What if this was all in his head and she didn't feel the same way? He could push her away without meaning to.

Brooke's perfectly manicured eyebrows raised ever so slightly. 'Sure,' she said quietly.

And that confirmed it for Jordan.

Brooke sensed something had changed between them too and she was ready to talk.

But that caused his throat to close up and Brooke stole his breath away as she turned and jogged out the door.

Chapter Thirty-Eight
BROOKE
Monday 30 October 2023 – 08:02 a.m.

As she stepped into the early morning sunshine, Brooke sensed a chill creep up her spine. Things weren't right with Jordan. She knew that and was kicking herself for allowing these feelings, or whatever they were, to get in the way of the more important issue: Amber's death.

Brooke knew she had no right to just swoop in and … and what?

Fall in love with Jordan? Was that what was happening?

There was no way that was possible. It was just a fleeting crush. The only reason she was experiencing these *feelings* was because she was vulnerable right now and they were working closely together for the first time, just the two of them. That was all it was. Nothing more.

Then why did she feel as if her heart was trying to escape from her chest every time she laid eyes on him? What the hell had changed in the past few days? She couldn't even pinpoint the exact moment it had happened. Had these feelings been there all along, or had they developed gradually over the last few weeks, months, or years?

When she'd arrived in Cherry Hollow a few days ago, she hadn't considered Jordan as anything other than a friend, but since Amber had died, they had been speaking more often on the phone. But that hadn't meant anything because they were best friends, and she was just being a good friend to him.

Except … she wasn't exactly being a good friend to Amber right now, was she?

But Amber was dead.

'Fuck,' Brooke muttered as she hurried away from Jordan's house. She knew things must be off because she never swore. Plus, what had he meant just now when he said they needed to talk about … *you and me*? Brooke felt as if she were back at school again, pulling apart every word a boy said to understand and decode any hidden meaning.

Brooke sent Emma a quick text asking after Linda and to call her if she needed anything. No immediate reply came so she broke into a jog, warming up her legs before she increased her speed. She planned to do a couple of miles around the town and then head to her mum's house. She'd shower later.

She needed to run to clear her head, but putting one foot in front of the other didn't seem to be helping as much as it usually did. In fact, with every step, the tension and worry increased, and her head was so fuzzy, full of questions and doubt.

Brooke increased her speed again, determined to punish her body. She wanted every muscle fibre focussing on running, wanted every brain cell to only think about the lactic acid building in her legs and not the dull ache in her heart.

By the time Brooke had run four miles and finished at her mum's garden gate, she was so out of breath that she thought for a second she might have a panic attack. Her face was boiling hot, sweat poured down her back and her legs were like rubber. She gripped the gate, bent over at the waist and sucked in a lungful of air. Tears streamed from her eyes.

She could barely see straight as the world around her swam in and out of focus.

No … No …

This was not a panic attack.

Brooke repeated those words over and over, but it was no use. She had no control over her body as she collapsed to the ground, curling into a foetal position, protecting her head with her arms.

'No, no, no, no …'

She knew panic attacks didn't last forever, although at the time that's exactly what they felt like. She'd had many in the past, her first one being at twelve years old right after she'd finished burying Kieran's body at the bottom of Beaker Ravine …

'Brooke!' Her mum's voice pierced the darkness, but she couldn't find her way back to the light. 'Brooke! It's okay, darling, I'm here, I'm here, just focus on my voice.'

Her mum stroked her back and hair over and over with her warm hands. She spoke to her in a soothing voice, but Brooke couldn't work out the exact words.

Hours passed, or it may have been minutes until Brooke was able to uncurl herself and look up at her mum.

'M-Mum,' she sobbed. 'I'm so sorry.'

Her mum leaned down and the women hugged and cried, sitting in the gravel at the bottom of the garden path for the next ten minutes. Brooke allowed the tears to flow, expelling every ounce of remorse and regret onto the ground beneath her.

Thirty minutes later, Brooke had taken a shower and dressed in some clean clothes her mum had laid out for her. They were not her usual style, not anymore. It appeared her mum had kept the clothes Brooke used to wear while she'd lived here and kept herself locked away, so they were shapeless and dingy, but Brooke had changed her mind about showering later and hadn't wanted to go back to Jordan's looking like a hot, sweaty mess.

Brooke towel-dried her hair and ran her fingers through it, separating the wet strands. She then dumped the damp towel in the wash bin and stepped out of the bathroom.

And there it was.

The door to her old room; her prison.

Brooke turned to head downstairs where she knew a strong cup of sugary tea was waiting for her, but something made her pause. Something made her turn around, walk up to the door and push it open. She scanned the room. Everything was different, but at the same time it was the same.

In place of her old boyband poster above her bed was a flowery photo in a large frame. Instead of her pink bedspread there was a quilted blanket draped over her single bed, and where the blackout curtains used to hang, shielding her from the sunlight and outside world, were a pair of bright yellow curtains. Four years ago, when she'd finally left home, she'd cleared the room out, glad to be free of it, but now she was back, almost as if it were calling to her. Had the room missed her?

Brooke shuddered as she stepped further into the dungeon, because that was precisely what it felt like despite it being bright and airy.

The room seemed smaller than she remembered, or maybe it was because the walls were creeping ever closer, surrounding her from all sides, squeezing …

A dark shadow loomed overhead, creating eerie shapes on the walls and across the floor.

A large, claw-like hand reached out to touch her …

'No,' she said to the empty room.

The walls stopped edging closer.

The creepy hand sunk back into the corner.

Brooke walked up to the curtains and looked down on the street below, seeing the drainpipe she'd climbed down as a child and later as an adult when Amber, Jordan and Tyler had come to steal her away in the middle of the night. Sunlight poured into the room, giving it life and colour and temporarily blinding her. The room may have looked different, but it was still a room and it no longer held power over her. It was time to take a stand against The Fear.

Brooke heard a knock behind her. She turned to see her mum standing in the doorway, her eyebrows raised but a smile across her lips.

'I wasn't sure I'd ever see you in this house again, let alone this room.'

Brooke looked from one side of the room to the other, taking note of the worn, stuffed teddy bears piled high in one corner. Her mum had saved some of her childhood things. 'Yeah, well, it's time to put the past behind me.'

Her mum smiled. 'It's so lovely to see you back here.'

Brooke allowed a few beats of silence to pass. 'Mum, I need to talk to you about something. It's about Amber.'

'What about her?'

'Did you have a problem with her?'

Olivia frowned as she took a step into the room. 'No, of course not. Why would you ask me that?'

'Emma told me what you said to her, about the town being better off without Amber. It almost sounds as if you're glad she's dead.'

Olivia gasped. 'Oh, Brooke, no, that's not what I meant at all.'

'Then what did you mean?' Brooke opened the nearby wardrobe door and a pile of old clothes tumbled onto the floor.

'I only meant that Amber was causing a bit of grief in the town. Rumours were spreading. People were afraid that a creature was after them. Did you know we even had a newspaper reporter come and interview some of the residents? He published a piece in the paper about Cherry Hollow being haunted by a demonic creature. Now that Amber has … gone … things seemed to have calmed down, but I never for a second wanted her to die. I know how much you loved her, and she loved you.'

Brooke picked up one of the items of clothing; a plain white t-shirt that had been worn so many times it was practically grey and see-through.

'Someone in this town murdered Amber and I'm trying to find out who.' Olivia remained silent for several seconds while Brooke began piling clothes on the bed. 'Why have you kept all my old clothes, Mum? I thought you took them to charity or threw them away?'

Her mum shrugged. 'Some things I just couldn't bear to part with. They reminded me of you.'

Brooke nodded, but it seemed an odd response. 'Do you have some black bins bags, Mum? Most of this can get thrown away. Surely you can use this wardrobe for other things now, like when guests come to stay.'

'Yes, I'll get some now.'

Brooke picked up another top and froze when she realised the significance of the piece. She'd been wearing it that day at the ravine. There was a small brown stain, faded over the years, but she knew exactly what it was ...

Blood.

Kieran's blood.

Chapter Thirty-Nine
ALEX
Tuesday 31 October 2023 – 11:35 a.m.

The house was cold, but not in relation to temperature. His mum hadn't returned home so he'd spent the previous two nights by himself. He had declined Jordan's offer of staying at his because Alex wanted to be alone. He hadn't seen or spoken to his mum since he stormed out of the hospital on Sunday, but the hospital had called him early this morning, asking if there was anyone who could come and collect Linda and bring her home because Emma had left shortly after Linda had woken up and not left a contact number.

Alex called Jordan, who dropped everything to help him. Alex then called his mum, but her phone was switched off. He didn't leave a voicemail because he didn't know what to say to her except to ask where she'd been for the past two days. No one in his family was speaking to one another. Even Linda hadn't been able to look him in the eye and form a decent sentence other than stuttering a few apologies at him.

Once Jordan had wordlessly helped Linda upstairs and into bed to continue resting, he made a swift departure, but not before telling Alex to call him straight away if he needed anything else. Alex thanked him and closed the door.

And now the house was cold.

Alex wandered around downstairs aimlessly for several minutes, attempting to summon the courage to go upstairs and face Linda. What was he supposed to say to her? He didn't even know what had happened between her and his mum after he'd left, but the fact his mum hadn't been home or been in contact or been there when Linda was discharged was a bad sign. But it was also inevitable she'd found out the truth. It should have come from Linda, but he was glad he'd told her himself. Maybe now she would begin to pull herself together and it could be just the two of them again, the way it was always supposed to be ... if she ever came home.

Eventually, he filled a glass with water and climbed the stairs, taking his time on each one, and found himself standing in the doorway of the main bedroom. Linda was tucked up in bed, propped up with pillows, staring blankly at the open window. The curtains were blowing gently in the breeze. Her face was white and there was an emptiness to her that made Alex uncomfortable. She'd always been the solid rock in the middle of the sinking sand that was this family, but now she was crumbling before his eyes.

And it was his fault.

No. It was *her* fault.

'Linda,' he said. She turned and laid eyes on him but didn't respond. 'I'm sorry I told my mum about ... what happened, but it was the right thing to do.' He set the glass down on the table beside the bed and stepped back.

Linda took a long, deep breath and held it for almost ten seconds before she spoke. 'I should have told her when it happened. It was wrong of me to make you keep such a secret for so long. I'm sorry.'

'What happens now? What did mum say to you?'

'She was angry ... I don't think she will ever forgive me. Once I'm strong enough, I'll leave this house and file for divorce.'

Alex raised his eyebrows. 'Won't you even fight for her?'

Linda smiled faintly. 'I don't think I'd win, Alex.'

Alex nodded, knowing it was true. 'Can I do anything?'

'Please tell your mum that I'm here, so she knows to avoid the house if she doesn't want to see me. I'll be out of here tomorrow.' Alex nodded again, keeping the fact his mum hadn't been here in two days to himself, and backed away from the room. 'Oh, and Alex ... Thank you ... for saving my life.'

Alex remained quiet as he closed the door. He stood in the hallway for several minutes before making his way downstairs, putting on his shoes and leaving the house. He didn't know where he was going, but he knew he had to leave.

Something was calling to him.

Chapter Forty
JORDAN
Tuesday 31 October 2023 – 18:10 p.m.

Later that day, around six in the evening, Jordan and Brooke were cooking dinner in Jordan's kitchen. He'd had a text from Alex earlier, thanking him again for picking Linda up from the hospital this morning and dropping her off at home. He'd been more than happy to help, especially when Alex told him that his mum was uncontactable and hadn't been seen since Sunday.

However, Brooke revealed that Emma had been staying at Brooke's parents' house in her old bedroom since Monday night. Jordan messaged Alex the news so that he didn't have to worry about her whereabouts, but Alex hadn't responded yet. For now, things appeared to have died down, so Jordan and Brooke were enjoying a quiet evening together, sipping wine and cooking steak and chips.

'Are we having any sort of green vegetables with this meal?' asked Brooke, topping up her wine glass.

Jordan smirked at her. 'Not unless they are deep fried.'

'Let me get this straight … you'll drink vanilla lattes, but won't eat a vegetable?'

'I eat them … just not with steak and chips.' Jordan stabbed the sizzling rump in the pan with a fork and turned it over. It sizzled and spat. 'Plus, chips are vegetables.'

Brooke grimaced. 'No, they're not.'

'I can assure you that they are.'

'Agree to disagree?'

'Deal.' Jordan clinked his wine glass with hers.

They were smiling and enjoying themselves. It was almost like they were back to the old ways, before all the strange awkwardness that had appeared out of nowhere. But as Jordan watched and listened to Brooke talk about her day with her mum and dad, he couldn't help but notice the way her eyes gleamed in the bright lights of the kitchen and admire the way her lips moved as the words flowed out of her mouth with ease. His heart started that annoying palpitating thing again. They hadn't attempted to talk about their awkward situation, but Jordan could feel the tension climbing the longer the evening wore on. They'd probably have to talk about it at some point—

'Jordan? Hello! You're phone's ringing.'

He jumped. 'Sorry. Shit. Where is it?'

Brooke pointed to the phone on the kitchen table. He grabbed it. 'Hello?'

'Hello, is that Mr Evans?'

'Yes. Speaking.'

'Mr Evans, this is the local fire department. I'm afraid there's been a fire at your place of business.'

Jordan's mouth gaped open and fear gripped his insides to the point he almost doubled over. 'W-What? Are you sure?'

'Quite sure. We've managed to put out the blaze, but I'm afraid the building is almost completely destroyed. We're still at the property now, so if you'd like to come down, we can have a chat. The police are here too.'

'Um, okay ... Why are the police there? Has anyone been hurt?'

'No, Mr Evans, but they believe the fire wasn't an accident.'

'Someone burned down my business?' At these words, Brooke sprung to her feet, setting the wine aside. She grabbed Jordan's hand as he finished speaking.

'We believe so.'

'I'll be there in ten.' Jordan stared at Brooke, who shook her head.

'I can't believe it. Who would do this?'

'Maybe whoever it was that killed Amber.'

'Do you think they meant for you to be inside at the time?'

'It's a possibility.'

Jordan grabbed her hand. He had a feeling he wouldn't be letting go of it for the rest of the evening.

Chapter Forty-One
EMMA
Tuesday 31 October 2023 – 18:30 p.m.

Emma had turned up at Olivia's door late Monday night, tired, cold and trembling, so Olivia had kindly ushered her inside, claiming she could spend the night in Brooke's old room seeing as Emma refused to go back to her home. When asked where she'd been since Sunday, Emma replied she'd slept in her car because she didn't know where else to go.

Emma had barely said a single word since she'd been here, other than 'thank you' when Olivia had brought her tea, food and clean clothes. All the words she wanted to say kept getting lost and her head ached at the thought of explaining everything to Olivia, who meant well but couldn't possibly understand what she was going through. Olivia, however, graciously allowed Emma her space.

Because today was a difficult enough day already, but now Emma had lost her wife, alienated her son and was too afraid to go home and face them. She didn't know where she was supposed to go from here or what she was supposed to do next. She was floating in limbo.

It was the evening of Halloween.

Two years ago today, the unthinkable had happened.

Phoebe had always loved this day; the dressing up, the sweets, the games, but now all that was left in Emma's head was the memory of that tragedy. She couldn't remember before when she'd been happy because her grief was too great, too raw, and it had spent the past two years eating away at every part of her, including her personality. It had grown so that it completely consumed her and stole all the happy, precious memories she had of her daughter and replaced them with the awful memories of that fateful day.

Phoebe had appeared to her as a vivid hallucination ever since then. Was Phoebe a real-life nightmare? Was she the same as what The Creature had been to Amber? Had she only been there to torment Emma further?

Earlier this Tuesday morning Emma had taken herself for a walk. She hadn't had a destination in mind when she'd set off, but she'd found herself at the edge of Beaker Ravine. No one had told her the way; her feet had found the path by themselves, and she'd put one foot in front of the other and somehow ended up by the fallen tree that spanned the deep chasm.

She understood why no one came here anymore. It wasn't a safe area by any means, but her curiosity was too great to ignore. Before she knew it, darkness closed in, signalling the end of the second worst day of her life. She stared across the expanse towards the other side.

And what she saw had made her scream and collapse to the ground …

Now, standing in Brooke's old bedroom, Emma's body was numb. She couldn't remember how she got back from the ravine. It was as if someone else had taken over her body because the last thing she remembered was looking across the wide gap and seeing her daughter on the other side, smiling and waving at her.

'Mummy!' she'd called. 'Come on, Mummy. Join me.'

Emma sobbed at the memory as her phone, which she'd left on the side table, sprung to life. She glanced at the number. It was private. She let it ring out.

Ten seconds later, it rang again.

And again.

Next, she heard heavy footsteps pounding on the stairs.

Then loud knocking.

'Emma! Emma!' Olivia's voice was bordering on hysterical, which caused Emma's feet to unstick from the floor. She wrenched the door open.

'What's wrong?'

'Your house,' gasped Olivia. 'It's on fire!'

Emma's heart plummeted to the bottom of her chest and her lungs constricted so much it was as if all the oxygen had been sucked out of the room.

'Emma? Did you hear me? Come on, I'll drive you over there.'

Olivia grabbed her arm and pulled her down the stairs. Emma followed. Her feet were on autopilot, almost tripping over themselves. Before she knew what was happening, Olivia had pushed her into a car and they were travelling down the road, going much faster than the thirty miles per hour speed limit.

As Olivia guided the car around a street corner, Emma's eyes locked onto the eerie orange hue in the distance, just over the brow of the road. It was made even more prominent by the growing darkness of the autumn evening. Since she'd heard the shocking news, the darkness had engulfed her as well, gripping her insides and not releasing its hold.

Emma leaned forwards as far as the seatbelt would allow, clenching the edges of the passenger seat with so much force her nails dug into the thick material, leaving miniature crescent shapes when she removed them. The belt dug into her shoulder, but her brain barely registered the sting.

'What's going on?' she asked. 'Why are you stopping?'

Olivia slowed the car to a stop and applied the handbrake, blowing out a breath. 'I'm sorry, Emma, but I can't go any further. They've cordoned off the whole road.'

Emma looked again and, sure enough, saw the yellow crime scene tape stretched across the road, along with several police officers dressed in uniform patrolling the area. They had stern looks on their faces as they held up their hands, stopping the throng of pedestrians and onlookers from passing through. It looked as if the entire town had turned up to watch the events unfold.

Emma flung open the car door, leaving Olivia in the car, and sprinted towards the nearest police officer, a petite woman with black hair tied neatly in a bun. 'That's my house!' she screamed as she grabbed the flimsy tape and shook it.

The officer stepped in front of her. 'Ma'am, I'm going to have to ask you to please step back. The fire brigade is tackling the flames as we speak and—'

'My son! Where's my son? My house is on fire. I demand to be let through! Please!'

The officer nodded. 'Okay, one minute. Wait here.'

Emma watched, her patience waning by the second, as the officer spoke to her colleague nearby, who then stepped forwards, taking over the situation. He was exceptionally tall, and Emma had to crane her neck to look at his face as he spoke.

'Ma'am, I can take you a little closer so you can speak to Detective Williams. He's in charge. We don't know where your son is, but—'

Emma's world crumbled and she let out a garbled shriek. 'No! Alex! Please, let me through.'

The officer waved her through and lifted the yellow tape to enable Emma to duck under.

'Come with me. Everyone else needs to stay back.' He lowered the tape again and nodded at his female colleague. 'Make sure no one else comes through. I'll be back in five minutes.' He then turned to speak to Emma, but she was already halfway up the road.

Emma had never run so fast in her life. She didn't care her lungs were burning and felt like they might explode at any moment. She didn't care her legs were filled with so much lactic acid she could barely feel them.

As she reached the brow of the hill, the devastating reality hit her like a punch to the face as she saw her home being ravaged by flames. Thick plumes of smoke billowed into the air. Police lights pierced the gloomy darkness, illuminating the surrounding houses on the street in red and blue tones. The sirens had stopped blaring now, but she still had ringing in her ears on top of her pounding heartbeat.

By the time she arrived puffing and panting at the edge of her street, her legs were ready to collapse underneath her, but she pushed forwards. She could hear the officer running to catch her, telling her to stop, but she ignored him. There was no way she was stopping now.

There it was …

Her home …

The home that, less than a week ago, she'd moved into with her wife and children; the home that was supposed to have been a fresh start for her family. It was now engulfed in a blazing inferno of brick, wood and all her earthly belongings.

A fire engine was parked on the street, along with an ambulance and two police cars. Numerous people wearing an array of uniforms relating to one of the emergency services were milling about, but there was no sign of the only person she wanted to see.

Emma stared up at her house.

Huge jets of water were being hosed onto the flames by two firefighters, but even Emma knew that the house was too far gone to be saved. Only a crispy, black shell remained.

Her only thought was of Alex.

Emma had never felt more useless in her life. She sank to her knees and wept hysterically, screaming Alex's name over and over until a paramedic came and draped a silver foil blanket around her trembling shoulders.

Chapter Forty-Two
BROOKE
Tuesday 31 October 2023 – 18:25 p.m.

They arrived at the scene in record time, having driven over in Jordan's van. He hadn't broken the speed limit, but he had taken a few corners without breaking, causing Brooke to sharply inhale and clutch the edge of her seat. Her heart rate was through the roof as her head flooded with questions and confusion. Had whoever set Jordan's business on fire wanted to kill him too? Or had they only wanted to destroy his business? But it wasn't just his business; it was his livelihood, his legacy, all he had left of his father, and now someone had taken it all away, set it alight as if it were a piece of scrap paper, nothing of importance. It made her stomach swirl and clench to think there was someone in this town who hated her and her friends so much that they'd commit attempted murder and arson.

Jordan skidded the van to a halt as close to the scene as he was allowed. The street had been cordoned off with yellow police tape, and barricades were in place to stop traffic. Confused yet inquisitive parents and their children dressed up in costumes were milling around, searching for answers or a better view of the blaze. Some of the older children were attempting to dodge their parents so they could get a closer look, their mobiles held aloft in a feeble attempt to get a recording of the action.

Brooke jumped out of the van along with Jordan and rushed up to the nearest police officer who was doing her best to control the buzz of onlookers throwing questions at her every few seconds. Her hair was already frazzled and sticking out from underneath her police hat.

'Let us through. That's my business,' puffed Jordan to the police officer. The air was thick with smoke and, although they were still a least one hundred metres from the building itself, there was a warmth emanating from it.

The police officer must have recognised Jordan because she allowed him through with no further questions. Jordan grabbed Brooke's hand again so there was no doubt she was coming with him.

It didn't take them long to reach the front of the building, which now resembled a black, crispy shell. It was apparent this hadn't been a small fire. There was no way anything could have survived inside. The fire itself was under control, but the firefighters were still using their water hoses to douse the area in case a small spark set it off again. Wooden beams had collapsed inside, windows had exploded and half of the roof had collapsed, now merely a pile of rubble.

'Mr Evans?' asked a nearby firefighter. He appeared to be the one in control of the situation.

'Yes. What the hell happened? When did this start?' asked Jordan, scanning the area. Brooke looked too, not knowing where to rest her eyes. Everything was such a mess.

'We won't know where and when it started until we check the inside and the police conduct their investigation. The fire is under control, but the rest of the roof could collapse at any second.'

'How do you know it wasn't an accident?'

'We found this on the road as we pulled up.' The firefighter held up a large petrol can, which must have been completely empty because he was able to hold it at shoulder height for several seconds with ease.

'Someone wanted to make it clear it was arson,' said Brooke.

'Yep,' replied the firefighter, who Brooke recognised as Derek Blunt, someone she and Jordan had gone to school with. 'Any ideas who?'

Jordan stared at his ruined business. Brooke could tell he was brewing with emotion, but she couldn't distinguish whether it was anger, shock, or sadness. His grip on her hand increased.

Jordan finally shook his head. 'Someone doesn't want us here anymore.' He turned to Brooke. 'Whoever killed Amber burned down my business. They're trying to rid this town of the survivors.'

Derek coughed as he adjusted his helmet. 'You mean the Fated Five?' Brooke and Jordan turned in his direction. His cheeks turned red. 'Sorry, didn't mean it as dig or anything. That's just what you guys are known as around here. You didn't know?'

'It's a new one on me,' said Jordan through clenched teeth.

Derek held up his hand to pause the conversation as his walkie-talkie crackled. He lifted it from his pocket. 'Say again. Over … Right. I'll be over with reinforcements. On our way … Sorry guys, but I have to go. There's another fire over on the other side of town.'

Brooke sucked in a breath. 'Oh my God. Where?'

'Amber Walker's old place.'

Brooke let out a garbled cry. Jordan squeezed her hand tighter, and before she could react he was already dragging her back towards his van.

'There's nothing more we can do here. We need to check on Alex, Linda and Emma.'

They ran past the barricades and jumped into the van.

Once Brooke was buckled in, she called Emma but it went straight to voicemail.

'Emma's phone's off.'

Jordan slammed his foot down on the accelerator, skidding the wheels again as he took off up the road. The sirens of the fire engine were behind him. He was going to beat them there.

'What is going on? Two fires in one night, at the same time? Two people working together maybe?'

'No idea,' replied Jordan. 'But someone is targeting us.'

'But why burn down Amber's old house?'

Jordan shook his head. 'Call Alex next.'

Brooke nodded, her hands trembling as she scrolled through her contacts and pressed the call button. Alex's phone was on because it started ringing, but within ten seconds it went to voicemail.

'No answer.'

'Shit ...' Jordan said nothing else, his eyes focussed on the road again.

They were almost there, just a few more streets. Brooke had no idea what to expect as they turned the last corner. The road was cordoned off again and the police weren't letting anyone through. Brooke had a feeling of déjà vu.

'Turn right down there,' said Brooke as she pointed to a small alley. 'We can cut through and hopefully skip the barriers.'

Jordan yanked the steering wheel and the van hit a curb. Brooke grabbed onto the seat, steadying herself. Jordan stopped the van and they jumped out, running down the alley, neither saying a word but breathing hard.

Brooke was right. There was no barrier down here so they could squeeze through a small alley and appear just down the road from the house which was engulfed in a huge inferno. When Brooke caught sight of it, she gasped, raising her hand to cover her mouth. Half of the house had disintegrated and collapsed to the ground. The other half was still ablaze, crackling and roaring high into the sky, sending tiny sparks and embers drifting through the breeze.

Jordan and Brooke crept closer.

Brooke saw Emma first, crumpled on the ground, shaking like a leaf. She rushed up to her. She heard a 'Hey, how'd you get down here?' from someone nearby, but ignored the person as she skidded down by Emma's side, who had her face buried in her hands.

'Emma. I'm here. Where's Alex and Linda?'

Emma raised her head at the sound of a friendly voice, her eyes brimming with tears. 'I ... I don't know, but they've found a body.'

Chapter Forty-Three
ALEX
Tuesday 31 October 2023 – 18:31 p.m.

He'd allowed Linda some space and left the house earlier in the day. He didn't want to see or speak to anyone, so found himself wandering around town with his hands in his pockets. He'd brought his phone but had forgotten to charge it, so the battery was now dead. Harriet had texted him earlier asking if he wanted to meet up, but he'd ignored her message. He just wanted to be alone.

Something was still calling to him …

Today was always a difficult day: Halloween.

Years ago, it had been the best day of the year because he would dress up with his sister and take her trick-or-treating around the neighbourhood. Seeing her eyes light up whenever she knocked on someone's door to be offered sweets was a sight he'd never forget. He could see her so clearly now in his mind. The fact she had died on Halloween was a difficult thing to accept because now the day was ruined, tainted by his grief. It would never be the same again.

It was growing late and getting darker by the second. He recognised the area he was standing in as the field that led to the thick copse of trees and the path winding towards the ravine; a place he never wanted to visit again, but no matter how many times he walked around the village (he thought he was on number ten now) he kept finding himself by the danger sign.

Maybe The Creature was drawing him back to the ravine, the last place he'd seen his sister, but it hadn't really been her, had it? He knew that, yet the urge to see her again was too strong.

Something was calling him there …

Was it Phoebe or was it The Creature? Were they one and the same?

Just as Alex was about to push open the rickety gate, he heard wailing sirens in the distance. He turned towards the sound and listened. Then he saw it; thick black smoke billowing into the grey sky and an orange hue on the horizon where the town was located.

'Shit,' he muttered.

More sirens pierced the evening.

The more he stared at the orange glow, the more his chest constricted.

Home.

His house was in the area where the glow was emanating from.

A deep pit opened inside him as he saw another orange glow coming from the other side of the town.

Cherry Hollow was on fire …

Alex raced down the gentle slope of the field, his legs and arms pumping fast. He wasn't a runner and had never been good at any sort of cardiovascular sport, but he ignored the burning in his lungs as he directed his legs towards his house. The closer he got, the more he panicked. He could barely breathe as he ran down the street, dodging trick-or-treaters in their various costumes. Everyone was looking in the direction of the sirens and gradually inching their way closer to the commotion, probably desperate to see what was going on.

All Alex could think of was his mum.

No, she hadn't been at home when he'd left, but maybe she'd returned home to talk to Linda and something had happened …

Linda.

Alex had left her tucked up in bed …

'Shit!' he shouted as he ran.

Alex finally reached his road and skidded to a halt outside the crime scene barrier, frantically searching for a way through. A police officer held up his hand, stopping him from going any further.

'Hang on there. I can't let you through.'

'I live at that house! My mum could be in there!' he screamed.

His shouts alerted another officer, who waved him over. Alex ducked under the tape.

'Are you Alex Smithson?' asked the officer.

'Yes! Where's my mum?'

'She's being treated in the ambulance just down there. She's okay. She wasn't in the house when it went up.'

'What about my other mum … Linda?'

The officer shook his head slowly. 'I'm sorry, I don't know.'

Alex shoved his way past the officer and sprinted towards the ambulance. He saw Jordan and Brooke standing next to it. An older police officer was talking to them.

And then …

'Mum!'

Emma looked up at the sound of her son's voice and let out a guttural sob as she flung the silver blanket off her back and raced towards him. She threw her arms around him, but her legs gave out and they both sank to the floor, crying and hugging.

It was several minutes before Emma regained her composure and was able to form words that were legible. 'I thought I'd lost you. They … They've found a body. Oh, Alex, I thought it was you.'

'It's not me, Mum. I'm okay.'

'Why didn't you answer your goddamn phone? You're on it all day!'

'The battery died. I'm sorry. I've been out walking, trying to clear my head after we spoke. I made sure Linda was in bed and then … Mum … Where's Linda?'

Emma's face was filthy from the soot in the air, and her tears had formed miniature streaks through the dirt. She shook her head, telling Alex all he needed to know. She began to cry again, her shoulders shaking from the emotion.

'I'm sorry, Mum. I shouldn't have left her.'

She gulped and managed to control her voice as she whispered, 'There's nothing you could have done.'

'You don't know that.'

Above them, Jordan cleared his throat. 'I'm sorry to interrupt, but I think the police want to speak to you some more, Emma.'

Emma wiped her runny nose and eyes on her sleeve and took a deep breath, then nodded and gingerly rose to her feet. Alex grabbed her arm and kept her steady as he led her over to the ambulance again where the paramedic was waiting with the silver blanket.

Detective Williams was standing by the ambulance too, along with two younger officers who each held notepads like they did in the movies.

Alex stood silently beside his mum as the detective asked her some questions.

'When was the last time you saw your wife, Mrs Smithson?'

Emma gulped and sniffed loudly as more tears filled her eyes. 'Sunday. At the hospital. She'd recently been admitted for ... attempting to take her own life.'

'Sunday? You didn't see her yesterday or today at all?' There was a hint of accusation and surprise in his voice.

'No ... We ... I mean, we had an argument at the hospital and so I stayed away from the house for a while. I stayed with Olivia, um ... Mrs Willows so I could cool off.'

'Who dropped her back at the house after leaving the hospital?'

'I did,' said Alex, squeezing his mum's hand. 'Jordan drove me and dropped us at home. I made sure she was comfortable and then I left the house early this morning around ten.'

'And you didn't return after that?'

'No.'

'What were you doing all day?'

'Walking around town. I'd had an argument with my mum on Sunday, and me and Linda weren't exactly on speaking terms either.'

Detective Williams raised an eyebrow. 'So, you both left Linda, alone in the house, after she'd attempted to take her own life, to fend for herself?'

Emma wiped her eyes again, but her tone took a sterner note. 'Are you accusing us of something, Detective?'

The detective held up his hand in surrender. 'I apologise. Not at all. I'm just trying to work out the events that led up to this happening. Alex, you're the last person who saw Linda alive.'

'So, it is definitely Linda's body that's been found?' asked Emma, a wobble to her voice.

'Yes, we believe so. The body was found in the master bedroom. Everything is badly burned, but it looks as though she died in her sleep.'

'Wait … Are you saying Linda never even made it out of bed? What about the smoke alarms? Surely, she would have heard them and been able to escape? She might have been a bit weak, but she was able to walk. Unless … unless you think she set the fire on purpose?'

The detective shook his head. 'I'm sorry, but we won't know more until we've conducted a full investigation. We also have the matter of Fix It All burning down. The fact that two fires have been started within an hour of each other is too much of a coincidence to ignore.'

Emma gasped as she looked over at Jordan and Brooke. 'Was anyone hurt?'

Jordan shook his head. 'No. It was closed at the time, but the building is destroyed. There's nothing left.'

'What the hell is going on?' asked Emma, closing her eyes as yet more tears developed.

Alex put his arm around her. 'It's okay, Mum. We'll get to the bottom of this … together.'

Emma smiled as she looked up at her son.

And for the first time since his sister had died, he saw the remnants of his old mum rising to the surface.

Chapter Forty-Four
BROOKE
Tuesday 31 October 2023 – 18:45 p.m.

She watched silently as Emma and Alex huddled together in the back of the ambulance. Emma was trembling all over and, even in the evening darkness under the glow of the streetlights, her face was ghostly pale. Alex seemed to be handling the situation very well, and Brooke was pleased to see he'd stepped up and was taking care of his mother, even if they did still have some unresolved issues that wouldn't fix themselves automatically just because they'd been through yet another family tragedy.

Jordan was speaking to Detective Williams, giving him the details of when he'd last left his business. Brooke stood to the side, listening to the hustle around her. The firefighters had eventually managed to control the blaze, but Amber's old house was destroyed, bar the garage to the side. The roof had caved in and the brickwork was black, the rendering peeling away and stained with soot and grime.

As she scanned the area, she noticed one thing was missing.

Actually, two *people* were missing.

Brooke frowned as she walked around, scanning the area for any sign of them. She wandered over to the crime scene tape to see if she could spot them. Numerous parents and their children were gathered, all craning their necks to see if they could spot anything interesting.

'Brooke!' Her mum's voice rang out above the murmur of the crowd. Brooke spotted her sandwiched between two women and jogged over.

'Mum!' The women hugged over the top of the tape.

'What are you doing here?' asked Olivia. 'Are you okay?' She looked her daughter up and down, searching for any signs of trauma or injury.

'I'm fine. Jordan and I heard about the fire and rushed over from Fix It All. Mum, someone's not only burned down Emma's house, but they've burned down Jordan's business too.'

Olivia covered her mouth with her hands. 'Oh, my goodness! Who do they think did it? Has anyone been hurt?'

Brooke flicked her eyes over the women crowded nearby, knowing for a fact they'd been listening and waiting for a juicy piece of gossip all evening. 'I can't say now, Mum. I'm sorry. I was just looking for someone.'

'Who?'

'Lucy Forrester and Trisha Sharp. They're two of the biggest gossips in town. Why aren't they here? When did you last see them?'

Olivia shook her head. 'Not since our little disagreement on Saturday at the coffee morning.'

'I saw them earlier today,' said a familiar female voice.

Brooke glanced past her mum and saw Hayley from The Bean Café pushing her way through the crowds. She had a badly bruised right eye and Brooke felt a momentary pang of guilt that she'd decked her in front of her customers.

'Where and when did you see them?' she asked.

Hayley leaned forwards and kept her voice low as she spoke. 'They were walking towards Fix It All and they disappeared around the back. I didn't think anything of it, but about half an hour later I smelled smoke and saw it was on fire, so I called it in.'

Brooke held her breath for several seconds. 'Have you told the police about this?'

'No, I haven't managed to speak to anyone yet. I've just walked over from closing the café to see if I could speak to someone.'

'Okay, I think it's best if you speak to them as soon as possible.'

'No one's letting anyone through. How come you're so special that you're on that side of the tape?'

Brooke gulped back her snappy response, determined not to let Hayley rattle her again. 'I'm with Jordan.' Hayley scoffed but attempted to cover it up with a cough. 'By the way, I'm sorry I punched you.'

Hayley narrowed her eyes. 'No, you're not. I'm sure you loved humiliating me in front of my customers.'

'I acted irrationally. I shouldn't have done that.'

Hayley squeezed her lips together. 'It's fine ... I guess I said some things that were inappropriate ... I'm sorry too.'

Brooke gave her a small smile, knowing they'd never be best friends, but at least they'd buried whatever animosity they had under the bridge. 'I have to go now. I'll send an officer over to talk to you, Hayley. Mum, it's probably best if you head home. There's nothing you can do here now.'

'Okay, darling. I'd better get back to check on your father anyway. Call me if you need anything. Tell Emma the same.'

'Thanks, Mum.' Brooke gave her a one-armed hug and then jogged back to Jordan, who had just finished speaking with Detective Williams. Brooke stepped in front of the detective.

'Detective Williams, Hayley from The Bean Café needs to speak to an officer about something she saw earlier today outside Fix It All.'

The detective looked past Brooke towards the crime scene tape. 'Thanks, I'll send someone over now.' He walked away towards one of his junior officers.

Brooke grabbed Jordan's arm and pulled him closer. 'Lucy Forrester and Trisha Sharp aren't here. Hayley just told me she saw them outside Fix It All about half an hour before the fire started.'

Jordan ground his teeth. 'Let's go and knock on their door.'

'Shouldn't we leave that for the police to do?'

'I want answers … *now*.'

Chapter Forty-Five
JORDAN
Tuesday 31 October 2023 – 18:55 p.m.

While the detectives headed in one direction, towards the crowd of spectators to speak to Hayley, Jordan and Brooke walked swiftly in the opposite one, towards Lucy's house, which was located next door to Emma's. However, when they reached the garden gate and looked up, they realised Lucy couldn't possibly be inside because everyone in the vicinity had been evacuated from their houses to a safe distance. The house was dark.

'Maybe they're at Trisha's house,' said Jordan, already heading down the street.

Brooke had to jog to keep up with his pace. 'Please tell me you're not going to barge into her house and accuse her of arson and murder.' Jordan slid Brooke a look that made her roll her eyes. 'Okay, just checking!'

Trisha's house was only one street over and, from the looks of it, this street hadn't been evacuated as there were lights on in the surrounding houses. Jordan pushed the garden gate open and banged on the door, Brooke only a few steps behind him. There were lights on inside, but the moment he knocked, they were switched off.

'Subtle,' he murmured. 'Trisha, open the door. It's Jordan Evans. Can we have a quick chat?' No answer. 'I know you're in there,' he added.

A few seconds later, there was scuffling behind the door and the light turned on again followed by sounds of the deadbolt being slid back and keys turning. The door creaked open, and a pale face appeared.

'Jordan, how lovely to see you,' said Trisha in a high-pitched voice. Her eyes were wide, and black mascara stained the area below them.

Jordan managed to keep a lid on his temper. 'Hi … is everything okay in there?'

Trisha was still peering through a small gap, unwilling to open the door any wider. 'Yes! Sorry, just, um … doing some cleaning … and … it's a total mess in here.'

'Is Lucy Forrester with you?'

'No.'

A loud clatter of something hard being dropped emanated from inside the house, followed by a female voice that shouted, 'Fuck!'

Brooke stepped closer. 'Trisha, what's going on? Do you realise there's been a fire one street over?'

'A fire? Goodness!'

'Cut the crap, Trisha,' snapped Jordan, placing a hand on the door, ready to push it open.

'Excuse me?'

'Are you telling me you haven't seen the plumes of smoke or heard the sirens? My business has burned to the ground as well and someone saw you and Lucy walking around the back of it only a few minutes before it caught fire.'

A moment of silence filled the air.

Trisha's jaw clenched as she dropped her head and relaxed her shoulders, allowing the door to swing open, revealing the scene in the hallway beyond. Lucy stood further down the hallway dressed all in black and had a small can of petrol under her arm, trying to shove it into a black bag. She screamed.

'Trisha! What are you doing!'

'I told you our plan wouldn't work,' replied Trisha in a solemn voice.

Jordan stepped into the house, followed by Brooke, who closed the door behind them.

'Start talking,' said Jordan, doing his best to keep his voice calm, but inside he wanted to explode. The Bad Man was stirring.

'Look,' said Trisha. 'We never meant for anyone to get hurt, okay? We just wanted to scare her, that's all. She was losing it. She needed to be in therapy. Our kids were traumatised.'

Jordan cleared his throat. 'You're talking about Amber, right?'

'Of course I am. Who else would I be talking about? She was the only loony around here spouting nonsense. Anyway, one day we followed her to the ravine. She always went there. It was creepy. We tried to reason with her, tried to explain that she and Bethany needed to stop talking about The Creature. It was bringing bad press to the town. But she freaked out and started yelling stuff about Alex and Harriet bullying Bethany. It was all nonsense.' Trisha laughed and wiped away a tear that leaked from her left eye, smudging the mascara even further. 'They'd never do anything of the sort! She said she was going to go to the police about them if they didn't stop.' Trisha glanced at Lucy, who was taking tiny steps backwards towards the kitchen at the back of the house. Trisha turned back to Jordan. 'I swear, I only shoved her a little, but she was too close to the edge, and she slipped and …'

Jordan squeezed his fists at his side. As he felt Brooke's warm hand on his arm, he relaxed, but only a little. 'You're lying,' he said through clenched teeth. 'Amber's body was found directly underneath the fallen tree. She didn't slip off the edge and tumble to the bottom.'

Trisha rolled her eyes. 'Fine. Whatever. What difference does it make? She was standing on the tree like a freaking loony. We were just trying to talk to her and then when she started threatening to tell the police about Alex and Harriet … I just bumped the tree a little bit. How was I supposed to know she'd lose her balance and fall?'

Jordan's face turned red. 'Why didn't you say anything to the police? Why didn't you say it was an accident?'

Trisha laughed. 'You're one to talk! After what you and your gang did all those years ago …'

'What?'

'Oh please! You don't think everyone in this town bought Tyler's crap confession tapes, do you? There are several of us who think you were all in on covering up Kieran's death, but Tyler took the fall for the lot of you.'

Brooke's grip on Jordan's arm tightened. 'Who thinks that?' she asked.

'Does it matter?'

'Yes.'

'Your mother, for a start,' spat Trisha.

Brooke gasped. 'That's not true!'

Trisha rolled her eyes. 'Believe whatever you want, Brooke. The fact is, none of you were wanted in this town after

Tyler's confession came out. Amber and her liar of a daughter started spreading rumours—'

'How dare you call Bethany a liar!' shouted Jordan.

Brooke pulled him back towards her. 'Trisha, Alex and Harriet have confessed to bullying and stalking Bethany, but this isn't about them. You killed Amber and made it look like she took her own life and even wrote a letter, didn't you?'

'What letter? What are you on about?'

'You didn't write it?'

Trisha's mouth dropped open. 'God, no! We just covered up our footprints at the edge of the ravine, that's all.'

Brooke frowned as she leaned in close to Jordan. 'You don't think Amber actually wrote it, do you? Trisha said that she was standing in the middle of the tree. Why would she be doing that?'

Jordan shook his head. 'She wouldn't do it.'

'Maybe not consciously ... maybe The Creature made her do it.'

'But the note ... The handwriting didn't belong to her.'

Brooke stared at him. Jordan opened his mouth to speak, but his words had vanished. Nothing made sense. Trisha and Lucy may have killed Amber, but if Amber hadn't written the note, and they hadn't written the note ... who had?

'Maybe no one wrote it,' said Jordan. 'It was old, wasn't it? The note. It looked as if it had been decaying under the floorboards for years.'

Brooke gasped. 'Why didn't I think of that before? It clearly doesn't have anything to do with Amber's death. It never mentions her or Bethany or anyone by name. Alex said he found it down between some wooden joists in the floor. So, the question is, who was the previous owner of Amber's house?'

Jordan shook his head.

Brooke took a deep breath, but as she did her eyes caught movement in her periphery vision.

Trisha bolted down the hallway towards the back door.

Lucy, who'd been hovering in the kitchen the whole time, grabbed a knife from the sideboard and hurtled herself towards Jordan, who didn't see her coming because he was facing away from her.

Brooke saw Lucy charging down the hallway, the knife held firm in her right hand like a spear.

'Jordan!' she yelled as she shoved him as hard as she could to the left, but due to his size and weight and her small stature, she barely moved him more than a few inches.

It wasn't enough.

He didn't react in time.

Lucy stabbed him in the side with the knife just as there was a knock at the front door.

Chapter Forty-Six
EMMA
Tuesday 31 October 2023 – 19:37 p.m.

Emma sat in the back of the ambulance, sipping on a sugary cup of tea, while a young paramedic kept an eye on her vitals. There was nothing physically wrong with her, so she'd refused to be taken to the hospital and had asked if she and Alex could leave the area as soon as possible. Olivia had called and told her that she and Alex were to come and stay with her once she was allowed to leave, but the police still had a few questions, so she and Alex were patiently waiting for Detective Williams to return. He and another officer had walked up the road with frowns on their faces about half an hour ago and hadn't returned yet.

'I wonder what's going on?' she asked Alex, who'd borrowed a phone charger from one of the paramedics and was now glued to his screen, back to normality.

'Huh?'

'The detective spoke to a woman down the street and then headed up that way over half an hour ago. I wonder what's going—Oh, my God!' Emma chucked her silver foil blanket off again and set her plastic cup of tea down before jumping down from the back of the ambulance. The paramedic sighed in frustration at the stubbornness of his patient but didn't bother calling her back. She was in no danger of fainting anymore.

Alex looked up from his phone as he heard her feet hit the tarmac. 'Mum! What are you—Oh, shit!' He followed his mother and jogged to keep up with her, as she was already halfway down the street.

Emma stopped and watched as Trisha and Lucy were led towards her, their hands pulled behind their backs, held tight by an officer each. They weren't putting up a fight, but they also weren't going quietly. Trisha was complaining the cuffs were too tight, and Lucy was shouting that the officer was touching her.

'Medic! We need a medic at 28 Brightly Road. A civilian has been stabbed,' the officer who was leading Trisha called out.

Emma stood open-mouthed as the commotion erupted around her. The paramedic who'd been tending to her needs ran past her carrying his bag and headed up the road.

'What's going on? Trisha, Lucy … what …'

'Please, Mrs Smithson, step back,' said Detective Williams, who'd just joined the commotion.

'Are they under arrest?'

'Yes. We're taking them to the station now for questioning.'

Emma ran up to the women and stood right in front of them, blocking their paths. Fury radiated throughout her body as she screamed at them. 'Why did you kill Linda? You burned down my home! What the hell is wrong with you?'

Lucy laughed. 'What are you on about? We didn't burn down your house or kill your wife.'

'Please, Mrs Smithson, step back. No questions—'

Emma pointed a stiff finger towards her smouldering home. 'You burned down my house!' she screamed again.

'No, we didn't!' shouted Trisha. 'Clearly, your wife set the fire, you idiot.'

'By setting herself alight in her own bed?'

'How the hell should I know? You're both crazy! You have no daughter, Emma. Phoebe doesn't even exist.' Lucy cackled again, which set Emma's teeth on edge and caused the tiny hairs on her neck to rise.

Emma punched Lucy square in the jaw.

'Mrs Smithson!' shouted Detective Williams. 'If you do not step back and remove yourself from this situation, I will have you arrested as well.'

Emma shook her hand, attempting to quell the sharp pain in her knuckles, but it had been worth it.

'Wow, Mum, I never knew you could throw a punch,' said Alex.

Lucy shrieked and shouted, 'She just assaulted me! Did you see that? She just assaulted me!' But the officer who was holding on to her merely pushed her forwards and past Emma, not saying a word.

Trisha glared at Emma, her eyes blazing. She opened her mouth to say something, but abruptly closed it as she was also shoved from behind by the officer leading her.

Trisha and Lucy kept their heads bowed as they were led towards the police cars.

Emma turned and ran down the road towards Trisha's house, remembering that someone had been stabbed. As she arrived at the gate, she saw the front door of the house was wide open and Jordan on the floor with Brooke standing over him, sobbing, her shoulders shaking so badly she could barely remain upright.

'Brooke!' Emma shouted. Brooke looked up and saw her. 'What happened? Is Jordan—'

That was when she saw the expanding pool of blood spreading out across the laminated hallway floor. It looked exactly like a red rose had melted.

Chapter Forty-Seven
JORDAN
Tuesday 31 October 2023 – 20:15 p.m.

The pain in his side didn't register, not at first. As he sensed the blade sliding into his torso, he also felt Brooke slam into him, but she merely bounced off his solid body. It hadn't been enough to shield him from the attack. He wasn't fast enough.

Then the burning sensation took over and spread as he grabbed the handle of the knife, slipping to the floor. The last thing he heard was Brooke screaming his name and the front door exploding off its hinges, followed by heavy footsteps and more shouts, this time from men and women in uniform.

When he opened his eyes, the first face he saw belonged to Brooke. Her mascara was smudged. Her hair was a mess. Her face was red and puffy, but she was the most beautiful creature he'd ever seen. She called for a nurse, grabbing his hand so tight it hurt. He glanced at his hand surrounding hers, both of which were covered in blood, most of it now dry.

He knew it there and then. There was no denying it anymore.

Jordan opened his mouth, but the words stuck in his throat. He coughed.

'Don't talk. I'm just glad you're awake,' said Brooke, as tears spilled from her eyes and slid down her face. 'They're taking you into surgery any minute now.'

He tried again. Whatever drugs were in his system were threatening to pull him back under, but this couldn't wait another moment.

'I ... I l-love you,' he managed before another wave of heat and pain engulfed him.

Brooke tutted. 'Shut up, silly. Let's talk about this later when you're not delusional from pain and drugs.'

Jordan squeezed her hand as hard as he could, which caused stars to dance in front of his eyes. 'N-No, you shut up and l-listen ... I-I love you.' Then, using the last of his strength, he grabbed her jacket and pulled her towards him, crashing her lips against his in a heated kiss.

He tasted blood in his mouth, but he didn't care. Nor did Brooke as her body sunk closer to his and she let out a soft moan that made all the little hairs on his neck stand up.

Jordan eventually admitted defeat and slumped back against the bed, unable to extend the kiss any longer for fear of slipping into unconsciousness. Brooke just stared at him and opened her mouth to speak but was interrupted by a nurse, who sniffed loudly behind her.

Jordan and Brooke turned to look at her. The nurse was weeping and smiling at the same time. 'Oh, my goodness,' she said, 'I think that's the most romantic thing I've ever seen.'

Jordan smirked as he closed his eyes. 'Just didn't want to die without kissing you first.'

Brooke rolled her eyes. 'God, you're so dramatic.'

The nurse stood by the side of the bed as she administered more medication. 'I'm afraid I'm going to have to break you two lovebirds up. Jordan needs to be prepped for surgery now. You're free to wait in the waiting area,' she told Brooke.

Brooke squeezed his hand again. 'I'll be here when you wake up. I promise.' They looked down at the blood covering both their hands. 'And you can never break a blood oath.'

One month later – 1 December 2023

Recovery had been long and painful, but Jordan was back on his feet as of a week ago. Brooke had handled everything while he'd been out of commission, including helping him put his house on the market, applying for insurance money for losing his business and looking after Morgan while he'd been recovering in the hospital. The knife had, miraculously, missed all his vital organs. There had been a lot of blood, which had made the situation look a lot worse than it was. The paramedic had worked fast, and they'd rushed him to the hospital, saving his life.

He spent a week in the hospital and was then allowed home to continue to recover. The police had been in and out of his hospital room, asking him questions to corroborate the chain of events.

Trisha Sharp and Lucy Forrester were arrested for arson for both properties and for the murder of Amber Walker, although it was looking likely that the murder charge would be reduced to manslaughter as they were sticking with their story of it being an accident. Both, however, were adamant they had not burned down Emma's house, arguing the case that they had no qualms with Emma or her family.

The evidence wasn't there to either confirm or deny this, except that the same type of petrol had been used to start and fuel both fires. The only other evidence Detective Williams had was Linda Smithson's toxicity report, which had come back with a large dose of sleeping tablets in her system that were available to buy over the counter at any local pharmacy, including the one located in Cherry Hollow. Therefore, her death was ruled as death by suicide, but how she'd started the fire remained a mystery.

Jordan managed to sell his home quickly, and, thanks to the insurance money, he and Brooke bought a small country house in the New Forest close to where his mother now lived. The sale hadn't been completed yet, but they were due to move in within the next couple of months.

In the meantime, Brooke quit her job in London and moved in with Jordan while they waited for their house to complete. It was a huge decision, moving in together so quickly after officially becoming a couple, but if Jordan had learned anything over the last few years it was to never take anything for granted, and if he felt something was right, to grab hold of it with both hands and never let go.

The idea of leaving Cherry Hollow had come up one evening while Brooke had been visiting Jordan in the hospital. He'd pointed out that, now he no longer had a business to run, there was nothing tying him to the town apart from his family home. Brooke agreed and even though her parents still lived there, she didn't feel safe in the town anymore and it had nothing to do with The Fear. It seemed that Trisha and Lucy had gotten their wish after all; they'd driven the last of the remaining Fated Five out of the town.

It wasn't the ending Jordan had in mind. Amber was still gone, but her death had brought him and Brooke together, something they'd never imagined was possible. Jordan hoped that, wherever Amber was, she was happy for them; that they'd finally found happiness with each other, despite having lost so much.

It was the first day of December and winter had well and truly settled in Cherry Hollow. The first frost of the year had arrived overnight, leaving every leaf, tree and plant tinged with tiny white crystals. The sunshine added to the beauty of the early morning, as Jordan and Brooke strolled hand in hand through the local graveyard. Jordan was carrying three bouquets of flowers cradled in his free arm and walked with a slight limp still. Morgan was on a lead, which Brooke held on to with a firm grip.

They stopped at their first destination.

Kieran's grave.

Jordan let go of Brooke's hand, took one of the bouquets and laid it down on the grass, then stepped back beside her. They bowed their heads in unison and spent a few seconds in silence.

'Goodbye, Kieran. You were a pain in the butt, but your laugh always brightened our lives,' said Jordan, squeezing Brooke's hand.

'Yeah, I remember the time he told that really rude joke and everyone found it offensive, but he started laughing so hard that eventually we all joined in and then forgot what we were even laughing about in the first place.'

Jordan chuckled. 'I'll never forget the time he pranked Tyler and me with a bottle of ginger beer. He told us it was real beer and, at the time, neither of us knew what beer tasted like and we started acting drunk and silly. Then he goes and says it had no alcohol in it.'

Brooke laughed out loud. 'He had a great sense of humour.'

Jordan nodded as he looked down at the grave. 'It's a shame he never got the chance to grow up. He'll always be twelve years old.'

'He probably still would've acted like a big kid.'

'That's true.'

'Goodbye, Kieran.' Brooke kissed the tips of two of her fingers, stepped forwards and pressed her fingertips against the cold stone.

Jordan and Brooke walked in silence to the next grave, located on the far side of the graveyard. This one belonged to Tyler Jenkins, who had no one in the town to tend to the grave so it was overgrown and the headstone was covered in moss, the carved lettering fading already. Jordan set the second bouquet on the grave and stepped back, repeating the process.

'Goodbye, Tyler. Man … you really fucked things up for everyone, but I'm sorry we weren't better friends to you. I hope that, wherever you are, you're at peace.'

'Thank you for sacrificing yourself for us,' added Brooke, copying the kiss-on-her-fingers gesture.

'Do you remember the time Tyler tried to impress Amber and me with his French pronunciation? He kept speaking French for weeks and all we did was laugh at him because he didn't get a single word right.'

Jordan snorted. 'He was always such a show-off.'

Brooke sighed and they took a few moments to collect themselves.

Jordan squeezed her hand. 'One grave left.'

Brooke's eyes filled with tears as she followed Jordan through the graveyard towards their final destination. The hardest one of all.

Amber's grave.

Brooke stayed back several paces, allowing Jordan to place the last bouquet by himself. He knelt on the ground and placed a hand on the frozen soil.

'You were the only good thing in my life at one point,' he said in a quiet voice that only he could hear. 'You were my whole world. I'm sorry I let you down. I'll always love you. I promise.' Jordan straightened up and took his place next to Brooke. He took the dog's lead, allowing her the freedom to approach the grave by herself.

Brooke sobbed as she sank to the ground. 'I'm so sorry I never came to visit you here after I left. The one time I do visit … it's to your grave, not your house.' Brooke wiped her eyes and runny nose on the sleeve of her coat. 'You have no idea how sorry I am, Amber. I wish I had listened to you, believed you. I was afraid. I was only thinking about myself.' She glanced behind at Jordan, who gave her an encouraging smile. 'I never expected to fall in love with Jordan. I don't even know what to say, other than I'm sorry I wasn't a better friend.' Brooke kissed her fingers once again, which were soaked with her tears, and pressed her fingertips to the grave. 'We'll make sure Bethany is okay. Sean's a great father, but we'll be there for her too. I love you. Goodbye, Amber. Thank you.'

Brooke wiped her eyes and nose once again before rising to her feet and taking her place next to Jordan, grasping his hand as tight as she could. They smiled at each other.

They spent one minute in silence before turning and walking out of the graveyard, leaving their three best friends, and Cherry Hollow, forever.

Epilogue
ALEX
One month later

It hadn't taken his mum long to make the decision to buy Jordan's house. She'd wanted to stay in Cherry Hollow. For what reason, Alex didn't know, but he didn't care where they lived as long as he had her all to himself. It was just the two of them now and he'd have done anything for his mum, even kill for her.

He knew she'd never forgive Linda for the part she'd played in Phoebe's death, but she deserved to know the truth about the woman she'd married. Watching Linda lie to his mum day in, and day out, for two years had been agony. Linda had deserved her ending. Besides, she'd tried to end her life before anyway, hadn't she? He'd just given her what she'd wanted all along. Peace. They'd both got what they wanted out of it.

All it had taken was crushing up a load of sleeping tablets into a glass of water and placing it beside her bed. She'd drunk it down without question. It had been too easy. Had she known what he'd put in the water? Had she noticed that the water had been flaked with white powder residue? Maybe she'd known his plan and had gone along with it willingly, or maybe she hadn't, but it had worked and that's all that mattered.

Alex had learned more than gossip from Harriet and Alex the First because Alex was a good listener and an expert at reading between the lines, so when Harriet had let it slip her mother had purchased fifteen gallons of petrol in one go, a flicker of a plan began to emerge. So, he'd watched, and he'd waited, and, sure enough, while he'd walked around town for hours on end, he'd seen Lucy and Trisha set fire to Fix It All and do a terrible job of covering their tracks too.

He'd worked fast and had managed to grab a jerrycan of petrol and pour it around Linda who was still fast asleep. He'd taken a match and watched everything burn for a few seconds before sneaking back out and returning to the hills, out of sight, waiting for the perfect time to return like the prodigal son. It hadn't been a perfect plan, but he was sixteen … and he'd taken the opportunities that had arisen.

It had all worked out for the best. His mum, while she still cried herself to sleep on occasion after having lost her wife, at least seemed content. Alex had done it for her. All for her. He bet she'd even thank him if she knew the truth. And now everything was back to the way things used to be. Just him and his mum.

No Phoebe.

No Linda.

Even his dad was gone …

It had been too easy to simply push him off the bridge. The man had been so drunk he couldn't even stand up straight, so all it had taken was a gentle push and … he'd never even seen his own son sneaking up behind him …

Alex was thrilled with his own performance of the grieving son. Of course, his mum had been too devastated at the time to bother asking questions about his dad's death. Even Linda hadn't investigated it because she had her own issues to deal with. His dad had simply died in a tragic accident or a possible death by suicide (the police still hadn't determined which it was) from drinking too much due to the loss of his daughter. It was just one of those things.

Alex hummed as he washed the dishes, eager to please his mum. He could see her through the kitchen window, kneeling next to a flower bed in the garden, clearing all the weeds. It was freezing outside, but her cheeks had a warm glow about them.

As he wiped his hands dry on a towel, Alex turned and started putting the dry plates away in the cupboard. Once he'd finished, he called out to her. 'I'm just heading into town for a bit. Do you need anything?'

'No, thanks, darling. See you later.'

'Bye, Mum.'

Alex left the house and jogged down the stone steps.

As he did, a cold wind whipped around his shoulders. Turning his jacket collar up, Alex hummed again as he walked.

Behind him, The Creature followed.

It wasn't finished with him yet.

Cherry Hollow: The True Horror Story Continues …

By Stephen Mallow
Date: 15 January 2024

You might remember my visit to the picturesque town of Cherry Hollow, located in the heart of the Lake District, last year. You may also remember I swore never to return to the town after seeing something that haunted me to my very core at Beaker Ravine where three of the Fated Five lost their lives.

Well, I have had to break my promise and will be returning to the town very soon because of the curious incidents that have gone on recently.

On Halloween night in 2023, two fires erupted in the town. One of the buildings destroyed was the local plumbing supply business owned and run by none other than Jordan Evans, one of the last two surviving members of the Fated Five.

The second building that burned down belonged to a new resident and her wife, who tragically lost her life in the blaze. Arson? Murder? Or suicide? The evidence suggests that the woman set the fire herself, yet the plumbing building was burned down by two of the town's long-standing residents who wanted to drive the last of the Fated Five from the town, which they succeeded in doing.

Jordan Evans has left Cherry Hollow, along with Brooke Willows.

Does this mean it's the end of The Creature's reign …?
It seems not.

This reporter is dying to know more about the secrets this town is keeping.

I've been sent an anonymous email.

Amazingly, yet another body has been discovered at the bottom of Beaker Ravine in a tiny cave, but here's the juicy bit …

The remains are aged at over forty years old, having been down there since roughly 1980.

So, the question remains: who does the body belong to?

Someone knows the truth.

Come with me back to Cherry Hollow to find out …

****

The third and final book in "The Darkness Series" is called "The Darkness That Came Before" and is set for publication on 1st February 2024.

Sign up to my newsletter via my website to be kept up to date with its release, be the first to see the cover and more!

www.jessicahuntleyauthor.com

****

Order the final book in
"The Darkness Series"

The Darkness That Came Before

Available to Order from Amazon

Out on 1st February 2024

Did you like this book?

I really hope you enjoyed reading The Darkness That Binds Us the second novel in "The Darkness" series.

If you have, please consider leaving me a review on Amazon and Goodreads, share a review on your social media pages and tag me, share my book to any book clubs you may be a part of or recommend my book to friends and family.

Reviews are massively important, especially to self-published authors. They help find other readers who may enjoy the book and spread the word to a wider audience.

For a FREE Novella — My Bad Self, sign up for my monthly newsletter at:

www.jessicahuntleyauthor.com

Connect with Jessica

Find and connect with Jessica online via the following platforms.

Sign up to her email list via her website to be notified of future books and her monthly author newsletter:

www.jessicahuntleyauthor.com

Follow her page on Facebook: Jessica Huntley - Author - @jessica.reading.writing

Follow her on Instagram: @jessica_reading_writing

Follow her on Twitter: @jess_read_write

Follow her on TikTok: @jessica_reading_writing

Follow her on Goodreads: jessica_reading_writing

Follow her on her Amazon Author Page - Jessica Huntley

www.ingramcontent.com/pod-product-compliance
Lightning Source LLC
Chambersburg PA
CBHW051321190726
48290CB00001B/252